— AN ASSASSIN'S CREED SERIES —

LAST DESCENDANTS

TOMB OF THE KHAN

BY

MATTHEW J. KIRBY

SCHOLASTIC INC.

ᴜld like to thank several people for their ongoing encouragement and help bringing this project to life. All my friends at Scholastic—Michael Petranek, Samantha Schutz, Debra Dorfman, Charisse Meloto, Monica Palenzuela, Lynn Smith, Jane Ashley, Ed Masessa, and Rick DeMonico—continue to enthusiastically support my career, for which I am grateful. I still feel like the luckiest kid in the world to work on Assassin's Creed with the uber-talented team at Ubisoft—Aymar Azaïzia, Anouk Bachman, Richard Farrese, Caroline Lamache, Holly Rawlinson, and Andrew Heitz. With regard to the research for this book, Eric N. Danielson generously provided me with valuable information about the Southern Song and Fishing Town. However, any mistakes or inaccuracies are totally on me. Finally, I would like to thank my family and friends, especially Jaime, who makes it possible for me to disappear into other worlds for weeks and months and bring back stories.

Photo credit: John Speed/Wikimedia

All rights reserved. Published by Scholastic Inc., *Publishers since 1920.* SCHOLASTIC and associated logos are trademarks and/or registered trademarks of Scholastic Inc.

The publisher does not have any control over and does not assume any responsibility for author or third-party websites or their content.

This book is a work of fiction. Names, characters, places, and incidents are either the product of the author's imagination or are used fictitiously, and any resemblance to actual persons, living or dead, business establishments, events, or locales is entirely coincidental.

ISBN 978-0-545-85553-2

10 9 8 7 6 5 4 3 2 1   17 18 19 20 21

Printed in the U.S.A.   40
First printing 2017

Book design by Rick DeMonico

For Charlie, whose inventive mind will make history.

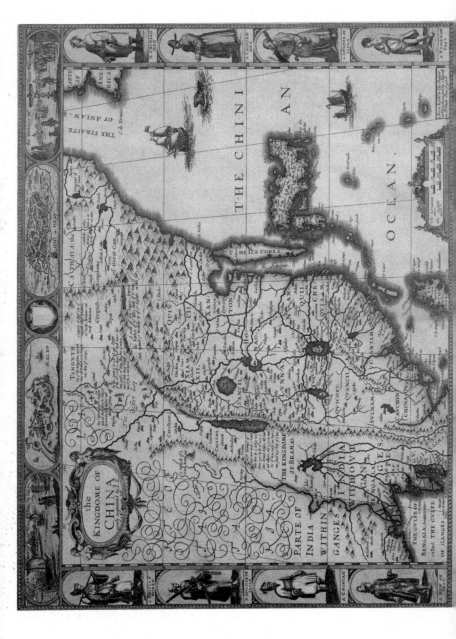

CHAPTER ONE

China, 1259 CE

Natalya held her breath and waited for the explosion.

From the high fortress walls above her, the Song artillerymen had just launched another barrage of iron bombs from their *fei yun pi-li pao*, their metal thunderclap cannons. The glowing red shells arced high through the night sky overhead and then hurtled downward toward the Horde of the Great Khan.

She palmed her ears and took cover behind the ramparts the Jin engineers had raised, and though the earthworks shuddered with each impact, shaking loose dirt into Natalya's eyes, the sound loud enough to shatter her ears like porcelain, the defenses held. Thus far.

The air, hot and humid between the strangling hands of

summer, quieted then, thick with the smoke of black powder that stung Natalya's eyes and nose.

No, *his* eyes and nose.

The eyes and nose of Natalya's ancestor, Bayan, a Buryat warrior from the far northern steppes. But experiencing the memories of a man had been the least disorienting aspect of this simulation. Bayan's Mongol culture had been completely foreign to her, their war of conquest across Asia and Europe deeply unsettling. And yet those invasions had introduced the DNA of her Mongol ancestors into her Russian and Kazakh family tree. The story of the Mongol conquest was in some ways the story of Natalya's ancestry.

Next to Bayan, a younger warrior trembled, his eyes turned upward as if he feared the earthworks would collapse upon them. Everyone in the Khan's army had seen what damage the Song weapons could inflict, tearing men and horses asunder with iron and fire.

Natalya felt Bayan stepping in front of her on the stage of her mind, and she retreated into the shadows, allowing his memory to play out.

"Steady," Bayan said to the younger warrior. "This is just for show. They want to make sure we remember our defeat at the Xin Dong Gate today."

The young warrior tightened his lips and nodded. "It's quite a show."

By his speech and the look of him, he was a Tangghut conscript and had likely done little fighting. He wasn't a Mongol of the steppes. He hadn't participated in the training exercise and great hunt that was the *nerge*. Bayan remembered his own first experience with it, the awe-inspiring line of warriors eighty miles long, marching and riding forward with discipline, unbroken, the right and left flanks reaching slowly ahead until they had enclosed a massive circle many miles wide, followed by a methodical constriction, driving all game inward until the herds of terrified animals at the center could be dispatched at the leisure of the Great Khan. The exercise had taken months, and had trained Bayan and the tribes of the steppes for war.

This young soldier would find his courage or he would perish, either at the enemy's hands, or the Horde's for cowardice. Bayan would instruct the captain over the warrior's Arban unit to pay the Tangghut special mind.

"What is your name?" Bayan asked.

"Chen Lun."

Bayan then asked for the names of the man's captain and commander, after which he said, "Stand firm, Chen Lun. Just as Ögedei Khan conquered the Jin, so Möngke Khan will defeat the Song. We will *nothing* this city and kill every man, woman, and child within it."

The warrior bowed his head. "Yes, sir."

Bayan left him then, and walked along the bulwark inspecting several of his own troops, pleased by their stalwart and strong appearance in the face of the Song artillery, and in spite of the heat and disease in this place. To the west, beyond the Khan's defenses, the mountain rose high and black into the night, the distant lights of Fishing Town atop it. Not even Alamut, the fortress of the Assassins in Persia, had resisted siege as successfully as this bastion had. Its location, with wide rivers and steep slopes on three sides, gave it an undeniable natural advantage, augmented by the Song engineers of war.

But another shadow rose up before the mountain, a terrace

on Saddle Hill, which the Khan had ordered his engineers to raise. Bayan assumed the structure would eventually facilitate an assault, or offer a better vantage on the city. Some thought it a foolish display of the Great Khan's pride, but was it truly pride if shown by the Scourge of God, the Emperor of the World?

At the appointed hour, Bayan retreated east to the barracks at Lion Hill, joining the nine other commanders of his Mingghan unit in the *ger* of their general. The large, round tent, enrobed in felt, was sweltering inside. Several of the other commanders coughed, and a few looked sallow and weakened, though they did their best to hide their infirmity. Bayan wondered how many troops they would lose to the plague before the end of this.

"We have new orders," General Köke said. "Wang Dechen is leading an assault on the Hu Guo Gate. Tonight."

"Wang Dechen?" one of the commanders asked.

"Yes," Köke said.

Wang Dechen was the Great Khan's most trusted general, his commander-in-chief. Here at Fishing Town, Wang Dechen controlled four of the Horde's Tumen, each ten thousand strong, both upon the rivers and upon the land. For him to personally lead an assault meant the attack was of critical importance.

Köke continued. "With our defeat at the Xin Dong Gate, the Song won't be expecting a fresh attack so soon, and not under cover of darkness. Wang Dechen wants only the fittest at his side. You each know the health and status of your Jagun."

"Mine is prepared." Bayan wiped sweat from his brow as it escaped from beneath his cap and helmet. "All of my men stand ready to fight."

Köke looked around the ger. "The rest of you?"

Several additional commanders offered their units in whole. Those whose soldiers had been more ravaged by disease volunteered only some of their Arban, smaller companies of ten men. Köke accepted them all.

"Muster your warriors and meet at the south bulwarks in one half hour," he said. "You will be given further orders there."

The commanders dispersed, and Bayan hurried toward the barracks. As he marched, Natalya felt a renewed surge of fear, and complete exhaustion. This would be the fifth battle she had endured with her ancestor in the Animus simulation, and she needed a break from the blood and the death.

"I can't," she said, pushing her way in front of Bayan's mind. "Victoria, I can't do this."

A moment passed, the battle drawing nearer.

"Victoria?"

Are you okay, Natalya? asked a woman's voice inside her mind, tinged with a slight French accent.

"No, I'm not. I think I need a break."

Well, your neurovitals are stable, though your pulse and blood pressure are slightly elevated.

Um, you think? Natalya wanted to say. What else could anyone expect from her blood pressure right before medieval hand-to-hand combat?

"I need a break, Dr. Bibeau," Natalya repeated, more firmly.

Are you sure? You know how hard that will be on you.

Bayan had just reached the barracks, and Natalya felt his exhilaration for battle mounting.

"I'm sure," she said.

A moment of silence. Natalya imagined irritation in it.

Of course. Stand by.

Natalya braced for what she knew was coming, just as Bayan had braced himself under the Song artillery fire, only Natalya expected a very different kind of explosion.

Terminating simulation in three, two, one . . .

The world around Natalya, the Mongol war camp, the stars, the humid heat on her skin, the smell of smoke and blood, all of it blew apart in a mind-fire that blazed through her for several excruciating moments. When the pain abated, it left behind ashes where her thoughts had been, and she found herself in the formless void of the Memory Corridor, a staging ground and transitional space meant to make adjustment to the simulation easier. Natalya couldn't imagine it being more difficult.

Take a few moments. Decompress.

Natalya wouldn't be able to really decompress until she was out of the simulation altogether, but she worked to clear her mind of Bayan's memories by taking hold of her own. Thoughts of her parents and grandparents, and the life she'd had before Monroe had found her and caught her up in this whole mess. Victoria had trained her to latch on to specific memories, like the sound of the bells ringing at her grandparents' Russian Orthodox Church, or the smell of *shchi* simmering on the stove while the spicy *manti* dumplings steamed. These were the details that made up who she was and helped her find herself again when she got lost in another life.

After a few moments of this, she took a deep breath to prepare for the worst of it, and said, "I'm ready to come out."

Very good. Parietal extraction in three, two, one . . .

Natalya's mind, stomach, skin, all of her seemed to turn inside out, as if exposing her raw nerves to the air. She didn't scream anymore, but she groaned until the sensation passed, and then Victoria lifted the Animus helmet away. Natalya stood in the center of a waist-high metal ring, tethered to it by a harness around her torso. Metal clasps secured her feet to small platforms on jointed supports beneath her, her arms and hands strapped to a kind of exoframe, a fully articulated skeleton that matched her subtlest movements. Unlike Monroe's setup, this type of Animus allowed Natalya's body complete range of motion within the simulation, without her actually moving anywhere. Victoria helped her unstrap from it all.

"Remember to breathe," the woman said, guiding her out of the ring.

Natalya stepped through, her legs wobbling a bit. Depending on how much and what type of movement she performed within the simulation, this new Animus could leave her physically exhausted. Waves of nausea drowned the pain, and she tasted bile rising. "I need a bucket," she said, closing her eyes. Keeping them open only made it worse.

"Right here," Victoria said.

Natalya turned toward the doctor's voice and opened her right eye the slightest bit, just enough to find the bucket through the blur of her own eyelashes. Then she heaved and heaved until her stomach was empty and she was out of breath.

"Done?" Victoria asked, smoothing her hair, sounding very gentle.

Natalya stumbled toward a cot in a corner of the room, gasping, feeling heavy. "Done."

She heard the sloshing bucket being carried away by one of the Abstergo technicians, felt badly for whoever it was, but only for a moment. After all, Natalya was the one going through hell.

She shielded her eyes and tried to open them a sliver. "How long was I in there this time?"

"Three hours, eleven minutes," Victoria said, taking a seat next to her.

"It felt like longer," Natalya said, but then, it always did.

"Would you like to sleep?"

Natalya opened her eyes a little more and turned toward the woman. Victoria's pixie haircut had grown out just a bit in the weeks since Natalya and the others had come to the Aerie, but the doctor's large teeth and smile remained the same.

"I think so," Natalya said.

"Very well. We'll debrief later."

Victoria took a hissed breath and stretched as the woman got up from her rolling chair and walked across the room. She went to a sleek glass cabinet from which she drew a pale blue fleece blanket, which she spread over Natalya.

"You rest now. We'll keep an eye on things."

Natalya nodded, or thought she nodded, but couldn't quite tell as sleep overcame her, and her eyes closed again.

When Natalya awoke, she was alone, but she was pretty sure someone, somewhere, would be watching her. She sat up in the soft light of the room, head pounding. She could expect that to last at least a day, though in the very beginning her headaches had lasted longer. The others experienced them, too. Victoria had reassured them all that each of their Animus machines had been calibrated and coded to their individual neurometrics, and that eventually the headaches should stop.

Should, not *would*.

Natalya rubbed the back of her head, up near the crown, where the Parietal Suppressor had bombarded her brain with waves of electromagnetic pulses designed specifically for her. Those waves didn't bother her at all while she was inside the simulation. The on and off part was the problem, which was why the others usually spent longer in the Animus than Natalya did. Sean would probably live there if he could, but then, he experienced things Natalya never would.

One of the techs had once suggested there was another, even more invasive version of the Animus out there, but Abstergo would never use it on kids. Natalya was glad for that. The CT scans and fMRI's and the Suppressor were invasive enough.

The door to the room opened with a *whoosh*, and Victoria walked in wearing her white lab coat, carrying her ever-present tablet. The room lights awoke fully at her presence, and Natalya squinted.

"How are you feeling?" Victoria asked.

"Better," Natalya said. "But I still feel like someone went all Lizzie Borden on the back of my head."

"Really?" Victoria said with a frown. "That should lessen with time."

Should.

"Do you feel ready to debrief?"

Natalya looked around the room, all white panels and glass and curves and computer monitors, the contours of the Animus ring like something from the bottom of the sea that had been shaped and polished by thousands of years of waves.

Natalya got to her feet. "Yeah, I'm ready."

"Good." Victoria extended her arm, gesturing toward the open door. "Shall we?"

They left the Animus room and entered a wide corridor, with a line of doorways on the right-hand side, and on the other, a wall of glass that looked out into the dense pine forest surrounding the Aerie facility. The trees were an aspect of this place that Natalya truly enjoyed. All she had to do was step outside and breathe in their scent and she often felt a little better.

Victoria led her down the corridor, and then toward a conference room. Once they left the labs and Animus rooms behind, the building opened wider, allowing golden evening light in through the glass ceiling and multiple glass walls and windows. The place had an almost prismatic effect in certain places, with each of the Aerie's five buildings constructed in much the same way.

When they entered the conference room, Isaiah rose from his chair to greet her, his green eyes vivid, his blond hair swept back. "Good to see you, Natalya. I understand your simulation continues to prove quite stressful."

"That's one way to put it," Natalya said.

"Are you holding up?"

"So far."

"Please." Isaiah gestured to one of the seats around the conference table, which looked as if it'd been cut from an enormous slab of obsidian. "Let's talk."

Natalya picked a chair opposite Isaiah, and Victoria took the one next to hers.

"The Mongol Khans were often quite merciless." Isaiah sat back down. "Especially during their invasion of southern China."

Natalya didn't really like to dwell on it, but the Mongols followed a pattern of psychological warfare and terror. First, they would offer to spare the city if its rulers would submit to the supreme sovereignty of the Great Khan and pay him tribute. If the rulers agreed, having heard rumors of Mongol invincibility, the city was usually spared any bloodshed. If the rulers of the city refused, however, the slaughter and destruction that would inevitably follow turned Natalya's stomach.

"I understand why that would be so distressing for you," Isaiah said.

"We all do," Victoria added.

Isaiah folded his hands on the table, his fingers long and narrow. "I wish there were some other way to learn what we need to learn."

So did Natalya.

"Would you like to call your parents?" Isaiah asked.

Natalya thought about doing that all the time, but she usually only allowed herself to call them every two or three days. And they visited most weekends. But she never told them about this kind of thing. She didn't want to worry them or stress them out.

"I think I'm okay."

Victoria laid a hand on Natalya's forearm. "Then can we ask you a few questions about the simulation?"

"Sure." Better to get it over with.

"How is the Parietal Suppression going?" Isaiah asked. "Dr. Bibeau tells me you're still having painful side effects."

Natalya nodded.

"That is to be expected," Isaiah said. "The electromagnetic waves temporarily silence your parietal lobes, the part of your brain that orients your perception of time and space. This allows for a deeper and more rapid acceptance of the simulation, but it can be quite disorienting for you."

He offered this same explanation every time, almost word-for-word, as if they hadn't had this conversation before. "The headaches aren't quite as bad," Natalya said, hoping to move on.

"That's good to hear." Isaiah tilted his head a fraction of an inch to the left. "Have you seen any sign of it?"

"No."

"Are you certain?"

Natalya didn't like the way he always second-guessed her. "I think I would recognize a dagger with the power to destroy the world."

"Perhaps you would," Isaiah said. "Perhaps you wouldn't."

She knew he was impatient, and truthfully, she felt impatient, too. The Piece of Eden was the entire reason she was here. It was the reason all of them were here at the Aerie, and Owen and Javier were wherever they were. The relic had to be found. But Natalya still wasn't sure who she wanted to find it first.

"We know Bayan came into contact with it at some point in his life," Victoria said. "It's only a matter of time."

"What if he came into contact with it as an old man?" Natalya asked. "I still might have a long way to go."

"If we had Monroe's Animus core, with all his research, we could be more targeted in our approach." Isaiah's eyes seemed to flash, and his jaw muscles tightened. "But unfortunately, we still don't know where he is, so for now, you will have to take Bayan's life one day at a time."

"One battle at a time," Natalya said. Isaiah and Victoria hadn't mentioned the Ascendance Event recently. They knew Monroe had found something unique in all their DNA. They just didn't know exactly what it was.

"What is the current situation in the simulation?" Isaiah asked.

Natalya filled him in on the mountain assault, and the Mongol Horde's very rare defeat. "Everyone's sick," she said. "Cholera or malaria or something."

Victoria swiped and tapped her tablet screen. "Some sources claim Möngke Khan died of an infectious disease during the siege."

"He hasn't yet," Natalya said.

Isaiah had started drumming his fingers on the obsidian table, his nails clicking. "Can you go back in tonight?"

Natalya paused a moment before responding, rubbing her temples. "No. I'm done for the day."

Isaiah looked at Victoria, sharply, and Victoria looked back at him for a moment before shaking her head, as if Natalya wasn't there to see any of it. But it didn't matter. They couldn't force her, and there was no way she was going back in right away.

Isaiah rapped the table with his knuckles, once. "Fine." He rose to his full height. "I trust you'll get a good night's rest. And tomorrow—"

"Tomorrow I go to war," Natalya said.

CHAPTER TWO

Owen wasn't afraid. But he wondered if he should be.

He sat on the cot next to Javier, their backs against the bare, chalky Sheetrock wall of the storage unit that Griffin used as a lair. The Assassin had his back to them, facing the computer monitor as he communicated with his superior.

"You're sure this location is compromised?" Griffin asked, his voice the low rumble of a diesel engine, the dark skin of his shaved head reflecting the light of the single bulb hanging in the center of the room. "I've taken precautions."

"Quite sure," the man in the computer screen said. Owen had seen his face once before; haggard, with thick graying hair and a beard. Gavin Banks, a leader in the Assassin Brotherhood.

"Rothenberg says a Templar strike team could be on its way there right now."

Javier glanced at Owen, his eyes narrow, his neck muscles tense. He seemed more worried than Owen did.

"And you trust this informant?" Griffin asked.

"I do," Gavin said. "You need to burn everything and clear out immediately."

Griffin nodded. "I've already scouted a new location—"

"No," Gavin said. "Proceed to rendezvous alpha twelve. Rebecca Crane will meet you there with further instructions."

"Rebecca?" Griffin paused. "All right, then."

"Good luck. Gavin out." The screen cut to black.

Owen took one breath, and then Griffin stood. "Each of you suit up and load what you can in a backpack. Hurry."

Owen and Javier glanced at each other, and then they both bounced off the cot, rushing to the crates and cases stacked on the storage unit's metal shelves. They'd done this once before, when Griffin had led them to Mount McGregor in search of the first Piece of Eden. They pulled on their leather jackets and hoods, and then they snatched up a variety of weapons: throwing knives, darts, and small grenades that delivered everything from poisonous gas to electromagnetic pulses that could drop a helicopter from the sky.

Owen watched Griffin packing up his own gear, including the Assassin's gauntlet he'd never even let Owen touch. When they'd finished with their packs, Griffin walked to the computer and pulled up a command prompt.

"Be ready, and remember your training," he said.

Owen didn't think he would ever forget the grueling exercises

Griffin had put them through over the past few weeks, training them in basic combat and free-running.

The Assassin shook his head at the screen. "We'll have three minutes."

"Until what?" Javier asked.

Griffin didn't answer. He typed a command, hit enter, and then marched to the storage unit's roller door. The metal rattled and clanged as he heaved it upward by the handle.

The sun had set outside, but it wasn't fully dark yet, the time of day when everything became its own gray shadow, but you could still just make out the faint details. Griffin led them toward the storage unit next door where he kept his car, but before he could open the padlock, distant headlights rounded the corner at the far end of the row, moving fast.

"Is that—?" Owen asked.

"We leave the car," Griffin said, and he ran in the opposite direction. "Move!"

Owen bolted after him, with Javier at his side, and they raced a few hundred yards. Then Griffin launched himself upward and climbed onto the storage units' roof. Owen did the same, still a bit surprised at the natural abilities he'd gained from the time he'd spent in his Assassin ancestor's memories. He heard Javier come up behind him, and the three of them raced along the roof without making a sound.

"What happens in three minutes?" Javier asked.

"Twenty-three seconds," Griffin said.

Owen looked back over his shoulder. He could see the lights from the vehicle approaching their storage unit. Then he noticed there were other lights, all converging on that location from different directions, including lights in the sky.

"There's a helicopter coming," he said.

"I hear it," Griffin said. "Keep low—"

A thunderous explosion behind them sent a wave of heat against the back of Owen's neck and pressed against his ears. The sudden burst of light illuminated the rooftop they ran across, as well as the rooftops of the neighboring rows, where Owen spotted a dozen scattered figures crouching and moving slowly toward them. They wore black fatigues, and helmets that gave them the ability to find and track difficult targets.

"Templars," Owen whispered, and all three of them dropped to their chests.

"Seems Rothenberg was right," Griffin said. "And they came prepared."

"You blew up your own hideout?" Javier asked, a thick column of smoke rising up into the sky. Owen could smell burning plastic.

"Standard procedure," Griffin said. "There won't be anything left for them to trace the Brotherhood."

"They'll just trace *us*," Owen said.

"No, they won't. Follow my lead." Griffin slipped away, up and over the roof's peak.

Owen and Javier did the same, and when the three of them reached the far edge of the roof, they dropped to the pavement, into the opposite alley from which they'd ascended. The darkened aisle appeared empty.

Griffin pushed up his sleeve and made some adjustments to his gauntlet. "Arm yourselves."

Owen steadied his breathing as he tugged his pack around and pulled out a few throwing knives and grenades. Javier withdrew his crossbow pistol. The Assassin turned his wrist upward, and with a simple flick, a hidden electrical blade erupted from the gauntlet, six or seven crackling inches in length. In the next moment, Griffin retracted it, but Owen could still smell the coppery ozone it left behind.

"We need to make sure we're not being followed, then head to the rendezvous." Griffin looked to his right and left. "Stay sharp. This is not a training exercise."

He led them at a trot away from the site of the explosion. Owen honed his focus the way he'd learned to do, the way his ancestor had done, extending his senses into the ground beneath his feet and the air flowing around him, listening to the echoes off the walls to either side. They kept to the edges of the alley, passing storage unit after storage unit. Before long, they came to the end of the row, a chain-link fence just a dozen feet beyond it.

But before that, Owen sensed something.

He focused the whole of his perception ahead of them, listening, smelling, feeling, sensing the presence of agents just around the corners to either side of the alley, waiting like the teeth of a bear trap. Griffin and Javier didn't have the same level of ability Owen possessed, but even they seemed to be aware of the agents. The three of them slowed to a silent halt. Owen readied a couple of EMP grenades, and Javier loaded his pistol crossbow with bolts. Griffin crouched into a fighting position, and then gave a nod.

Owen leapt ahead and threw the EMP grenades to either side before ducking into a roll, and even though the explosions were silent, the effect was not. The Templar agents bellowed and scrambled to pull their helmets off, their weapons on the ground, all their electronics fried.

There were eight of them, four on each side. Javier came around the corner firing darts laden with neurotoxin, and one of his targets collapsed. Griffin launched at the nearest agent, electrical hidden blade humming, and took him out with a jolt stronger than any Taser, then fought his way through two more.

Seconds in, and half the Templars were down, leaving four still on their feet. Owen pulled out a smoke grenade, preparing to give Javier and Griffin some cover, but he stalled in arming it. His hand was shaking, and he stared at his quivering fingers, unable to work the trigger, with the distant realization that he was afraid, only his body had known it when his mind didn't.

"Owen!" Javier shouted.

Owen turned as a heavy blow caught him from behind, driving the air out of him, and he stumbled forward a few steps before he could spin to face his attacker. The woman had her helmet off, and she held a length of rebar like a baseball bat.

This is not a training exercise.

Owen spread his stance as she charged, and managed to duck the first swing, landing a blow in her side with his fist, but the agent was faster and better. Her sharp elbow caught Owen in the face, blinding him with stars. He expected the rebar to follow, but then Griffin was there, and the woman went down with a smoldering burn where the Assassin's blade had caught her in the neck.

Something thudded behind Owen, and he turned to see that Javier had just stunned another agent with a shot from his crossbow. Owen finally got his hands to work the smoke grenade, and in the cloud that exploded from it, Griffin took down the last two Templars. "Hurry," he said, coughing a bit. "By now the others will have noticed that these agents have gone silent."

They climbed the fence and raced across a vacant lot littered with empty cans and weeds, dodging the roving spotlight from the helicopter overhead, until they reached a busy street. There, they all stashed their weapons back in their packs and tried to disappear into the crowd. Owen adopted the hunched posture of someone on his way home from a long day at work, eyes slightly downcast. Griffin had once mentioned the Assassin ability to hide in the open, but neither Owen nor Javier understood exactly what that meant. They weren't even really Assassins, in spite of what they'd just done. Owen was only staying with Griffin to help his friends and find out what really happened to his dad.

Griffin looked back over his shoulder. "Let's take a cab."

"A cab?" Javier said. "Assassins take cabs?"

"Exactly," Griffin said. "Hide in plain sight."

He whistled between his thumb and finger, and a white sedan with a checkered stripe down the side pulled over to the curb. The three of them piled into the back seat, and Griffin gave the driver some directions. As they pulled into traffic, Owen craned his head and looked out the back window, toward the vacant lot and the storage facility beyond it.

His hands were still shaking, and he balled them into tight fists.

What had happened to him back there? He'd simply frozen up, and if that agent had come at him with a gun or a knife instead of that rebar, she might have killed him. Instead of getting easier with Griffin's training, this whole situation actually seemed to be getting harder.

For the first few days and weeks after the Draft Riots simulation, Owen had felt confident in his abilities. Powerful, even. But now he wondered if that self-assurance had been false. Just the echoes of his ancestor in his mind. Varius had been a skilled Assassin, and after living in those memories, Owen had felt capable, too. But now that the weight of Varius's mind had mostly lifted from his, Owen realized that maybe he wasn't all that powerful on his own. He was still just a teenager, and those Templar agents had been sent to either capture him or kill him.

They stayed quiet for most of the drive. Eventually, Griffin had the cabbie drop them at a corner, where they waited a moment before climbing into a different cab and heading toward the suburbs. Owen figured it was all to make sure they weren't being followed, and it seemed to work. The lights of the Templar helicopter faded from view, and eventually vanished behind city skyline behind them.

Griffin had the cab drop them at a nondescript house on a quiet street, as if that were their destination, and after the vehicle had pulled away they set off on foot, following behind Griffin.

Javier turned to Owen. "You okay?"

"Yeah," Owen said.

"That was wild," Javier said.

"You did good," Owen said, feeling a bit envious of the composure and skill Javier had demonstrated.

"You both did," Griffin said. "But those agents were playing with kid gloves. We'll debrief when we reach the rendezvous."

A mile or so later, they reached the outskirts of the development, where the road turned to dirt and gravel, and the land turned to open farms. A few miles on, through empty fields and pastures fenced with old wood, rolling hills to either side, they rounded a bend, and a large house came into view among the trees.

"Whoa," Javier said.

The place appeared to have been abandoned a hundred years ago. It rose two, maybe three stories, clad partly in wooden siding, and armored in other places by rounded wooden shingles like scales, all of it gray, split, and weathered. A front porch sagged along the house's face, and at one corner an angular tower climbed up above the roofline, a round, blackened window at the top like a cyclops' eye, a sharp, wrought iron crown upon its peak. Boards stretched across most of the other windows and the front door.

"This is it," Griffin said.

Owen looked at the house again. "This is it?"

"Kinda got an Addams Family vibe to it, doesn't it?" Javier said.

Owen agreed, but Griffin ignored him. "Come on."

They marched directly toward the front door along a flagstone walkway, the weeds and grass to either side knee-high. This place set Owen's skin crawling. He saw no lights inside, and no sign of any Rebecca Crane.

"This is the rendezvous?" he asked.

"Yes," Griffin said.

They reached the front porch, and the wooden steps groaned beneath their feet, all cracks and loose, rusted nails.

Owen shuddered. "But where—"

Then the front door opened.

Javier yelped, and Owen jumped backward and almost tripped down the stairs.

"Griffin." A woman stood in the dark entryway. "I've been waiting for you."

"Rebecca," Griffin said. "Good to see you back in action."

Apparently, the door only appeared to be boarded up. The woman motioned them all forward. "Hurry, inside."

Griffin led the way, and Owen followed him, peering back at Javier. They came into a foyer, and the interior of the house matched its exterior. Faded wallpaper peeled away from the walls, doorways stood at angles other than right, and the smell of dust and mildew soured the air. A staircase Owen would have a hard time trusting led up to the second floor, and a hallway reached into impenetrable darkness beneath it. There were empty rooms to either side of them with cobwebbed chandeliers.

Rebecca closed the front door and secured it with an electronic lock that was definitely not original to the house, and Owen realized the place was probably much more secure than it looked.

"You're later than I expected," she said. "Did you have any trouble?"

"Templars staged a raid as we were leaving," Griffin said. "Had to come the long way."

"Sorry," she said. "But at least you're here."

"What is this place?" Owen asked.

Rebecca looked around and up at the ceiling. "It's what it looks like. Mostly."

"So it's a haunted house?" Javier said.

Rebecca smiled, her teeth barely visible in the darkness. "The only ghosts here are the ones you carry in your DNA, Javier."

"You know my name?"

"Of course we do."

Owen didn't like that, or the way she said it.

"So what's the plan?" Griffin asked. "Gavin said you'd have orders."

Rebecca nodded. "This way."

She walked away from them, toward the black hallway under the stairs. The three of them followed her, but before she'd gone too far, she opened a door to the right.

"Watch your step," she said, apparently intending them to walk through it. "The staircase goes down to the basement."

Griffin led the way without any hesitation, followed by Javier. Owen reached his hands out to either side until he found a handrail, and then slowly inched his way forward, his eyes trying desperately to find something in the darkness to latch on to, even inventing things if they had to. His toe found the edge of the first step, and then the next one down, and the next, one at a time. Beneath him, Griffin's footsteps thunked and echoed. Above him, Rebecca closed the door to the staircase.

"Lights coming on," she said. "Shield your eyes."

Owen closed his, but through his eyelids he could tell when the stairway lit up around him. Upon opening his eyes, he discovered that this area of the house was in the opposite condition of everything else above. The walls were smooth, covered in gray paneling, and at the bottom of the steps they entered into a room that better fit Owen's idea of what an Assassin's hideout should look like. More than the storage unit anyway.

There were several computers, a large glass conference table, and an entire wall of weapons, clothing, and armor. Over in a far corner of the room, Owen noticed a reclining chair much like the one Monroe had used with his Animus.

"Is that your baby?" Griffin asked, nodding toward it. "Here?"

"No," Rebecca said. "This is something else. New Abstergo tech. Shaun got hold of a processor and blueprints in Madrid. I used them to build this machine."

"Shaun?" Javier asked.

"We have a friend with that name," Owen said.

"Oh?" Rebecca cocked her head. She had short brown hair, with olive skin that reminded Owen of Natalya. "Is your friend also a cynical egotist who thinks he's smarter than everyone else?"

Owen stammered. "Um, no."

Rebecca shrugged. "Must be a different guy, then." She turned to Griffin. "You still remember how to run the Animus?"

"Of course," Griffin said. "Why? You're not staying?"

"No. I'm needed elsewhere."

"What could be more important than this?" Griffin asked. "We're talking about the Trident of Eden. One of the prongs has already been found. The second—"

"I know that," Rebecca said. "But trust me, there is a hell of a lot going on in the world right now, and the Brotherhood is spread way too thin. I have my orders. For now, you'll just have to manage on your own. This location is secure, and I've set everything up for you. It should be plug and play. Think you can handle that?"

Griffin stood there a moment, eyes narrowed, and Owen felt a tension between the two Assassins. Griffin seemed unsettled and angry. Apparently, things weren't always harmonious in the Brotherhood. But the moment passed quickly, after which Griffin nodded, and his shoulders visibly relaxed.

"Fine," he said. "I know it's not your choice."

"It isn't," she said. "But it really isn't Gavin's, or even

William's. The Templars took away that choice when they almost wiped us out fifteen years ago."

"What are my instructions?" Griffin asked.

"Rothenberg says the Templars are currently after the second dagger, which was last seen in medieval China. We need to get to it first." Rebecca turned and pointed at Owen. "Through the ghosts inside his DNA."

CHAPTER THREE

Sean couldn't wait to get back into the Animus. Victoria had started imposing durational limits on his sessions, and yesterday, she hadn't let him into a simulation at all. That had been pretty frustrating, but Sean had managed to get through the day, and as soon as he finished his breakfast this morning, he'd be back in the ring.

"Morning," David said through a yawn as he walked into the lounge that served as their space for eating and relaxing. "They bring the muffins out yet?"

Sean nodded toward the buffet counter. "Banana nut today."

David stopped mid-stride. "Never mind."

"You don't like bananas?" Sean asked.

"I don't like the nuts," David said, pushing his thick, white-framed glasses up as he headed toward the hot plates.

His older sister, Grace, walked into the room then, her dark, curly hair pulled to the back of her head. She was fifteen, almost Sean's age, and over the past few weeks he'd been getting to know her better than he had her thirteen-year-old brother. Grace and David almost hadn't stayed at the Aerie. Their dad had actually taken them both home for a few days, but then they'd come back. Sean hadn't asked what that was all about yet, but maybe he would soon.

For him, there was never a question of staying. The lawsuit settlement from the accident a few years ago had barely covered Sean's hospital bills, and his parents needed the money Abstergo paid them. Being a paraplegic cost them over seventy thousand dollars a year. But even without that, Sean would have wanted to stay, for himself.

"Morning, Grace," he said.

"Morning." She went straight for the coffee. "Victoria going to let you in today?"

Sean scooped up some of his scrambled eggs. "She said she would."

"Where'd you leave off? Tommy back from London?"

"Yeah. I finished with that investigation and came back to another riot."

"Tommy Grayling seems to like a riot," she said, coming over to sit next to him.

"I wouldn't say that."

"All right." Grace took a sip of her coffee and looked at him over the rim of her mug. "You seem to like a riot, then."

Sean smiled. "I like the action, that's true. But mostly, New York City in the nineteenth century just had a lot of riots."

"You seen Natalya today?" David asked as he sat down with a plate more bacon than eggs.

"Not yet," Sean said, but he didn't mind. Things were still awkward with her, and he got nervous whenever she entered the room. He never should have said anything. He should have just left everything between Tommy and Adelina behind in the simulation. But it had been more confusing back then, who was who and what it all meant. He wasn't even sure how much he really liked Natalya, or if that was just Tommy flowing through his mind, in love with Natalya's ancestor.

"Why does Victoria limit you anyway?" Grace asked.

"She says I could become too dependent on it." Sean pushed his nearly empty plate away.

"Like an addict?" David asked.

"Something like that," Sean said. But he didn't see it that way. It was true that he'd spend every waking moment in the simulation if he could, but that didn't make it an addiction. How can you be addicted to air?

"You know there's nothing wrong with you, right?" Grace said. "And I don't mean the simulations."

Sean looked at her rich, brown eyes. She sounded completely sincere, in the way that few people did when they said that kind of thing. They'd learned about disability politics, and they meant well, but they didn't get it. It actually seemed like Grace might understand.

Sean knocked on the armrest of his wheelchair. "To me, there is something wrong with this."

"That's not what I mean," she said. "You're—"

"Good morning," Natalya said as she walked into the room.

"Good morning," David said. "Missed you last night."

"I wasn't feeling well." Natalya grabbed a bagel and a yogurt.

Whatever Grace had been about to say hung in the air for a moment longer, and then dissipated like the steam from her coffee. Sean was glad to let it go.

"You still getting those headaches?" Grace asked Natalya.

She nodded. "Aren't you guys?"

"Mine go away in a few hours," Grace said.

"Mine too," Sean said. They'd been pretty bad, at first, but not anymore. They were worth it to him anyway.

Natalya took a seat at the table, across from Sean, and he felt his stomach tighten just a bit. If there was one thing he could change about his experience at the Aerie, it would be his attraction to her.

"Have you found the Piece of Eden?" David asked, chewing on a bacon strip.

The table grew quiet. They all knew why they were there. They all knew what had happened in Monroe's simulation of the Draft Riots, back before Abstergo had found them and told them the whole story. They all knew what was at stake if the three prongs of the Trident of Eden were found and combined. But that wasn't something they talked about often, or openly. It was still a bit like talking about aliens, or wizards.

"Not yet," Natalya said calmly.

"How's the China simulation going?" Grace asked.

Natalya stared at the bagel on her plate. "It's hard. There's a lot of death."

"That would be hard on anyone," Sean said, trying to help, but it somehow came out sounding dismissive.

Natalya just nodded without looking up.

He wanted to escape, quickly, before things got more awkward. "Tommy awaits," he said. "I think I'll head out."

"See you this evening," Grace said.

David gave him a nod, and Sean rolled his wheelchair backward from the table, and then pivoted toward the door. Anytime he left a group this way, by himself, in his chair, he could feel them all trying not to watch him go. People told him that was just in his head, but there was always this silence behind him, like they were afraid to talk until he was gone, like they had to wait and be respectful or something as he struggled. He hated it, and was glad to reach the door, at which point David started talking about the simulation of his great-grandpa's memories as a World War II pilot with the Tuskegee Airmen.

Sean left the lounge and wheeled himself toward the Animus rooms. The Aerie had five separate buildings, all connected by a network of enclosed glass walkways through the trees. He and the others kept mostly to the same two buildings: the main reception area (where they went when their parents came to visit or take them out for a few hours), and the building they were in now, where they ate, slept, and explored their genetic memories. Sean didn't know what Abstergo did in the other parts of the facility.

When he reached his Animus room, Victoria was already there, and he rolled in as casually as he could.

"Good morning," he said.

She got up from her computer and smiled. "I can always count on you to be the first one here, Sean."

He didn't know if that was a compliment, or a dig, or some combination of the two. "Can I go in today?" he asked.

"Of course," she said. "But I think yesterday was a useful and necessary break for you, don't you? I might build a few more such days into your schedule."

Sean wanted to argue with that, but decided to save it for later. Right now, he just wanted to get into the simulation, and he was afraid if he put up any kind of fight, or seemed too eager, the doctor would change her mind about today.

He wheeled himself over to the Animus ring, and Victoria seemed to have finally learned not to offer to help him. His legs were one thing, but his arms were strong enough to get him most anywhere he needed to go. He got into position and put the brakes on his wheels. Then he lifted himself into the Animus ring and down into the harness, where his legs dangled above the exoframe platforms. From there, Victoria clasped his feet in place and strapped in his arms and hands, then hooked him up to all the machines that monitored his brain and his heart.

She was moving slowly today, but he said nothing, keeping outwardly calm and patient with each of the straps.

"There," she finally said. "I think we're ready."

"Okay," he said. "New York City, here I—"

"Actually . . ." Victoria moved away from him toward one of the computer monitors. "We won't be sending you back into Tommy Grayling's memories again."

"What?" Sean spun himself around within the ring to face her. "Why not?"

"It doesn't seem to be a healthy environment for you anymore—"

"What do you mean? How is it unhealthy?" Sean heard the answer to that question in his own voice, the impatience and anger, but it was too late to stop it.

Victoria folded her hands in front of her waist. "I know we've disagreed about your use of the Animus, Sean, but—"

"That's because you don't understand," Sean said. "You want to stop me."

"Please let me finish—"

"I don't want to let you finish," Sean said. "I want to go into Tommy Grayling's memories."

The door to the room *whooshed* open, and Isaiah stalked in wearing a black suit made of a fabric that seemed to absorb light. "I think you ought to listen to Dr. Bibeau, Sean. And show her the respect she is due."

Sean hadn't seen the Aerie director in over a week, and this sudden appearance stopped him from speaking, distracting him from his anger.

Isaiah nodded toward Victoria. "Please continue, Dr. Bibeau. I believe Sean will listen now."

She made eye contact with Sean, and though he glowered at her, he kept his mouth shut.

"I was going to say that we believe the benefit of the Grayling simulation has plateaued. The Animus isn't here for your entertainment. We would like to give you a range of experiences, in different ancestors."

"Why?" Sean asked.

She looked down at her security blanket of a tablet. "It is too early to go into more detail, but suffice it to say, we believe—"

"Why?" Sean asked again.

Victoria turned to Isaiah.

The director regarded them both with a sober expression. "We may as well tell him. I think he's mature enough to handle it."

"Handle what?" Sean asked.

Victoria pulled up her tablet again, hugging it to her chest like a shield. "There have been some interesting changes in your neurology. Specifically in your motor cortex."

"My motor cortex?" Sean did not want to leap too far ahead of them, but it was hard not to hope where they might be going. "What kind of changes?"

"Let me be clear," Isaiah said. "We are not talking about restoring your ability to walk with your own legs."

Sean felt himself retracting a bit from them. "Then what are you talking about?"

Victoria cleared her throat. "The Animus simulation is activating your motor cortex in ways it hasn't been since the accident that left you paralyzed. Essentially, that part of your brain has been starved of input from your legs. Until now."

Sean looked down at the exoframe supporting his feet and legs. "So what's that doing?"

"We're more interested in what it *could* do," Isaiah said. "The Templars, through Abstergo, have interests in multiple industries, including medicine. We're hoping that we might use the data we're gathering from you to better understand the brain of a paralyzed patient."

"What could you do with that?" Sean asked.

"Eventually"—Victoria cast a sidelong glance at Isaiah—"at some point in the future, we *might* be able to develop uniquely neuro-responsive prosthetics."

"What does that mean?" Sean asked.

"Right now," Isaiah said, "responsive prosthetics are quite limited. They take months to learn to use, they're unwieldy, and they're unavailable to those with spinal cord injuries. We're hoping to develop something new. Something revolutionary. A prosthetic that the patient would *already* know how to use, because we will have programmed it to their unique neurology. The prosthetic will already know how to be a part of that patient's body."

Sean felt as though his heart, his breathing, and everything in him had stopped, even though the computer monitor chimed through the silence with his vitals. "I could walk again?"

"Not with your own legs," Isaiah said. "With a prosthetic. But I want to caution you that we are still many years away from that." He pointed to the floor. "We're in the basic science stage here. For now, *you* are the basic science stage."

"So what do you want me to do?" Sean asked.

Victoria stepped toward him. "We want to observe you in a wide range of genetic memories. As many ancestors as we can. We want to study the total flexibility of your motor cortex. We've learned everything we can from Tommy Grayling."

"Oh," Sean said.

He'd become attached to the giant policeman in a way he never had with anyone else in his life. Sean had learned Tommy's beat, and he'd become friends with his fellow patrolmen on the Broadway Squad. He'd been with Tommy through brawls and injuries and heartbreak. He'd retired from the force and gone to London with Tommy as a Pinkerton agent, and he'd learned about himself with and through Tommy's strength.

"Can I still go into Tommy's memories? Sometimes?"

"Perhaps," Isaiah said. "When it doesn't interfere with the research."

"We'll notify your parents about all this, of course," Victoria added.

Sean didn't really need to think about it. He would help Isaiah and Abstergo however he could. It was just hard to say good-bye to a life that felt as though it had become his own. But he finally nodded, to himself as much as Victoria and Isaiah.

"Okay," he said. "Then who's next?"

Victoria swiped her tablet. "We're going to go back a little farther in your ancestry. Ireland, late eighteenth century."

"Okay," Sean said. "Okay, let's do it."

"Excellent," Isaiah said, smiling. "You, Sean, are destined for great things. We're going to make history, the three of us."

Sean was almost embarrassed how much it meant to hear that. After the accident, it didn't seem as though anyone expected anything from him, and any achievement, no matter how small or normal for someone who could walk, made him a hero. It felt good to be valued for something real, and something only he could do.

"Thank you," he said.

"Thank *you*," Isaiah said. "And now, I'll leave you in Dr. Bibeau's capable hands." He strode across the Animus room and out the door.

Sean adjusted himself in the harness, and waited patiently as Dr. Bibeau went about rechecking all the equipment connections. Then she returned to the computer monitors and went to work. Sean looked up at the ceiling, listening to her tapping and typing, excited by what this new simulation would be like, and what it might mean.

"All right," Victoria said a few minutes later. "I'm preparing to bring the Parietal Suppressor online. Are you ready?"

"Ready," Sean said.

Victoria came over and placed the helmet over his head, enveloping him in a shroud of sight and sound, cutting him off from the rest of the world. Compared to Monroe's Animus, the first time using this machine had been like stepping out of a horse and buggy and into a Ferrari.

Can you hear me, Sean? Victoria asked.

"Yes."

We're all set out here. Are you ready?

Sean took a deep breath. This was the only part about the Animus he didn't like, but he closed his eyes. "Ready."

Try to relax. Loading the Memory Corridor now . . .

Once, on vacation, when Sean was five years old, he fell into a river swollen with spring rain. The raging current swept him away before anyone could grab him. His memories of the incident came mostly from what his parents had told him later, but partly from what he actually remembered. The part he remembered wasn't much, but it had stayed with him. A feeling of total powerlessness against this *thing*. This living wall of water he couldn't fight that tumbled him and pulled him and completely overwhelmed him.

That was what the Parietal Suppressor felt like.

His uncle had been fishing farther downstream and managed to snatch Sean from the river. But his uncle wasn't here now, and this wasn't a river. The torrent was inside Sean's own head.

The Memory Corridor flashed into existence around him, blinding at first, but quickly settled into a formless glow, like a foggy day where you can't find the sun.

Parietal insertion in three, two, one . . .

The wave smashed into him.

CHAPTER FOUR

G race felt the same way Sean did. Or, at least, the same way she assumed he might feel. She didn't really know, because they hadn't exactly talked about it, but she thought he might be here at the Aerie for reasons similar to hers, even though people on the outside probably wouldn't find their connections obvious.

She watched him as he left the lounge, and then David started talking about his simulation in the memories of their great-grandpa, who'd served with the 302nd back when the military was still segregated, flying his P-51 Mustang.

"They have three colored lights under the tip of the right wing, to flash code signals to the ground. Red, green, and amber." He grinned, and then said, "the ultimate flight simulator," for maybe the fiftieth time.

"Red, green, and amber?" Grace said. "This isn't some computer game. We're not here to have fun."

"But it is fun," David said. "Why do you have to ruin everything, Grace?"

Grace was only half listening to him, thinking instead about Sean, and watching Natalya as she stared at the door, probably thinking about Sean, too. Grace didn't know exactly what had happened between them, but Sean got fidgety and quiet whenever Natalya was around. It was obvious he liked her, but Grace couldn't tell how Natalya felt about him. That girl kept so much to herself she was like a tortoise. You could see her head and her feet and that was about it.

So they sat there, and Grace sipped her coffee, letting David ramble until his eggs got cold.

"What about the racism?" Natalya finally asked him.

David got quiet. "I get mad about that. We get harassed by some of the white fighter squadrons, even though we're better than they are. Some of the white bomber squadrons refuse us as escorts. It doesn't matter how well we fly, people assume we can't be good pilots because we're black."

"I'm sorry," Natalya said.

David just nodded.

Grace didn't point out that David was speaking in the present-tense "we." That happened to all of them. It could still get confusing for her if she didn't work hard to keep it straight. She assumed that was partly what Victoria's weekly therapy sessions were for.

Natalya turned to Grace. "What about your new simulation?"

David smirked. "Grace is a gold miner."

Natalya eyebrows went up. "Really?"

"A gold *trader*, actually," Grace said. "He's from West Africa in the fourteenth century. His people were important in the medieval kingdoms of Ghana and Mali. That's what my dad says anyway."

"Wow," Natalya said. "Can we trade ancestors?"

"Sure," Grace said. At least Natalya's ancestor was supposed to have contact with a Piece of Eden. "I'd rather be doing what we came here to do."

Natalya paused. "And I'd rather not kill people."

Grace could see it wasn't meant as an attack against her personally. It was true that the thought of killing people in the simulation didn't bother Grace as much as maybe it should. But then, at least one of her ancestors, Eliza, was an Assassin. Victoria hadn't let Grace get anywhere near those genetic memories again.

"You really trust them?" Natalya asked.

"Who?" Grace asked.

"Isaiah and Victoria."

"I know they're offering us the chance to do something important," Grace said.

"Is that why you came back?" Natalya asked.

The answer to that question was more complicated than a simple "yes," but that was all Grace gave her.

In the beginning, with Monroe, Grace's only goal had been to get her and her brother home safely. Then the Templars had caught them, or rescued them, depending on which way you looked at it. The agents had brought them to this Abstergo facility and explained everything. How the Templars has been waging a secret war with the Assassins throughout all of history.

They'd explained the Templar mission to achieve a stable and peaceful world, where progress could be encouraged and driven forward.

Of course, then Grace's parents had come, and her dad had taken them both home immediately. David had objected, and Grace had, too, a little. But that was just how their dad was. He was a welder, and he'd been laid off more than once. He wasn't inclined to trust any corporation of Abstergo's size and wealth. Right after they got home there'd been another gang shooting, this one just two blocks away. Grace's parents did their best to keep the family safe, and Grace did her best to steer David away from trouble, but in the wrong place at the wrong time, none of that mattered. So their dad had sent them back to the security of the Aerie, and if David didn't start taking this seriously, Grace worried Abstergo would kick them both out of the program.

"Can we get going?" David asked, his plate empty.

"Sure," Grace said.

"You coming, Natalya?" David asked.

She shook her head. "You go on ahead."

So they said good-bye to her and left her in the lounge, making their way through the glass walkways to the Animus hall. She left David in his room with a tech and went to her own. A tech waited for her, too, but no Victoria.

So Grace waited.

And waited.

It was some time before Victoria came in, a little out of breath.

"So sorry, Grace. It's been a somewhat complicated morning. Are you ready to venture to West Africa?"

The waiting had left Grace irritable. "The Piece of Eden isn't there."

"You've only spent a few hours in those memories," Victoria said. "Timbuktu was a major hub of trade."

"It just seems like a waste of time," Grace said.

Victoria sighed and rubbed her forehead with her thumb and index finger. "I know you're impatient. But there is no other way. The data we pulled from Monroe's files is incomplete. If we had his Animus core, we would know exactly where to send you."

"So you haven't found him?"

"No."

"What about Owen and Javier?"

"You would know if we had. But the information we do have leads us to conclude that some of your ancestors had contact with the prongs of the Trident. We're doing the best we can with what we have, correlating with historical data, cross-referencing with your friends, trying to narrow it down. That all takes time."

Grace stepped into the ring and climbed into the harness. "I wish I could take Natalya's place. She doesn't even want to go. And she's the best bet right now, isn't she?"

"I admit, it would be nice if we could send you into her memories. But this Animus is much faster, and more stable and reliable than using Helix."

"So I just have to wait and do nothing."

"Not *nothing*."

"If feels like nothing."

"Why does it feel that way?"

Grace noticed a change in Victoria's posture as she switched from scientist-mode to shrink-mode. The woman's head now tilted a little, her eyes very soft and earnest. But Grace wasn't in the mood for therapy.

"Never mind. Let's just do this. West Africa, it is."

Victoria hesitated. "Are you sure? We can talk about this."

"I'm good." Grace readied herself. "Maybe I'll find something this time."

"If you're sure," Victoria said, turning slowly toward the computers. "I'll bring up the simulation where you left off yesterday." Then she hooked Grace up to the exoframe and all the hardware, established her baseline vitals for the day, and placed the helmet over her head.

Are you ready?

"Ready."

Loading the Memory Corridor in three, two, one . . .

Brilliant sparks flared in Grace's mind, and in the next moment she was standing in that familiar void of misty forms that came in and out of view without ever settling on anything fully recognizable.

How are you doing?

"Just fine."

The simulation is prepared. Just say the word.

Grace closed her eyes, waiting for the Parietal Suppressor to break through the wall around her mind like a battering ram. "Ready."

Parietal insertion in three, two, one . . .

The battering ram hit her, and it felt as if it split her skull right open, but that feeling gradually passed, replaced by a very weird sensation of floating, of being everywhere and nowhere at the same time. It was like there wasn't any difference between her and the world around her. The boundaries between her thoughts, her body, and the matter that made up the universe had become smudged and blurred.

Loading genetic identity in three, two, one . . .

The walls around Grace's mind returned, and the entire weight of the world slammed back into place. She staggered a bit, and looked down at her ancestor's body.

Masireh was a slender man. He wore sandals, and robes, with a sash around his waist, and a dagger. A cap covered his head, and he stood outside Grace's consciousness. She felt him waiting there, and though it was still difficult for her, she had become practiced at opening the gate to allow him into her thoughts.

It helped that she already knew him from the day before. His wife and his children. His trade and his world. He was actually a lot like her dad.

Take a few moments to—

"I'm ready."

Okay then. Loading full simulation in three, two, one . . .

The gray of the Memory Corridor became saturated with shades of tan and brown, and a breeze carried sand into Grace's eyes and mouth. The fine grit of it collected in the creases near her eyes. Then she was standing in a street of Timbuktu.

The buildings around her seemed to have been sculpted from the desert, their smooth walls made of mud brick and sand. Palm fronds and grasses thatched their roofs, and over the top of them, Grace could see the mosque, its tower studded with wooden beams, like the spines of a cactus. A white sun pressed down on all of it with the heat of a clothes iron, and Grace found it hard to breathe.

A camel bellowed behind her, and she hurried out of its way. The beast carried its owner's load of salt, which had become a very lucrative commodity, though not as lucrative as Masireh's gold trade.

Grace turned full access over to him, and he resumed walking toward his destination, a meeting with a merchant from Marrakech. Masireh carried with him the hope for a possible new trade relationship with this merchant. Such would give him more direct access to the Spaniards and other Kafir kingdoms to the north. There were some who opposed doing business with Jews and Christians, but Masireh tempered his own faith with pragmatism.

Along the way, he passed through the luxury goods market and stopped to admire a bolt of fine silk from Persia. The red fabric flowed and slipped between his fingers almost like water, and he made a plan to purchase it on his way home.

The Marrakech merchant had lodged himself in an inn at the edge of town, and while it might have been more fitting for the man to present himself at Masireh's home, the offense was forgivable in the interest of business.

When Masireh reached the inn, its keeper directed him around the back toward a pavilion where the merchant and several of his men had situated themselves.

"Do you know him?" the innkeeper asked, his left eye narrowed.

"I know of him," Masireh said, and walked toward the meeting.

The merchant was a solidly built man, dressed in very fine robes, with much lighter skin than Masireh's, and a lengthy beard. "Peace," Masireh said as he approached the pavilion.

"Welcome, I am honored," the merchant said, and bade Masireh to sit upon a very fine cushion. "I have heard of your high reputation, both the quality of your gold, and the integrity of your dealings."

"You humble me," Masireh said.

The merchant's men moved to stand at the edges of the pavilion, stationed along the sides and corners, forming a circle. That didn't seem to bother Masireh, but it gave Grace a twinge of misgiving.

"Please," the merchant said, pointing toward a pot upon a charcoal brazier. "Let me offer you some tea."

Masireh bowed his head. "I thank you."

The merchant poured, and Masireh drank, and for the next hour their conversation circled wide around the true reason for their meeting, discussing instead where the merchant had recently traveled, and how he found the journey from Marrakech. Only after they had boiled the tea leaves three times did they turn to the matter at hand.

"You have regular buyers?" Masireh asked.

"I do," the merchant said. "And they are eager to make an agreement with me to obtain your gold."

"I am eager to do business with them," Masireh said.

"There is only one requirement upon which they are quite insistent."

Masireh leaned forward. "And what is that?"

The merchant hesitated. "I trust you, Masireh. It pains me to even bring this matter to you, but my buyers would like assurances that your supply of gold will meet their needs. It would do them no good if your mines should fail tomorrow, leaving them to seek a new source of gold elsewhere."

"I take no offense," Masireh said. "But I assure you, my mines will continue to produce gold long after I am gone, and my grandchildren are holding meetings like this one with your grandchildren."

"For myself, I believe you. But my buyers insist that I inspect the mines, myself."

Grace felt another twinge, but this time, so did Masireh. He shifted on the cushion, which had started to feel less comfortable. The pavilion had become quite hot as well, shaded though they were.

"I'm afraid that isn't possible," Masireh said. "The locations of the mines of Wangara are closely guarded secrets. I believe you know that."

The merchant nodded. "Indeed I do. And I would not ask such a thing were my buyers at all moveable on the question."

"Then they will be disappointed," Masireh said, blinking. His vision had become somewhat blurry, possibly from the brightness of the sun. Grace knew otherwise, and if she could have, she would have gotten Masireh to his feet and walked him quickly away before it was too late. But she knew doing so would change the memory, which would desynchronize her from the simulation, kicking her out. With the Parietal Suppressor bombarding her brain, desynchronization was an extremely unpleasant experience.

"Is there nothing I can do to persuade you?" the merchant asked.

"Nothing." Masireh felt as though someone had wrapped a blanket around his head, and even though Grace wanted to scream, his words came very slowly. "I . . . hope this won't be an . . . insurmountable obstacle."

The merchant smiled at him. "I think we can come to an arrangement."

Masireh looked down at his empty tea cup, and only then realized he had been poisoned. As he slumped to the carpet, he watched the shadows of the merchant's men closing in upon him, and then the shadows swallowed him.

"He's unconscious," Grace said, floating in a darker void than the Memory Corridor.

Yes, he is, came an unfamiliar voice.

"Who're you?"

This is Anaya. I'm a technician. We've met before. Dr. Bibeau is with Natalya at the moment. Are you okay?

"I'm fine," Grace said. "We just have to wait a minute." This had happened before. When her ancestor was sleeping or unconscious, the simulation lapsed into a kind of nothingness, but with the way time flowed faster in the Animus, it never lasted long. But now Grace was actually worried about Masireh, and eager to find out what had happened.

It looks like he's coming to, Anaya said.

Grace focused back in, and a brilliant night sky stuffed with stars soon drove the smoky gray away. The Milky Way stretched overhead like a dust storm in space, and Grace realized Masireh was lying on his back. Once again, she opened the door of her mind and turned what was hers over to him.

Masireh tried to sit up, but found his hands and his feet were bound. His movement seemed to bring someone toward him, though. The desert sand whispered against the person's sandals, and a moment later, the merchant stood over him.

He'd been eating something, and he kept chewing for a moment. "I'm sure you know what happens next," he finally said.

"You release me and then you crawl back to Marrakech to face your disappointed buyers," Masireh said.

The merchant laughed. "There are no buyers. You know that."

Masireh smiled back at him. "Yes, I know that."

"You're going to take me to your mines."

"No, I'm not."

"Then we will kill you."

"I would not be the first Wangaran to die this way. I shall not be the last."

Grace felt Masireh's heart pounding, even if outwardly he tried to remain calm. He had no idea where they were, but given the night's darkness, he'd been unconscious for hours, and they might have taken him miles from Timbuktu. After they'd poisoned him, they'd likely just rolled him up in the carpet and thrown him over a camel. His wife was probably wondering where he was. His sons would be out looking for him throughout the city.

"You won't be able to show your face in Timbuktu again," Masireh said. "Where would you even sell the gold?"

"I have partners," the merchant said. "It will be easily done."

"I wonder if they know they're dealing with the sort of man who would poison another man's tea."

"It wouldn't matter," the merchant said. "Gold is gold. And you will take us to your mines. I will not ask you again."

"Then you are learning," Masireh said.

The merchant drew a knife from within his robes that Masireh recognized as his own. Then the merchant bent down and sliced the blade across Masireh's cheek. A quick, casual stroke, and Masireh felt the hot, sticky flow of his blood, and then the pain.

"I won't give you an easy death," the merchant said.

"Is death ever easy?" Masireh asked, licking the side of his mouth where his blood had run. Grace could taste the iron.

"I admit," the merchant said, "you are braver than I expected you to be."

Masireh said nothing. In truth, he did not think himself brave, and Grace felt his terror, even as she tried to reassure herself that he would live through this. He had to, or else he couldn't have passed this experience on in his genetic memory. But what would he go through before then?

"I am going to get some sleep," the merchant said. "But I don't think you will. You will spend the night thinking about what I will do to you tomorrow, and then in the morning, I will do something much worse if you don't take me to your mines."

"How long will I have to contemplate?" Masireh asked.

"Five hours until dawn," the merchant said. "Plenty of time."

Before Masireh could say anything more, his captor walked away, reopening the view of the stars, and Masireh lay there studying them. Since he had just cleverly learned the hour, he was able to find his position before long. One didn't traverse the shifting deserts without a constant map. It seemed they were ten miles west of the city, heading toward the great river basin where the earth's riches were found.

Masireh tested his bindings again, but found them unyielding, and the cords had begun to dig into his wrists. He craned his neck in all directions, and found his ties were staked to the ground. There was no escaping them.

The merchant and his men had set up a camp a few yards away, but without tents. They lay around the fire, their murmurs occasionally marked by laughter, their camels a shield from the wind. Masireh looked back up at the sky, offered a prayer to Allah, and after that, Grace followed him around as it seemed he paced the confines of her mind, thinking within her thoughts.

CHAPTER FIVE

fter Grace and David left, Natalya took as long eating
her breakfast as she could, long enough to wonder if
Isaiah or Victoria would come looking for her. They
didn't, and eventually she sighed and made her way
slowly toward her Animus room, stopping along the way to step
outside and admire the trees and breathe the fresh air from a
small, unlocked balcony.

The slanted morning light hit the pine needles on the forest
floor, and a light breeze set the tops of the trees swaying as if to
music. Something gentle, like the third movement in Respighi's
Pines of Rome, a piece her dad always liked. She closed her eyes
and smelled the air, felt the goose bumps rise on her arms from
the chill. If she wanted to, she could climb down from the balcony and take off running into the woods, down the mountain.

Why did that feel like it would be an escape? Natalya really wasn't a prisoner here. None of them were.

That's what made this experience confusing.

Monroe had said the Templars were ruthless and not to be trusted. That they sought to dominate and control the world, repressing free will. But that hadn't been the case so far. Natalya was here because she had seen the look on her parents' faces when Isaiah had told them about the compensation if she stayed. Her mom and dad would never have *made* her stay, but participation in Abstergo's "research study" meant they wouldn't have to work quite so hard, not to mention the "educational benefits" they saw, so Natalya had reassured them that she wanted to stay, even though she wasn't sure at all.

When she thought about Bayan's simulation, she almost wished she had let them take her home.

Someone knocked on the glass door behind her, and Natalya turned. Isaiah stood inside, on the other side of the door, motioning as if to ask permission to join her.

She nodded, and he stepped out onto the balcony, breathing deeply through his nose.

"I made sure to have many areas like this built around the Aerie," he said. "Places of calm, for reflection and meditation."

"It's nice," Natalya said.

He stepped up next to her and leaned forward, resting his forearms on the railing. "I wondered if you would avoid the Animus today."

Natalya said nothing.

"It's natural," he said. "And I think I was a bit impatient yesterday, and hard on you. I apologize if that's the case."

Natalya shrugged.

"Do you need a day off?" he asked.

Natalya stopped and thought about that, a bit surprised that Isaiah had offered it. But she realized she'd reached her avoidance's point of diminishing returns, and that putting it off from here would just make it harder. "I can do it," she said.

Isaiah nodded. "When you're ready, then." He turned and reentered the building, leaving her alone on the balcony for another few minutes.

Then she followed after him, and soon reached her Animus room. Neither Isaiah nor Victoria was waiting there for her, which she found curious, considering how important her simulation had seemed to them yesterday. Maybe one of the others had found the third Piece of Eden in their simulation. If that were the case, it would certainly help Natalya to share some of the pressure.

Sometime later, Victoria came in, apologizing for keeping Natalya waiting. Apparently, Sean and Grace had needed some extra attention. Natalya put that aside to perhaps ask them about another time.

Victoria fixed her with Professional Compassion gaze. "Are you ready?"

"I'm ready," Natalya said.

"What you are going through is probably not unlike PTSD," she said. "Post-Traumatic Stress—"

"I know what it is," Natalya said. But maybe there was something to that. Last night, she'd woken up at three thirty in the morning all sweaty, thinking that a Song dynasty bomb had just gone off.

"You're experiencing trauma on two levels. Your level as an

observer, and your ancestor's level as a survivor. Perhaps we can talk about that later?"

Natalya nodded. "Maybe."

"It's important that you let me know if you start experiencing anything . . . unusual. Outside the simulation, I mean."

"Like what?"

"Flashbacks. Vivid dreams. That sort of thing. Okay?"

Natalya found everything about this conversation unsettling. "Okay."

"Natalya." Victoria positioned herself to make direct eye contact. "I . . . I truly do have your best interest in mind. I hope you know that."

The doctor's sudden intensity unsettled Natalya even more. "Thanks," she said, but it came out as a question.

"I once went through a very difficult time. The Templars brought me through it. We can help you. Remember that." Victoria pulled away. "And now, let's get you situated."

She went to the computer, Natalya climbed into the harness at the center of the Animus ring, and a few minutes later, an electromagnetic sledgehammer went to work on the back of her head, and shortly after that, she was sharing the stage of her mind with Bayan, about to launch a frontal assault on an impregnable fortress. Natalya was reminded of that saying, the one where an unstoppable force meets an immovable object, and she wondered exactly how that scenario was supposed to end.

She looked around her, at Bayan's Jagun now gathered at the bulwarks with three hundred other warriors, prepared to charge with Wang Dechen against the city gate, and for more than one reason, she turned her mind entirely over to her ancestor. She didn't want the pain of desynchronization, but more than that, she didn't want any part in the killing that was to follow.

Bayan took command, rallying his troops with silent gestures. Wang Dechen's strategy depended upon stealth, to catch the Song unaware, and Bayan hoped this night the Horde would finally breach the walls.

Despite the hour, the air had not cooled, and Bayan's sweat soaked into the silk lining of his armor as they waited for Wang Dechen to give the command.

The general paced before the assembled force unmounted, his helmet gleaming. Horses would only alert the Song of their approach, so a silent foot charge would bring the army to the gates, along with their hooks and ropes. They had only to wait until the moon had set.

Bayan noticed the captain of a nearby Arban, a man he knew, and remembered that Chen Lun belonged to his company. Bayan looked and found the Tangghut warrior among the ranks, appearing just as pathetic and frightened as he had before.

Natalya could only pity the man from behind the curtain of Bayan's disdain. She felt as Chen Lun did, and wanted no part of this, even though she knew Bayan's mind, and the world that had shaped it. She knew of Tengri, the Sky-Father, and Eje, the Earth-Mother, who had sent the Mongols out from the steppes to subjugate the world. She felt Bayan's surety, that if the gods did not want this conquest, the rule of the Great Khan would fail. Natalya understood, but understanding it did not mean she condoned it.

Before the moon had set, a dense formation of clouds had advanced across the sky, overcoming the stars and smothering the moon. Wang Dechen gave the order, and the signal flags went up, sending his order silently down the ranks. The Horde marched, leaving the safety of the bulwarks, keeping to the trees, and staying silent, following the rise and fall of the wet terrain.

When they reached the base of the mountain, Wang Dechen gave another order, and the signal flags spread the halt command down the line. Then the flags called the infantry forward, including Bayan's unit, followed by the archers, and the ascent began.

The trees and boulders strewn across the mountain's face made it difficult to maintain the customary order of their line, and the wet leaves of the undergrowth painted Bayan's face. The moon had yet to reappear by the time the infantry reached the city's outer stone wall, and Bayan knew then that Tengri was with them.

Wang Dechen sent another order by flag up to the front, ordering the infantry to prepare to assault, and the archers to ready their arrows. Bayan felt cold battle fire burning through his arms and legs, his sword eager for blood, and Natalya wished there were some way she could escape the confines of her own shared mind.

Dozens of trained throwers came forward with their hooks and lines, and with the grace and precision of herdsmen roping their sheep, they sent their lines high into the air, up to the top of the wall, where the hooks lodged in stone.

In simultaneous motion, the throwers retreated and Bayan's line advanced to the ropes, where his warriors took hold and planted their feet on the wall. From there, they began the slow march up the vertical face, while the archers below them kept their bows pulled, sighting for watchmen on the wall who might sound the alarm.

Bayan made sure his entire unit was on the ropes before he took a line in his hands. The penalty for desertion was death, meted out not only to the deserter, but often to his commander as well. His first warriors had not yet reached the top of the wall, but they would soon, and Bayan ground his boots into the stones, which were slick with moss in places.

He had heaved his body ten feet off the ground when a warrior fell from above with a cry. Bayan looked down at him in confusion, and then five more warriors fell from ropes to either side, smacking into the ground with heavy thuds.

An arrow struck the wall near Bayan's left foot with the spark of metal against rock, and the twang of its flexible shaft. It had not come from the Mongol archers, nor had it come from overhead. The missile had come from the trees to the northwest.

Bayan looked, and he heard the next volley more than he saw it in the faint light, and then half the men on the ropes fell, pierced and screaming. There were so many of them, they landed on top of one another with the crack of breaking bones. A moment later, arrows rained down on them from the top of the wall as well.

Over the sounds of dying men, Bayan heard Wang Dechen's command, "Pull back to the line!"

"To Wang Dechen!" Bayan shouted to his men. Then he dropped to the ground, already smelling blood in the air, arrows whispering in his ears.

The Song devils had somehow known of the Horde's advance and circled a force around them, outside the wall. Bayan took cover behind a pile of bodies as his warriors descended, and near his hand he noticed Chen Lun's open eyes and bloody face. Bayan looked away from those eyes and scanned the forest, searching for their attackers, until the last of his men had reached the ground, and then he bolted with them toward the safety of the trees.

The forest gave them some cover, but arrows from the wall above and the dark woods to their left still managed to find occasional flesh.

Bayan ordered his men to stand firm, then searched out Wang Dechen and found him glowering a short distance away, a smear of blood upon his helmet.

"Our numbers are reduced by a third at least," Bayan said.

"Some of the ropes are still in place." Wang Dechen pointed through the trees. "If our archers could drive the enemy back from the wall, a few of us could reach the top."

"And what of the enemy at our flank?" Bayan asked.

"Take your company and march toward them. Engage them and draw their fire."

"Yes, General," Bayan said. He still wondered how the Song had managed their maneuver, but now was not the time to solve that problem.

He ducked back through the trees to his men, and after a quick scout he found three of his Arban captains and ordered them to round up what they could find of their units. A few minutes later, he had twenty men assembled, not a high number, but enough to accomplish what the general wanted done.

To Natalya, the new objective seemed like a suicide mission, but Bayan felt no hesitation and she could admire his bravery, even if she deplored what he was doing.

As Bayan crept forward, advancing on the enemy bowmen, he wished the moon would reappear. The Horde had lost the advantage of surprise, and the darkness now gave a new advantage to the Song, who knew the terrain.

Bayan drew his sword, quietly, his hands slippery with either water, sweat, or blood, or perhaps all three. His men armed themselves as well, and they closed the distance without disturbing the foliage, until they caught sight of the first archer. He stood behind a tree, a shadow with a bow. The night and the forest kept the others hidden, but they had to be close by.

Bayan silently ordered his company to fan out, to create the illusion of greater numbers, and when they were sufficiently scattered, he gave the signal.

All twenty men howled, ripping the silence open at the belly, and rushed forward. Bayan charged the Song archer, who had spun around at the sound, a look of shock on his face as Bayan ran him through with his sword. A moment later, arrows came at them, but not well aimed. That meant Wang Dechen could stage his second assault on the wall without the pressure at his flank.

Bayan and his men ducked and weaved through the trees, rushing and retreating, never offering the archers an easy target. When Bayan spied another of the bowmen, firing arrows haphazardly, he circled wide around the enemy and rushed him, but before he reached his target a second shadow leapt out at him.

Bayan dodged the knife thrust and turned to fight his new attacker as moonlight suddenly filled the space between them, the clouds having retreated. Bayan saw the man was a veteran, his face creased with years of battle, but noted at the edge of his sight that the first bowman had raised an arrow.

Bayan ducked reflexively, but then one of his men was there, engaging the archer hand to hand. Bayan turned back to the veteran as the man bore down on him, and barely deflected another knife thrust with his sword. The enemy pulled back before Bayan could counter with a strike of his own.

Now it was Bayan's turn to charge, and with his sword, he had the longer reach. But the veteran proved extremely agile, escaping Bayan's blade again and again, each time coming close to landing an attack with his own weapon. In the closeness of their battle, Bayan noticed the man was missing most of his left ear.

A sudden, fierce swipe at Bayan's shoulder would have cost him his arm, had his armor not taken most of the attack. Bayan grunted and realized this old warrior was his better, but he refused to retreat, even if it meant his death.

He dodged away to prepare for another thrust and—

An explosion shook the ground and rent the forest with a blinding flash. The city had brought its artillery to bear on Wang Dechen, and Bayan knew the battle was now lost.

The veteran seized the moment of distraction to attack, but Bayan had expected that and prepared for it. He feinted away, as if caught by surprise, drawing the veteran forward, and then spun around with his sword, driving it into the man's side, almost to the hilt. Within her mind, Natalya wanted to cry out.

It was a killing blow, the veteran's death almost instant, and Bayan jerked his weapon free of the fallen body.

The horn of retreat cut through the wood then. Bayan called to his men, and they withdrew from the fighting, pulling back to the main body of the Horde under scattered arrow shot. When Bayan reached the front line, he found it in chaos. Fallen, burning trees sent smoke and flames up into the sky, warriors racing back and forth, a group of them clustered around something on the ground.

When Bayan drew near them, he realized they surrounded Wang Dechen. The general had been terribly injured, with a ragged opening of armor and flesh across his chest, and a head wound pouring blood.

"Help me!" Bayan shouted, even though he knew either injury would be fatal. "We have to get him to safety!"

Two of the men bent to assist him, while the rest of the Horde fled back down the mountain. No Song forces left the safety of their fortress to follow them. It seemed they were aware of the Mongol false retreat, something for which, in this case, Bayan felt grateful.

When they drew near the bulwarks, runners saw them coming and raced into the camp, so that by the time Bayan reached the general's tent, the shaman already waited for them inside, wearing his mask and feathered headdress. He ordered the general placed on the ground before him, and he removed Wang Dechen's clothing and armor, administering to his wounds, all while he chanted and called on the gods and ancestor spirits.

"You must open the belly of an ox and place him inside it!" the shaman finally cried.

Several warriors rushed from the tent, and some minutes later, Bayan heard the bellow of an ox just outside. He then assisted the shaman in carrying the general from the tent. The beast already lay on its side, insensate, its throat cut. A large group of warriors had gathered, and one of the other commanders took his sword and opened the ox's belly, its intestines spilling out onto the ground. The sight of it filled Natalya with a different kind of horror than she had experienced in battle. This was a mix of revulsion and utter confusion, even though she knew that to Bayan, this ritual was not at all strange.

"Wang Dechen!" a voice shouted.

All turned to see the Great Khan rushing toward them, clad in golden armor, and all assembled there bowed low to him as they parted to let him through. His sixteen-year-old son, Asutai, strode beside him.

"He was injured by the Song artillery, my lord," Bayan offered, his head also down.

Möngke went to his general's side. "Help me with him."

Without hesitation, Bayan reached forward, and with the shaman and the Great Khan, they pushed Wang Dechen's body into the belly of the ox. After that, the shaman resumed his chanting and began to beat on his drum and dance.

"To lose him would be to lose my left and my right hand," the Great Khan said.

Bayan wasn't certain if Möngke was speaking to him directly, so he kept his head bowed and said nothing, his own hands and arms covered in oxblood.

But the Khan turned toward him. "Were you there?"

"I believe I know what happened, my lord."

"Tell me."

Bayan lifted his head. "The Song knew we were coming. Somehow they flanked us from outside the gate, and we were unaware until their arrows rained down. Wang Dechen tried to launch a second attack, but their cannon fire wounded him."

Möngke nodded, his whole body quivered with terrifying rage. "Get him to the temple at Jin Yun!" he shouted as he stormed away.

Bayan turned back to the general inside the ox. The rhythm of the shaman's drum had become frantic, his head shaking back and forth wildly as he crouched and danced. All watched him, hoping and praying as men brought a wagon and loaded up the ox with the general inside it, then rolled away toward the temple to the south.

Natalya felt Bayan's doubt, the first he had experienced since she had begun this simulation. Perhaps the gods were turning against the Great Khan, to take his greatest general from him. Perhaps they were not pleased with him for staying in this place through the hot and fetid summer months. It was said that some had advised against it, but Möngke had rebuffed them. Perhaps this was punishment for his arrogance. There had to be an answer for it. There had to be a reason.

These and other disturbances harried Bayan's mind. The question of where the Song archers had come from, in particular, refused to be ignored.

For now, though, he went to find Boke and make his report, after which he would see to his men and learn which of them he had lost.

How are you doing? Victoria suddenly asked, and Natalya felt a flood of gratitude at the sound of the doctor's voice. *Do you need another break?*

"Please," Natalya whispered.

It was the only way to get the blood off her hands.

CHAPTER SIX

Owen stood in the basement of the creepy Assassin house and pointed at the new Animus. "You want to send me to China?"

"Yes," Rebecca said. "The year 1259. The Templars recovered something from Monroe's data that leads them to believe Möngke Khan had a Piece of Eden."

"Möngke Khan?" Javier said.

Rebecca turned toward him. "The grandson of Genghis Khan. His grandfather was assassinated by Qulan Gal."

Javier folded his arms. "When you say assassinated . . ."

Griffin nodded. "One of ours."

"Monroe's data makes sense," Rebecca said. "The Mongol Empire continued to expand after Genghis Khan. It moved into

Russia and Persia. They were at Europe's doorstep, and most people at the time believed the Mongols were sent directly from hell as a punishment from God. It stands to reason the Khans had a little help from an incredibly advanced technology they couldn't possibly comprehend."

"I didn't even know I had Chinese ancestors," Owen said.

Rebecca nodded. "Most people would be very surprised at their own DNA. How interconnected we all are. Genghis Khan likely has sixteen million living descendants."

"So what happened in 1259?" Javier asked.

Rebecca walked over to the glass conference table. As she touched its surface, a hologram leapt up from the glass, like they did from Monroe's coffee table back in his warehouse. That seemed like a very long time ago to Owen.

The image before them now showed Earth, focused on an area of southern China. "In 1259, Möngke Khan attacked one of the last strongholds of the Song Empire." Rebecca pointed at a blinking point on the globe. "A place called Diaoyu Cheng, or Fishing Town. An impressive fortress. Möngke Khan died during the assault, which brought the expansion of the Mongol empire to a halt."

"So if he had one of the prongs—" Griffin said.

"It might be there," Rebecca said. "Or at least, that's the time and place we start looking."

Owen stepped toward the hologram, studying it. "So it's like New York. I'm going into the Animus to try to find this thing or figure out where it went."

"That's exactly right," Rebecca said. "Are you ready?"

"Sure," Owen said.

"What about me?" Javier asked.

Rebecca looked his way. "You sit tight for now."

"Sit tight?" Javier scowled. "Isn't there something I can do?"

"No," Rebecca said. "Not at the moment."

Javier obviously didn't like that, but if their positions were reversed, Owen wouldn't be happy, either. There wasn't anything he could do about it.

"How did Monroe figure all of this out?" Griffin asked.

Rebecca switched the hologram to an image of DNA, the double helix spiraling across their view. "There's nothing magical about the Trident. It's a piece of technology. Very, very advanced technology, but technology nevertheless. It seems the prongs put off a unique form of energy, or radiation, which interacts with human DNA. It leaves an impression behind, a genetic marker, and that gets passed on. We don't actually know what that marker is, but Monroe apparently figured it out. It's only a matter of time before the Templars do."

"Radiation?" Owen said. "It changed my DNA?"

"It seems so," Rebecca said. "We're still trying to analyze it."

"I wish Monroe was here to explain it," Owen said. He still didn't know what to make of Monroe. Who he was or where he stood.

"I'd like a word with him myself," Griffin said, but with frightening menace.

Rebecca switched off the hologram. "If you're ready, let's do this. I need to get going."

"I'm ready," Owen said.

They crossed the room to the new Animus chair, which

looked different from Monroe's design, much sleeker, and only slightly more comfortable. Owen sat down and settled into it.

"I've incorporated the new processor and blueprints," Rebecca said, "but there's a component to this machine I disabled."

"What component?" Owen asked.

"As near as I can tell," Rebecca said, hooking Owen up to various straps and wires, "Abstergo has developed a way to suppress the activity of the parietal lobes. That would make for an incredibly strong simulation, but I don't dare use it on you until I know more about it. It wouldn't do us any good to leave your brain damaged. So this will be a regular simulation, a lot like the ones you've already experienced. Got it?"

"Got it. I think I'm ready."

"Then let's do this." Rebecca began the process of hooking Owen up to the Animus.

"Good luck," Javier said.

"Wake me up if I'm drooling," Owen said.

Then Rebecca placed a helmet over Owen's head, covering his ears and his field of vision. It felt as if he had taken a dive into a dark tank of water exactly the same temperature as his body, filling his senses and cutting him off from the outside world.

Everything okay? Rebecca asked. *You read me?*

"Loud and clear."

I aim to please. There was a pause. *Okay, the Memory Corridor is loaded.*

"Punch it," Owen said.

All right, here we go.

Searing light flooded the emptiness of the helmet, painful for several moments, and Owen clenched his eyes shut. But gradually the pain subsided, and he opened his eyes, finding himself in the amorphous Animus waiting room. Nothing surprising about that. He'd been here before. He was surprised, however, when he looked down.

"I'm a woman."

Is that a problem?

"No," he said. "Just . . . an observation."

He settled into this ancestor, who was dressed in layers of black clothing, with embossed leather armor. She had a sword at her side, but also wore two gauntlets, one on each arm. One gauntlet held a hidden blade, and the other a wrist-mounted crossbow.

Owen held out both weapons in front of him. "She's an Assassin."

It would seem so. But we don't have any record of her from this time period.

"Is that normal?"

It's not terribly unusual. Templars steal or destroy our records whenever they find them. The passage of time doesn't help, either. Some records are simply hidden too well, even from us.

"I can feel her pressing down on me." That's how it was for Owen, like a weight on his mind to which he had to slowly surrender. "Is the simulation loaded?"

It will be in just a few more seconds.

Owen gave in enough to know his ancestor's name was Zhang Zhi. Her father was an Assassin, too.

Okay, it's ready. Just say the word.

"Word."

The void of the Memory Corridor appeared to catch fire and burn with electrical storm, scorching Owen's mind, but the mist gradually cleared with the pain, and he found himself sitting on a mat on the wooden floor. The walls around him appeared to be made of wood and bamboo screens, with a doorway to his right. It was a summer night, he knew that, and he grew more aware, from one moment to the next, as the full weight of Zhang Zhi settled over him.

The Mongols were at the gates. Her father had gone to fight them with the army. Cannon fire had filled the night. Her father had not returned.

Zhi tried to focus herself by practicing her Eagle Vision, a skill she had not yet mastered. Her father had trained her in the arts of hand-to-hand combat, various weapons, and the acrobatics Owen thought of as free-running. Zhi had achieved mastery of them all, but Eagle Vision continued to elude her. Even now, as she tried to extend her awareness, to discern the patterns in the air and the vibrations in the floorboards, she gained nothing from the exercise. She knew someone approached, their footsteps heavy, but knew nothing else about them or their intent. Given the events of the night, perhaps she did not want to know.

A moment later, a man cleared his throat in the doorway. She turned to see a soldier wearing lamellar armor of lacquered plates, his head bowed. "I am sent to bring you."

"Where?"

The soldier looked up. "To your father. It is not for me to say why."

Zhi rose to her feet. There were many reasons why her father would not have come himself, but each of them frightened her. She dug her heel into that fear and followed the soldier from the room and then from her father's house.

They followed the streets of Fishing Town, where life continued much as it always had, in spite of the siege, though at this time of night, everyone was indoors and asleep, the streets patrolled by soldiers. Fishing Town had all the food and water it needed. The only activities to have ceased in the last few months since the Mongols swept in were those connected with the larger countryside, such as trade.

They followed the main road out of town, the vacant Imperial Palace to the north, past the reflection of the moon in the Big Heaven Pool, toward the well-lit barracks, which seemed caught in a storm of commotion. Zhi's worry returned and increased with each step, her mouth dry, her chest hollowed out. The battle against the Mongols had obviously come to an end, but its aftermath remained.

"This way," the soldier said as they reached the barracks' perimeter. He led her to one of the inner buildings, and stopped at the doorway. "I'm sorry," he said. "Prepare yourself."

That confirmed what Zhi had almost kept herself from fearing. She entered the building, a single, large, rectangular room, and smelled blood. Doctors tended to wounded soldiers around the room, but she found her father among the dead.

General Wang Jian stood over him with somber reverence. Zhi dropped to her knees beside her father's body, at the general's feet, and wept.

Beneath the weight of the memory, Owen felt a suffocating swell of grief over the death of his own father. No one had summoned him the way they had Zhi. No general had paid his father honors. Instead, it was a cop in a suit who'd shown up at the door, sounding serious but not sad as he explained what had happened. Owen's father had suffered a ruptured appendix and died in prison.

That was it.

Gone.

No good-byes. No last I-love-you's. Just gone.

"He saved the city," General Wang Jian said.

Zhi sat up straight and wiped her eyes dry, and Owen did his best to dial back into her.

"What happened?" she asked.

"Our scouts discovered the Mongol army approaching," the general said. "We prepared for them. Your father took a hand-picked force down through the Feiyan Cave to attack the enemy flank. The northerners fell into the trap, and we repelled them. But a small detachment engaged your father and his men. The killing strike was nearly instant. He did not suffer. He saved the city."

Zhi looked down at her father's face. The deep creases. The scar where he had lost most of his ear in a battle many, many years ago. She felt tears returning, but restrained them until she could grieve in private.

"We will honor him," the general said. "I will personally see to his funeral and its expenses."

"Thank you," Zhi said. "He had great respect for you."

"Your father and I may often have been at odds, but I know he loved our people and our land." With a bow, the general went to see about his other men, the still living injured ones.

Zhi bent with her hands clasped tight in her lap and kissed her father's forehead. Then she took the gauntlet from his wrist, its hidden blade extended. Whoever had killed him had likely not had an easy time of it. She returned to the city, cradling that gauntlet, which would be her shrine to him in their home. *Her* home. The one she now lived in alone.

Only she wasn't alone when she arrived. From outside the door, she could sense that Kang was waiting for her, and she needed no Eagle Vision for that. Her father's old mentor smelled perpetually of fish.

"Come in," he said through the door. "We must talk."

Zhi marched in and found him on her father's favorite chair, the low one with the tall back and the round feet. The sight of this old man sitting cross-legged upon it infuriated her.

"I do not feel like talking," she said, standing near the doorway.

"If only your feeling could save our people," he replied, half his craggy face shadowed by the lantern beside him.

"He is gone because of you," she said. "You ordered him to—"

Kang actually laughed at her. "Is that what you believe? Because I think the Horde of the Khan would gladly take credit for his death."

Zhi wanted to blame him, and remain angry with him, but she knew he spoke the truth, and Owen found he identified with her. When his father died, he had wanted to blame his grandparents somehow. He was angry because they had never accepted his father, never allowed him to be anything other than the punk their daughter had dated in high school. But Owen had eventually admitted his death wasn't their fault.

"Come in all the way, Zhi," the old man said. "You cannot linger at the threshold forever."

She regarded him, and the only thing that moved her inward was the love her father had felt for his mentor. It was a love Zhi had never understood, but to honor her father, she would at least listen to what Kang had to say.

"There," he said as she took the barbarian seat opposite him. "First, I must correct you. I did not order your father to the wall."

Zhi stared at him. "You didn't?"

"No. I have always advised your father to leave the army to itself. Our Brotherhood works in different ways. But your father was never content to let good, brave men die, much to the credit of his honor."

She believed him, and with that revelation, much of her anger at the old man burned out, though its smoldering ashes remained.

"But his honor did not save him, did it?" Kang added.

With that, Zhi's anger flared up again.

"The mantle passes to you now," Kang said. "You must take your father's place. But how will you choose to honor him? Will you die a glorious death in a battle, as he did? Or will you find your own path?"

"I don't know what I will do."

"I did not ask the question expecting an answer tonight. I will leave you to think on it." He rose from the chair, took up his walking stick, and hobbled toward the door. "But I am now your Mentor, and I would see you not only honor your father's name, but the Brotherhood as well. You could save our people."

"How?" Zhi asked.

"Do what I cannot." From the doorway, the old man turned and said, "Be an Assassin."

Zhi sat in her chair long after he had gone, staring into the light of the lantern, remembering her father, maintaining a fragile belief that somehow he was not dead. Somehow, he would yet come home. The body she had seen was a mistake.

Owen remembered something like that, too. After the cop had left, and for the next two days, he begged his mom to take them to the prison for a visit. The police had made a mistake, and his dad would be there, alive. He finally stopped asking because it only made his mother cry, and eventually he had realized why. Denial never made anything better, and usually it made things worse when it finally imploded on itself.

Zhi came to that realization close to dawn, after the lantern had burned out, and she wept again as she lay down on her bed, holding her father's gauntlet, and when she finally made the decision Kang had asked of her, she fell asleep with tears in her eyes.

Owen fell into the simulation's gray nowhere. He'd been here before, with Varius.

Are you doing okay? Rebecca asked.

"Fine," Owen said, but it sounded as heavy as he felt.

Everything looks good from here. I'm going to turn things over to Griffin. I probably won't be here when you come out, so I'll say good-bye now. And good luck.

"Thanks," Owen said.

A moment passed, and then he heard Griffin's gruff voice in his mind. *You should be coming out of sleep soon.*

"Got it," Owen said.

Are you really doing okay? Javier is worried this simulation might be a bit rough for you.

"Tell him thanks, but I'm holding up."

Will do. A pause. *Looks like things are coming online.*

The charcoal smoke of the void cleared, and Zhi opened her eyes. It was late morning, another hot day, which she was glad for. Within the town, they had water and numerous pools, and shade, and the occasional breeze over the top of the mountain. Down below, the Mongols would have no relief from it.

She rose, washed her face, and drank some tea. Then she lifted a loose floorboard in her father's room and lowered his gauntlet into the darkness. After replacing the board, she went in search of the old man.

The city had been awake for some time, and by the soberness in the air she could tell that news of the previous night's battle had spread. Though Wang Jian had prevailed, the city would not be itself again until the Mongol Horde had withdrawn completely.

She left the main body of the town and followed the road, past the Big Heaven Pool, now swollen with the sky's blue, and past the engineers' workshop with its nine boilers, until she came to the Hu Guo Temple. Beyond it lay the Fishing Terrace, where legend said a giant had once pulled countless fish from the river below. Zhi crossed that stone plateau, and on its far side she found Kang sitting outside his hut, mending a net.

"I'm glad to see you," he said. "You reminded me of your father just now, as I watched your approach."

She didn't want to hear him speak of her father. For now, she had to hide her grief, even from herself, until after she had succeeded. "I have an answer for you."

"Oh?" he said without looking up from his knots. "And what answer is that?"

"I am going to kill Möngke Khan," she said.

His fingers ceased moving, and he draped the net over his knee. Then he looked up at her. "Say it again."

"I am going to kill Möngke Khan."

He smiled. "I believe you. And now your real training can begin."

CHAPTER SEVEN

S ean had just enjoyed a delicious meal, and his ancestor now stood by the fireplace, leaning against the mantel, staring into the flames. Recently remarried in his old age, he had come to his library for some quiet and solitude, while his young wife and his daughters had gone to their sitting room following supper. Brandon Bolster was an Englishman living on his estate in Ireland. He had a fine life, and Sean decided he could easily stay in this simulation for a long time, Piece of Eden or not.

The door to the library opened, and his son, Richard, walked in. "There's something you should see," he said. He hadn't eaten supper with the family, but then, his duties around the management of the estate often kept him away, sometimes for days.

"What is it?" Brandon asked.

His son held out a tattered piece of paper. "This was found nailed to one of the stable doors."

Brandon frowned and took the notice. It was written in a crude hand, with poor spelling, but made its meaning perfectly clear, even to Sean. "Not exactly the Ninety-five Theses, is it," Brandon said, chuckling.

Richard took the notice back and brandished it in front of Brandon's face. "This is serious, father. You can't ignore it. They've already killed cattle and torn down walls on some of the neighboring estates."

"I know that."

"Then what are we going to do?"

"What can we do? Are you suggesting we give in to their demands?"

"No." Richard looked down at the paper. "Not . . . all of them."

"Not *all* of them?" Brandon stepped away from the mantel. "But some of them?"

Richard shook his head. "I don't know anymore. When we converted that acreage to pasture, I knew it would upset some of the tenants and farmers, but I didn't think it would come to this."

"That is *our* land," Brandon said, snatching the notice from his son's hand. "We have a right to do with it what we will. And if we can make it more profitable by grazing cattle than raising crops, that's what we'll do, and damn these Whiteboy troublemakers to hell." He threw the notice into the fire, where it immediately burned to a black and fragile memory in ash.

"But we've taken their livelihood," his son said. "Some of them can no longer feed their families. We've given no thought to them."

Brandon inhaled deeply, calming himself. "And did we owe them a thought?"

"By law, or by honor?"

"Is there a difference?" Brandon asked.

"At times, I think there might be."

"I don't see it that way. What of the honor of this family? As stewards of this land, we have a duty to see it thrive, so that you and your children and your children's children will inherit a thriving estate. That is how our nation maintains peace and order."

His son looked down at his boots, and Brandon noticed they were caked in mud, like a common laborer. Richard hadn't bothered to remove them before coming into the house, but this was clearly not the time to note the oversight.

Within the current of Brandon's mind, Sean had let the memory carry him along, growing slowly aware of the situation his ancestor faced. In the wake of a changing economy in Ireland, many of the laborers, farmers, and tenants had found themselves without land to till, and secret societies had formed among the angry peasants. The Whiteboys, the Hearts of Oak, and others had been terrorizing the countryside, most recently in Brandon's county of Cork. They'd made demands for the use of the land, and threats of violence and destruction if their demands weren't met. Such was the notice Richard had found on the stable door.

"What would you have us do?" Brandon asked his son.

"Meet with them," Richard said. "Listen to them, and try to come to an understanding."

"Meet with them?" Brandon asked, feeling somewhat incredulous. "This is open rebellion! You would have us negotiate with these brigands?"

"They're farmers, Father, not brigands."

"They *were* farmers." Brandon turned away from the hearth, his back to his son. "This is what happens when good men find themselves angry and idle with drink in the pubs. This is not a people's movement. This is a mob."

Richard sighed. "The notice gave us until tomorrow night. I pray you will reconsider your attitude before then." With that, his son left the library.

"Empty threats," Brandon said to himself, feeling the heat of the fire against his back.

The next morning, after a sleepless night in which Sean found himself in and out of the gray void of unconsciousness, Brandon rose just before sunrise, dressed, and went for a walk about his land.

He took the north lane across the hill where his house stood, and followed it along the open pastures and fields, lined with their stone fences and hedgerows. Those walls were fairly new, built to keep his cattle enclosed. When he reached the edge of the hilltop, the road took a gentle dip down into a wooded glen. A blue morning mist filled it, swirling about the tops of the oak and yew. Brandon stopped here and sat upon the hedgerow, facing west, and he waited and watched.

Sean wasn't sure he had ever felt such contentment in his life, not even before the accident. It angered him to think there were some who sought to destroy this. His ancestor had inherited an estate that had been in his family for generations, and he had worked hard to improve upon it. What right did these drunk Whiteboys have to make their demands?

The light slowly changed as the sun rose at Brandon's back, lighting up the world, bringing the fields and hedgerows to life with vibrant color. Brandon would take the blue of this sky over any sapphire, and the green of these pastures over any emerald, and Sean felt the same way.

To his right, the mist down in the glen retreated into the shadows of the wood. As a younger man, Brandon had hunted there with his father, and he had then taken Richard hunting there in his turn. That was the order of things.

The sun was now high enough to warm Brandon's back. He closed his eyes for a moment, but then opened them at the sound of someone approaching.

Two herdsmen came down the road toward him carrying their staffs, a dog trotting at their heels, on their way to tend Brandon's flocks. They doffed their caps as they strode by, and bade him good morning, but Brandon noted something insolent in their eyes. Could they be members of this secret society? Working for him even as they plotted with the Whiteboys against him? That was the trouble with these things. Rebellion eroded trust and relations, sowing chaos, turning society against itself as surely as any pestilence or disease.

Brandon watched the herdsmen step through a gate and set off across the pasture, heading west. Where would they stand come evening, if the demands on that infernal notice hadn't been met?

Brandon rose from the hedgerow. He would not give in to such fears. He would not let these brigands turn him against his own. He refused to compromise the inheritance he had received and built upon, so he would stand against these rebels and give them no ground.

Within that memory, Sean stood with his ancestor. There wasn't even a risk of desynchronization, because he would have made the same choice. It was a drunk man with a car who had paralyzed him. Someone out of control. A man someone else should have stopped, but no one did. The way Sean saw it, Brandon was being that person, stepping forward to do what was right.

When Brandon reached the house, he called for his son, and a servant went to fetch him. Brandon waited in his library, and when Richard entered, he gave him the key to the cabinet where they stored the guns.

"Arm yourself and those you most trust," he said.

"Father?"

"We need to be ready, should the Whiteboys mean to make good on their threat tonight."

Richard held out the key. "This isn't war. You know these men."

"I thought I knew them," he said. "They severed ties with me when they nailed a threat to my stable door."

"They would argue that you severed ties with them when you evicted them."

"I won't have this argument with you, Richard." Brandon snatched the key back. "It seems as though you would simply step aside and let them burn this house to the ground as they have threatened to do."

"I would talk to them before it comes to that. I pray you will change your mind before nightfall."

His son marched from the library, and after he'd left, Brandon dropped into an armchair, already feeling tired. Sean stayed with him for the rest of that day as he made preparations. Brandon gave muskets to two groundskeepers, and a manservant who claimed to be a decent marksman. He tried to send his daughters and wife to stay with his sister in Kinsale, but they wouldn't hear of leaving him, and he had to admit that his wife was as good a shot as he was. He ordered the thatched roofs of the stables and barns wet down to prevent their burning too easily, and had pails of water arranged in every room.

Through all the preparations, Brandon's son remained absent. But as the family sat down to eat dinner, Richard finally walked in, and with a silent nod toward his father, he took his place at the table. Appetites proved light and the mood heavy. Each noise outside brought a general tension into the room until it was determined to be innocent.

After eating, Brandon's wife and daughters went to their drawing room, and he was about to go with them when his son laid a hand on his shoulder.

"Might we have a word in the library?"

Brandon nodded. "Certainly." He smiled at his wife, and followed his son, and when they were alone he asked, "Do you mean to fight, should it come to that?"

Richard stepped away from him, appearing affronted. "Of course I do. You're my father, and this is my home. Could you doubt my loyalty?"

"I hoped my faith would not be disappointed." Brandon stepped toward his son. "And it wasn't."

"We have our disagreements, but my place is at your side."

Now Brandon placed his hand on his son's shoulder. "Let's just hope the Whiteboy threat was idle."

"That is how I spent my day. Talking to those still friendly to us, trying to reassure them."

Brandon pulled his hand away. "What?"

"I didn't speak out of turn. I gave no promises or concessions. I simply tried to remind them of our goodwill."

Brandon could only admire his son's earnestness and optimism, and perhaps wish for some of it himself. "I'm sure your efforts were appreciated."

"Perhaps. Whether I did any good, however . . ."

Brandon smiled. "I judge a man by his intentions. Come, let's join your sisters."

They moved from the library to the drawing room, where Brandon experienced the same sensation of contentment he had that morning on the hill. Jane, his eldest daughter, was playing softly on the pianoforte, and the others were reading or conversing by warm lamplight. Brandon and Richard took seats for themselves, and they passed the next few hours pleasantly. When the time came for bed, his wife and daughters could not be persuaded to go up. They remained in the drawing room, while he and Richard barricaded the doors, and then patrolled the downstairs rooms, regularly checking the view from the windows.

Sean felt his ancestor's fear, and he shared in it. Everything was at stake. The constant tension gnawed at the older man's joints and muscles, causing unfamiliar pain for Sean as the night wore on. His previous simulation in the memories of Tommy Grayling had been a very different experience. Tommy was much younger and stronger than Brandon. But both men were brave and stubborn.

I think it's time to pull you out, Victoria suddenly said.

"What?" Sean asked. "Why?"

We have what we need from your motor cortex, and we're ninety-seven percent confident this ancestor never interacted with any piece of the Trident.

"Can I stay a little longer?" Sean asked. He wanted to see this memory through.

Victoria paused. *A few more minutes.*

"Thanks."

So Sean stayed in the simulation, and two hours before dawn, the watchmen alerted Brandon to a mob that was on its way up the road. That roused the household, and everyone took up positions, preparing for whatever was to come. Brandon ordered a gunman to each corner room, and through his own window, he could see the ruffians rushing forward in their white shirts, a few of the cowards in white hoods.

Some of them carried pitchforks and scythes, and many of them held torches. When they reached the house, they didn't even call for a parley. They just howled and hurled bricks.

Some of the projectiles broke through the windows, scattering shattered glass over the furniture and floor. Brandon had ordered those armed with muskets to exercise restraint as long as possible, fearing the way gunshot might inflame the mob.

"Let's hope their objective is only to intimidate," Richard said at Brandon's side.

"Let's hope."

But then men with torches marched toward the house. Brandon took aim at one of them, waiting, barely breathing.

With a cry, the assailants threw the torches at the broken windows, trying to land the flames inside the house.

At that, Brandon pulled the trigger, his ears ringing from the explosion. Richard fired his gun next to him, as did the groundskeepers on the opposite corner of the house.

A few of the torchmen fell, their bodies struck by lead balls, and their compatriots pulled them away from the house, while the rest of the mob roared with fury, brandishing their weapons, but now hanging back.

"Maybe they're thinking better of this," Brandon said, reloading his musket.

"I saw Michael Dooley out there." His son shook his head. "He was one I talked to today. He shook my hand."

"I'm sorry." Brandon passed his son the powder horn. "But now you know what we're dealing with."

Richard nodded and loaded his weapon, and they prepared for the next wave.

None came at first, though the mob leered and screamed. Brandon saw familiar faces among them, too. Farmers he'd known for years. But not the herdsmen he had seen that morning, and he took some small comfort from that.

"They're trying to torch the stables," Richard said.

Brandon looked and saw that some of the mob, no doubt frustrated, had turned their destructive intentions onto some of the other buildings, but the wet thatch refused to catch fire. Brendan hoped they wouldn't enter the stables to kill the horses. He looked back at the main body of the mob, which had gathered tight, as if conferring. "Do you think they're giving up?" Richard asked.

"Not likely. They're up to something."

A few moments later, his fears were borne out. The mob spread out in a line, and someone gave the order, and they all charged as one. Brandon took aim and fired, but his hands shook and he missed. Richard managed to hit one of them, and so did one of the groundskeepers, but the flood came on. Brandon looked at his son.

Not enough time to reload.

Not enough men for a fight.

A torch flew through the broken window, landing on the floor. Richard doused it with one of the pails in an instant, but the mob had reached the walls of the house. Pitchforks and torches broke more glass, and one of the curtains caught fire. Brandon and Richard retreated toward the middle of the room, and then Brandon heard one of his daughters scream.

"Jane!" Brandon shouted.

It's time, Sean, Victoria said, her voice clear over the chaos.

"What?" Sean said. "No!"

I'm sorry. Memory Corridor in three, two, one . . .

"No!" Sean shouted again, but the house went up in a different kind of blaze, a crackling white storm, and when it cleared, Sean was standing on nothing, in nothing.

"Let me go back!" he shouted.

You can't change the outcome, Victoria said. *These events happened over two hundred years ago. And remember, you know your ancestor survived, because he passed on his memories of this event after it happened.*

"But what about Richard? And my daughters?"

His daughters, Sean. Say it. His daughters.

That stopped him. "His daughters," he said more calmly.

Not yours. You have a different life. Take hold of it.

But Sean didn't want to take hold of it. He didn't want to return to his body.

Remember the good you're doing out here. We're learning so much from you.

Sean let out a long sigh. He went through the exercises Victoria had taught him, calling up the memory of his mom's pot roast, the cedar smell of his dad's woodshop. But with those pleasant memories came others from the hospital, horrible memories of tubes and pain and tortured nights. The bad ones were almost better at reminding him who he was than the good ones.

Are you ready for parietal extraction? Victoria asked.

"Yes," he said very quietly.

Okay. In three, two, one . . .

He felt the tsunami rage through his skull, spinning him, and then the water receded, and he was left battered and bloodied on the shores of his mind. He kept his eyes closed against the vertigo until Victoria lifted the helmet away. For a moment, he thought he might throw up, but the tingling in his cheeks went away, and this time he seemed to have avoided that particular embarrassment.

"How are you feeling?" Victoria asked, disconnecting him from the machines.

"Okay. Better than the last time."

"That's good to hear. It should keep improving."

He nodded, but waited until the spinning room had come to a complete stop before he tried to lift himself out of the harness.

"Do you feel up to talking?"

"Like, therapy?" Sean rubbed his hands through his hair. "Probably not."

"Not with me." Victoria paused. "With Isaiah."

Isaiah really didn't talk with them that often, although Sean assumed that was probably different for Natalya. The chat with the director that morning had been an exception, and Sean wondered what Isaiah could want now. Also, Victoria's hesitation suggested that maybe she wasn't happy about it.

"What does he want to talk about?"

"Your potential," she said.

CHAPTER EIGHT

G race knew that Masireh would not be able to free himself from the bindings. He would have to wait for the merchant to do that for him the next morning.

But such a release wouldn't happen unless Masireh revealed the location of his gold mines, something his honor would never allow. He could always give a false location, but they would discover it soon enough and kill him anyway, only he would die even farther from his home and family. Masireh needed to bring the merchant back to town, where he had allies, and there was only one way to make that happen.

The night grew cold, but the sand beneath Masireh's back continued to radiate the heat of the day for some time. Then, against his skin, Masireh felt the insects and crawling things that came out in the cool darkness to hunt. He ignored them, and he ignored the cold that gradually seeped into his skin until he was shivering. He did not sleep.

When dawn stretched its pale light over the desert, and the dewdrops gathered and vanished almost in the same moment, the merchant came to stand over Masireh.

"Did you sleep well?" he asked, stretching and yawning.

"Well enough for both of us," Masireh said.

"And will you tell me where your mines are located?"

"I can't," Masireh said.

The merchant pulled out the knife. "I warned you. I have been very patient, but that patience has reached its end."

"Don't berate yourself," Masireh said. "No one could possibly have the necessary patience."

"And why is that?"

"Because I don't have the answer to your question."

The merchant pointed the knife at him. "What do you mean?"

"I said it plainly. I don't have the answer. I don't know where the mines are."

"You are lying."

"I wish that I were. For my sake, not yours."

The merchant lowered the point of the knife by an uncertain inch. "Explain."

"It is an arrangement with my brother. He handles the mining. I handle the trade. He is safe, and I take the risk, should anyone try to force me to reveal the location of our mines. It works out very well for my brother."

"Not so well for you." The merchant looked angry now. The false geniality of his demeanor had fallen away, and Masireh now saw the coldness in his true eyes. "Or me. Now I will get nothing for killing you."

He lunged downward with the knife.

"Perhaps not!" Masireh said, almost breathless with sudden panic, and within the memory, Grace tried to shield herself from the blade.

The merchant had stopped, the knife halfway to Masireh's neck. "I already told you I am out of patience—"

"There is a map."

The merchant straightened back up, but the knife remained in his hand. "A map?"

"A map to the mines. Should anything happen to my brother, I am to open it."

"And where is this map?"

"With a trusted friend, back in town. It is sealed. He doesn't know what it contains."

The merchant rolled the knife tip against his thumb for several moments, and finally put it away. "Back in town?"

"Near my home."

"I can kill you there as easily as here."

"I don't doubt that. But if I do this, will you give me your word on something?"

"You think you're in a position to barter?" The merchant laughed, his genial mask returned. "I am curious, though. What is this request?"

"Don't hurt my brother. When you reach the mines, spare him."

The merchant turned away. "That will depend upon your brother."

Not long after that, the merchant's men came and pulled up the stakes holding Masireh to the ground. They did not loosen the bonds around his wrists, however, and after giving him a small amount of water to drink, they forced him by the point of a sword to march eastward, back toward town. Ten miles later, when the first of houses and buildings came into sight among the dunes, the merchant came to stand before Masireh, holding his knife once again.

"I know you are up to something, but I tell you this. If you stray, if you give me even the smallest of signs that you are lying or working to betray me, I won't use this on you. I will take it to your house and find your family. Do you understand?"

Masireh understood very well, which made his anger that much hotter. But he kept it contained, a lidded pot that did not appear to be boiling.

The merchant stepped closer. "Do you understand!"

Masireh nodded.

The merchant eyed him for a moment longer, and then he untied Masireh's wrists. "You lead the way, but know this. You may not see the knife at your back, but it will be there."

"This way," Masireh said, and walked toward the city.

They passed the pavilion near the inn where he had met the merchant and been poisoned. They passed the market, with the silk Masireh had planned to purchase. Along the way, many people stopped to greet him, and he nodded and smiled as if nothing was amiss, though they asked where he had been, because his family had been looking for him. Masireh did his best to convince them that all was well. The merchant had no trouble fooling those they met.

It was near midday when they reached the house Masireh had told the merchant about.

"Remember," the merchant said. "Your life and the lives of your family are in my hands."

"I have not forgotten," Masireh said.

The man who greeted them at the door seemed surprised to see them, but before he could speak, Masireh said, "Peace, my friend. I come with terrible news. It seems my brother has died in an accident at the mines."

"Oh?" said the man at the door.

"These associates of mine will swear to it," Masireh said.

"And what would you ask of me?"

"A map was entrusted to you many years ago. A map to my family's mines. I have come to claim it."

"I see," the man said. He opened his door wide, and ushered in the visitors. "Please, wait in my courtyard, and I shall retrieve it for you."

Masireh entered the man's house with the merchant and his guards. They came into a fine courtyard with a fountain and fruit trees. The air was cool and fragrant.

"It may take me some time to find it."

"We will wait," Masireh said, glancing at the merchant, who appeared irritated, but said nothing.

The next few minutes passed very slowly, and in total silence save the trill of the fountain. The merchant had a hand inside his robes, no doubt gripping the handle of Masireh's knife. He and his men stared hard at Masireh until the man of the house returned with the map, rolled and sealed.

"There is a protocol that must be performed before I give you this," the man said.

"What protocol?" the merchant asked, the first words he had uttered since entering the house.

"Your word is not enough. I must know that Masireh's brother is dead."

"How?" the merchant asked.

"Normally, I would see the body for myself."

"We will go to retrieve it," the merchant said. "But for that, we need the map."

"That is true. So I will give you this map, but you must leave me with some form of collateral."

"How much?" the merchant asked.

"Not money. Unless you have a caravan of gold outside, you couldn't possibly have enough. I would like something much more valuable."

"What?" the merchant asked.

"A life," the man said. "Masireh's life. Leave him with me. If you return with the body of his brother, I will release him to you. If you do not, his fate is in my hands."

The merchant folded his arms and seemed to be considering the man's offer. He looked at his men, and looked at Masireh, and Masireh did his best to appear frightened. At last the merchant nodded. "You have a deal."

"Excellent," the man said. He handed over the map, and the merchant took it.

Then the merchant turned to Masireh and he smiled. "Until we meet again." He nodded to his men, and they abruptly departed the house.

After they had gone, the man turned to Masireh. "How do you get yourself into these situations, brother?"

Masireh sighed. "Bad luck."

The revelation shocked Grace. She had given Masireh free access to the palace of her mind, and yet he had somehow concealed his brother's identity from her. As if his performance for the merchant had required him to conceal his brother's identity even from himself. Masireh had been extremely clever and disciplined and bold. All qualities Grace wished for herself, and the fact that she had his DNA within her was a good thing. She also wished she had a brother she could count on the way Masireh could count on his.

"One of these times," his brother said, "your luck will fail."

Masireh sat down upon the edge of the fountain and dipped his fingers in the water. "What map did you give them?"

His brother waved him off. "I marked a spot fifty miles away. There's nothing there."

"They'll be back."

"Of course they will. But we'll be ready." He turned toward the inner house. "Have you eaten?"

"Not since yesterday."

"Come then. We have preparations to make."

Grace? Anaya's voice carried over the sound of the fountain. *This memory seems to be winding down. I'm showing a low probability that this ancestor interacted with the Piece of Eden.*

"I think you're right," Grace said. But even without the Piece of Eden, this simulation hadn't been a waste of time to her, after all. She'd even enjoyed it, and felt that maybe she'd gained something from it, on a level she didn't understand yet, but was beginning to.

Are you ready to come out?

"I am."

Good. Isaiah would like to speak with you.

Grace knocked on the door, and Isaiah called her in. This was his office, but she had the impression it wasn't his *real* office. Like he had a bigger, better office somewhere else in the Aerie, but this was the office he used when he wanted to meet with her or one of the others. He sat at his desk, which didn't have anything on it. The room didn't have any kind of personal expression at all. Even the stark, black-and-white photos hanging on the wall seemed to have been picked for their universality and inoffensiveness. Some bridge in the fog. Some leaves on the ground. Some old wooden fence in a field.

"Please, have a seat," Isaiah said.

Grace went to one of the chrome-supported angular chairs facing his desk and sat down. "Anaya said you wanted to speak to me?"

"Yes. Victoria mentioned your frustrations."

"Oh."

"I wondered if I might help."

"How?"

"Why don't you tell me what's bothering you?"

Grace wasn't sure. This morning, she had simply wanted to be a part of the mission and find a Piece of Eden, to prove that she and David were valuable to the program. But after experiencing Masireh's memories, she wasn't quite as impatient with the trial and error of the Animus anymore.

"Let's start with what you told Victoria," Isaiah said. "You wish you could switch places with Natalya?"

"Does Victoria tell you everything?"

"Only what I need to know." He sat back in his chair, and the leather creaked. "Is that how you feel?"

"Sometimes."

"Why is that?"

"She's going to find one of the prongs of the Trident."

"And?"

"That's why we're here."

He got up from the chair and walked around to sit on his desk near her, his arms folded, his gold watch showing on his wrist. "Your dad initially refused my offer and took you and your brother home."

Grace nodded.

"But then he brought you back."

Obviously.

"I wonder what changed his mind?" Isaiah sounded genuinely curious. "He never really told me, and I didn't ask. But I doubt it was the money."

"No," Grace said. "It wasn't the money."

"Then what was it?"

Grace hesitated. The chair she sat in had a little bit of flex to it, such that whenever she shifted her weight, she bounced a little, so she tried to hold still. "He wants what's best for us."

"And what is best for you and your brother?"

"Education. Opportunity. A place we'll be safe and stay out of trouble."

"And you don't want to disappoint him?"

It was much more complicated than that, because it wasn't just about her dad, not really. It was also about her, and the expectations she placed on herself. But she just nodded her answer.

"Let me reassure you, Grace, that you are doing something very important. You may feel that if you don't find a prong of the Trident then you aren't valuable to us. But that isn't true. If you stay with us, things will happen, I promise you."

"What things?"

"Great things, and you will one day be at the center of it. You are intelligent, confident, and resourceful."

"Thank you." Grace appreciated hearing that, even if she couldn't tell if Isaiah really meant it.

"Abstergo is full of people like you. People who are driven. People who push themselves. Those are the people who change the world, Grace. I'm pleased that you would take Natalya's place if you could, but I wouldn't want that for you. You have your own place, and only you can fill it."

"Thank you," she said again, feeling more convinced of his sincerity. But he hadn't mentioned David. "What about my brother?"

"That is up to him," Isaiah said. "Now, off you go."

Grace rose from her chair, and with a nod she left the office, closing the door behind her. From there, she went to the lounge, where David and Sean were sitting and drinking sodas. Victoria often stressed that they should all drink something after the Animus, preferably something with sugar or fructose.

"Where you been?" David asked.

She pulled an orange juice from the refrigerator. "Isaiah wanted to see me."

"He wanted to see me, too," Sean said.

David pretend-sulked. "He didn't want to see me."

Grace tried not to worry about what that might mean. "What did he talk to you about?"

"My simulation."

She gulped some of her juice, realizing that she really was thirsty. "What about it?"

Sean looked out the windows, into the trees, but his gaze felt a lot more distant than that. "Injustice, I guess. Anarchy versus order." He looked back at Grace. "What'd he talk to you about?"

She downed the rest of the juice and went to grab a bottle of water. "Just making sure I'm happy here."

"Well, I'm happy here," David said. "We got in a dogfight over Italy today. It was—"

"We?" Grace said.

David looked at her. "Yes, we. Or they, or whatever. The point is, it was incredible. I'm telling you, best flight simulator ever—"

"It's not a game," Grace said. "How many times do I have to tell you?"

"It may not be a game but that doesn't mean it can't be fun," David said.

Grace shook her head at this too-familiar argument. If David didn't start taking the mission more seriously, would Isaiah continue to keep him at the Aerie? Grace didn't want to think about what could happen to David back in their neighborhood if she wasn't there to watch out for him. She turned to Sean. "Do you have a little brother?"

"I have a younger sister."

"And does she make your life a lot harder than it has to be?"

"What's wrong with having fun while we're here?" David asked. "Nobody else gets to do what we're doing."

Sean shrugged. "He's right about that."

Grace sat back and folded her arms. "And what would Dad say to you right now?"

David's expression changed. He dropped his defensiveness and his mouth opened as if something had just occurred to him. "Do you guys wonder what else is going on here?" he asked.

"What do you mean?" Sean said.

"We've only been in two of the buildings." David pointed out the window. "There's three more buildings out there. What do you think they're for?"

"Why don't you just ask?" Grace said, still feeling irritated with him.

"Maybe I don't need to," David said, pushing up his glasses.

CHAPTER NINE

K ang was nothing like Zhi's father. She had already known that, but as her training progressed, the differences became more apparent. Kang forgave no mistakes and tolerated no shortcoming. Owen felt sorry for her, watching the memory unfold, feeling the weight of her grief on his mind. Not only had her father just died, the ashes from his funeral fire still warm, but the man now training her only reminded her of what she had lost. That was how it had been with Owen's grandparents right after his dad died, especially his grandpa.

"Again!" Kang said.

Zhi executed the maneuver she'd been training, racing through the forest, dodging, flipping, climbing, stabbing her targets with her hidden blade, shooting her targets with the crossbow on her other wrist.

Above her on the stony bluff, Kang watched, thumping away the seconds with his staff, tracking her time. When she finished the course, Kang shook his head.

"Again! You must be faster!"

She stood there breathing hard, her muscles quivering, staring up at him. It did not seem possible to complete the maneuver any faster.

Kang pointed at the trees behind her. "I can see three places where you could have shaved a second off your time. You must seek new routes, use new techniques."

"Forgive me, Mentor," she said.

"You can ask the Khan for forgiveness for disturbing his sleep. Right before he tortures and executes you."

Zhi bowed her head.

"Would that honor the memory of your father?" Kang asked.

"No," she whispered.

"So," he said. "Again. Faster."

Zhi dug her fingernails into her palms, and stalked back to the starting point of the course. Along the way, she recovered the bolts of her crossbow, and focused all the anger she felt at Kang into the training exercise.

From the starting point, she leapt forward again, taking in the rocks and roots and branches and tree trunks in the space between her breaths, seeking the best, fastest course. Her blade flashed and the bolts from her crossbow sang, finding their marks, and through it all Kang's staff tolled her failure.

"You were only one second faster!" he shouted. "Again!"

Zhi wanted to shout back at him that she was trying, but she restrained herself, simply glaring at him instead.

"You hate me." Kang wore a thin smile, as if he enjoyed what he was putting her through. "But I am not the enemy. Möngke Khan is the enemy. Don't forget that."

It was an easy mistake to make.

"I would like you to come out of this alive," he said. "I would like for you to take your father's place in the Brotherhood."

"That is what I want as well."

"Then you must be worthy of it. You must prove your usefulness as an Assassin." He pointed the end of his staff at the course. "Again!"

Zhi ran the exercise several more times before she reached the level of proficiency Kang expected. He acknowledged it with a simple nod. The achievement took so much out of her, she experienced no satisfaction from it, and wanted only to collapse. Fortunately, Kang offered her a rare chance to rest.

So they sat on the Fishing Terrace together, eating cold fish and rice in silence. Zhi could see the confluence of the three rivers below them, the surrounding hills dyed orange by the setting of the summer sun. The warmth of it brought sweat to her forehead, with no breeze to carry it away.

"Does it not strike you?" Kang said.

"What?"

"That the survival of our empire depends on this piece of earth we sit upon." He knocked on the rock of the terrace. "One hill. One fortress."

"One man," Zhi added.

"Yes," he said. "But I wonder, are we just throwing pebbles at the river?"

"What do you mean?"

"Do we truly alter its course? Do any of us have that power? Or are we just causing ripples and telling ourselves we have made a difference to the current?"

"You will not discourage me," Zhi said.

"I don't mean to. Inevitability is not an excuse for inaction." He turned to her. "When will you take your action?"

"I'm waiting for you to tell me I am ready."

He laughed at her.

In spite of her exhaustion, she grew angry again. "You find that amusing?"

He shook his head. "I think you mistake me. I laugh at the both of us."

"Why?"

"Because I have been waiting for *you*. To show me you are ready." He laughed again. "It would seem we will both be kept waiting."

She didn't know how he expected her to show him she was ready, but she wasn't in the mood to play his games. She was tired, and it had been a very long day. She got up to leave.

"It is simpler than you think," Kang said behind her.

She stopped, about to respond, and then shook her head against it. Perhaps tomorrow she would feel like arguing with him.

"Good night," she said, walking away.

"Tomorrow at sunrise!" he called. "Don't be late!"

She kept going, past the workshops and the lake, into town toward her father's house. When she arrived she went to her father's room and pulled his gauntlet from beneath the floorboard, just as she had done every night since he had gone to the wall.

She cradled the gauntlet in her lap, smelling the leather and the oiled metal of its blade, and spoke to her father's spirit. She told him about her training, and about how much she hated Kang. She told her father how much she missed him, and she promised to honor him by killing the Great Khan and becoming an Assassin. Then she went to sleep, and as soon as her eyes closed they opened again, and somehow it had become morning, and she got up to repeat the day.

Owen experienced all of this with empathy for her. He had been there. But he admired her, too. For all Kang's criticisms, Zhi was strong, and capable, and skilled. Owen even hoped that the Bleeding Effect might carry some of her abilities across the boundary of the Animus into him. He had already acquired some skills from the time he had spent carrying the weight of Varius's mind, but he wanted more.

It was another hot morning as Zhi walked through town. She stopped to buy some breakfast and learned that the Mongols hadn't attempted another attack since that night, and many thanked her father, crediting him with the victory, though none knew of his true nature.

When she reached Kang's hut, she found him sitting outside, waiting. As she approached, he looked up at the sun. "You're late. The sun has risen."

"I needed rest."

"Not to worry. The Khan will give you plenty of time to rest when he wraps you in fresh buffalo fat, stakes you to the ground, and leaves you to the flies and maggots—"

"Enough," she said.

"Enough? Do you think the Khan—"

"Enough!" she shouted. "Do you think I don't know what the Khan will do? Do you think I haven't heard the stories? Do you think it matters to me?"

"What does matter, then?"

Zhi narrowed her eyes, furious and disgusted. "Do not mock me, old man."

"I do not mock you." He got to his feet and lumbered over to her. "What matters to you?"

She took a step toward him, close enough to smell the fish. "The memory of my father."

"And?"

"And? Right now, that is all I need."

Kang shook his head. "That is your failing. When you are able to put your own desire for vengeance aside. When you are as loyal to the Brotherhood as you were to your father. When you honor the Creed as much as you honor his memory . . . then you will be ready."

"It isn't for you to decide," she said.

"Oh, but it is. It most surely is." He returned to where he had been sitting before and lowered himself to the ground. "Your father was like you. He also put his honor before the Creed. He chose not to hide. He went to the wall that night even though I told him it was not his place, and look what happened. His death accomplished little."

Owen felt Zhi's rage erupt. She lunged at the old man, but before she could strike him, his staff caught her on the side of the head and knocked her to the ground. She tasted dust, and balls of lightning scorched her vision.

"You are more impulsive than he ever was," Kang said. It

seemed he had barely moved. "That is another thing you will master before I am done with you."

Zhi squinted and shook her head, then touched the spot where he'd hit her. A lump had already begun to swell, but through the pain, she knew Kang was wrong. "His death was not in vain," she said, nearly gasping.

"I suppose that's true. He may have won that battle, as everyone says he did. But he could have won the war."

Zhi would not stay there and listen to the memory of her father so diminished, especially not by a man he had trusted. She labored to her feet, her head still reeling in a way that disoriented Owen. Her honor was hers, not the Brotherhood's. They would never deserve a greater loyalty than what she gave her father. Her revenge was more important than any Creed. Kang couldn't stop her, and she realized she didn't need his permission. She turned to leave.

"Think on what I've told you," the old man said.

She ignored him.

"Sunrise tomorrow!" he called. "Do not be late!"

But she had no intention of returning.

Later that night, after the besieged town had gone to its restless sleep, Zhi dressed in her black lamellar armor, her cowl, and armed her wrist with her crossbow and bolts. Then she went into her father's room, and she sat with his gauntlet for some time.

When the night had fully left behind the day before and entered the hours of the empty black desert before dawn, she pulled her father's gauntlet over her wrist and cinched it tight. It fit her, just barely. Then she left the house and made her way to the Feiyan Cave. The bats for which it was named had long since left their lair on their nightly hunt, even as she entered their grotto pursuing her own prey.

A staircase had been carved into the rock at the entrance. It spiraled down the sides of a shaft of earth, while a stream from the lake followed its own, parallel course below, filling the cavern with sounds. Once Zhi had descended into total darkness, she awoke a lantern, and its light scattered the shadows of rocks and insects in all directions. She smelled clay, and damp, and the air felt cooler.

The cave had always been forbidden to her and other children of the town growing up, and it was claimed that a giant serpent lived inside it. Zhi saw no serpent now as she climbed downward, and eventually, the staircase became a level path. Someone had long ago opened this natural passage wider, to allow for soldiers and messengers to make secret entrances and exits from the fortress. She followed this path as it found its way down through the mountain, and when she reached the warning signs carved in the rock for the exit ahead, she extinguished her lantern and crept the rest of the way forward.

Her boots gently disturbed the bubbling stream at her feet before the water fell into a separate channel, diverted there so as not to give away the location of the cave. She felt along the slick walls with her hands until a sliver of night opened ahead, only slightly brighter than the darkness of the cave, and when she reached it, she paused.

Beyond that point, her purpose would truly begin. She hadn't fully left the fortress yet, but she was about to. She looked down at her father's gauntlet, and then she stepped through.

Outside, she smelled the ash of an old fire, and heard the forest alive around her. Behind her, through a trick in the shadows of the rocks, the crevice became nearly invisible, and she actually worried that she wouldn't be able to find it again on her way back.

If she made it back.

She certainly hoped to, but that was not required for her mission.

The mosquitoes, heat, and humidity were even worse down in the valleys and ravines, which if anything demonstrated the tenacity of the Mongols. Zhi passed the charred remains of the trees from the previous battle, but it seemed the steppe people had claimed their dead.

Zhi headed southeast, keeping to the shadows, free-running through the forest. She could almost hear Kang's staff thumping away the time at her from the fortress overhead, but she did her best to push that from her mind and focus on her silent movement toward the Mongol encampment.

She covered the miles quickly, and soon reached the first of the round tents the Mongols used for shelter. There were guards posted, but they were easily avoided, which was better than killing them. It would do her no good to risk alerting the camp until it was absolutely unavoidable.

She pressed inward, pausing, listening, watching. The patrols were regular and disciplined, which meant she only had to be patient, and she could get past them. The tents had been built in regular formations, their felt skins wrapped around wooden bones, and everywhere there were horses. Zhi had heard about the Mongol love for their herds, but she doubted the horses loved their riders for bringing them here in the summer with all the flies.

The size of the camp at first impressed her, and then shocked her, as did the grandeur of some of the tents. Hundreds and hundreds of trees had been cut to make room for thousands of tents, and it seemed the Khan and his noblemen had brought small palaces with them from the north. That vanity made it easy for Zhi to determine which tent belonged to Möngke. She simply had to find the largest and richest of them, which she soon did.

There were two soldiers guarding each of the entrances, and Zhi could see no way around them. From the shadows, she fired two bolts from her crossbow, almost simultaneously, and both guards went down silently, clutching their necks. She leapt over their bodies and raced into the tent, and then dove to the side for cover.

Lanterns hung from the thick timber frames above her, the ceiling beyond obscured by its height and the haze of smoke and incense. Silks and tapestries hung from the walls, while tall wooden screens, carved and inlaid with gemstones and precious metals, formed partitions that divided the tent into hallways and rooms.

Zhi had only moments before the guards outside were discovered. She moved to one of the massive wooden pillars and scaled it like the trunk of a tree until she attained a vantage point in the rafters, above the tops of the walls so that she could look down into the rooms. From there she could find the Khan.

That did not prove difficult, either. She soon located his dining hall, his throne, and then his bedroom. There were guards throughout the tent, but she could keep hidden where she was, and the wooden beams were wide enough for her to creep along unnoticed.

When Zhi reached a point directly over Möngke, she stopped for a moment and watched him from her perch. He seemed a large man, and strong. How many deaths could be laid at his feet, and the feet of his family before him?

A distant noise rose up, voices shouting alarm.

Zhi's eyes widened. She had to act. Now.

She leapt from the rafter, straight down onto Möngke's bed, her father's hidden blade buried instantly in his throat. The Khan's eyes shot open, and his mouth flew wide, but no sound emerged. Zhi made eye contact with the dying Möngke until the strength of his bleeding weakened, and she saw his body empty out its spirit and become a shell. Once he was dead, she dove from the bed and climbed back up into the rafters. That was when Owen noticed the dagger with the Khan's armor, near the bed. Zhi had no idea what it was, but he did. He'd held one very similar to it in the memories of Varius. The second prong from the Trident of Eden.

But Zhi now focused on escaping. She had to be quick, for once the Khan's dead body was discovered, there would be no place safe enough to hide within the tent.

The commotion outside had become louder, and many of the guards within the tent had either moved toward that entrance, or toward the Khan's bedroom, so Zhi made her way toward the opposite end of the tent.

She dropped to the ground as close to the exit as she could, and then stepped outside. The two guards standing there went down instantly, one shot by her crossbow, the other with her knife in the back of his neck.

But this time there were other warriors gathered to witness it.

They shouted, pointing. She heard swords being drawn, and knew arrows would fly next, so she ran, dodging between the tents, sometimes climbing up and over them, their felt coverings stretching a little beneath her feet, their wood creaking. The Mongols gave chase, rousing the entire camp.

Beneath Zhi's mind, Owen worried for her, silently begging her to move faster, just as Kang had done. Her only chance for escape would be the forest. Its edge lay several hundred yards away, through the enormous camp, a distance that seemed impossible, but she honed her senses and flew along the route her intuition mapped for her. In spite of her fear, with every step, she smiled, and with every breath she laughed. Her father's death had been avenged. His memory had been honored. His blade had done what it was meant to do.

Even if they caught her, she had succeeded.

CHAPTER TEN

After dinner that night, David lay in bed in his room, awake and thinking. Something about the Aerie had been bothering him since that afternoon. He hadn't mentioned it to any of the others, because it kind of involved them, but it went back to what Grace had asked.

What would Dad say to you right now?

She probably didn't think he'd taken the question seriously, but he had. He had thought about what his dad would say, and he realized that what his dad would say depended on what his dad knew, and right now, his dad didn't know very much. None of them did, not really, because they never asked. They were too busy thinking about their simulations. When he'd stopped to think about that, the Animus had suddenly seemed to be a distraction, and David then had remembered all the things Monroe had said about Abstergo and the Templars.

So then he had wondered: if Abstergo wanted them all to focus on one thing, the Animus, did that mean there were things the Templars *didn't* want them asking about? And what would those things be?

The first thing that came to David's mind was the Aerie itself, because he'd never even caught a glimpse of what was going on elsewhere in the compound. That struck him as odd, but Grace and Sean hadn't seemed curious about that at all.

But David was, and lying there in his bed, he decided to do something about it. Shortly after one, in the middle of the night, he got out of bed, pulled on some clothes, and crept from his room.

He'd never been out at that hour. The Aerie was quiet and dark, but still felt alive, breathing the air circulating through its vents. David could even hear an owl, or something out in the forest, muted by the glass.

He crept along the corridor, then down another, and another, working his way toward the walkway that connected this building with the next one over. He figured there were probably security cameras all around this place, and they'd catch him any minute, so he wanted to see as much as he could before then.

When he reached the walkway, its outer door was closed, but it wasn't locked. He entered the passage, and hurried through the elevated tunnel of glass, the woods above, below, and to either side of him.

On the far side, he entered into a new building he'd never seen before. It actually looked a lot like the one where he and his sister and the others lived, and David wondered if there were kids sleeping in some of these rooms, too. Maybe the compound housed whole units of Abstergo research subjects.

He pushed ahead and came to another walkway, but this one didn't open. An electronic keylock to the side had a lens for a fingerprint, and a touch screen for a code or password. David was about to walk over to it when he heard footsteps on the far side of the door, coming toward him.

He hurried away and down a side hall, where he yanked off his shoes and then hugged the wall. He heard the door open, and then a security guard strolled by without a sideways glance.

As soon as he'd passed, David tiptoed toward the closing door and barely managed to slip through before it hissed and clicked shut behind him. Now he stood in another, much longer walkway. Some distance away, it seemed to bend and disappear into the darkness of the woods. David put his shoes on and glanced backward at the locked door. The security guard made him wonder what exactly would happen if they caught him sneaking around like this. Would he get kicked out, sent home? His dad wouldn't be happy. He worried about drugs and gangs in the neighborhood, and the truth was that David did, too. But maybe Isaiah could do something worse than just kicking him out.

He decided he had already come this far, he might as well keep going and see as much as he could before they found him. So he hurried down the corridor.

The bend he'd seen ahead turned out to be a staircase that followed the mountain's slope some distance downward. He descended it and reached another walkway, but several yards on, it ended at a door that seemed to lead into the mountain. A part of the complex was underground.

David listened at the door before opening it, but heard nothing. So he pushed and found the door unlocked. Bright light filled the hallway he entered, and he had to squint for a minute until his eyes adjusted to it.

This part of the Aerie seemed much more alert. The corridor branched ahead in four directions, and David decided to keep moving straight ahead. The doors he passed all had those electronic locks on them, so he didn't really have an option to explore. He just kept going, creeping along, listening.

Eventually, the hallway opened wider and soon ended at a pair of open double doors. Beyond them, David entered a huge garage full of cars, SUVs, and vans like the one that had brought them to the Aerie in the first place. But one car in particular caught his eye, a vehicle the sable color of a shadow at night. The curve of its hood rose up from what looked like a small jet engine intake at the front, sweeping away to the sides over large wheels. The darkly tinted windshield wrapped around and over a sleek cockpit, while the rear of the car rose up subtly, like a panther shifting on its haunches in ambush.

The car was incredible. David moved toward it and couldn't resist trying the door. It opened, so he climbed into the driver's seat, which felt more like sliding into the pilot's chair of a spaceship, the console covered in touch screens and dozens of controls. He closed the door and grasped the flared steering wheel for a few moments, imagining himself driving it.

Then he decided he better not stay any longer. He was about to climb out when he noticed a massive door opening on the far side of the garage, and he ducked down low in the seat as several vehicles pulled in. They killed their lights as they entered and parked near him, and a woman wearing some kind of paramilitary gear climbed out of the forward van. Then Isaiah, still wearing his dark suit, marched through the double doors. He joined up with the woman from the van, and together they walked toward the vehicle where David now hid, shaking. But he was able to hear their muffled conversation through the car windows.

"They're teenagers, Cole," Isaiah said. "I don't understand the difficulty."

"The Assassins have obviously been training them," the woman said. "The one called Javier, especially, seemed quite capable."

David felt a prickle at the back of his head. They seemed to be talking about the Owen and Javier that he knew. It was pretty unlikely they'd be referring to other teenagers with one named Javier.

"This would be easier if it wasn't a containment mission," Cole said. "But either way, they've moved to a new location and we don't have any leads. There's a good chance they may now have access to an Animus."

"My concern, exactly," Isaiah said. "Which is why you'll be relieved to know this is no longer a containment mission."

"Sir?"

"The Assassins cannot be allowed to access those genetic memories, even if that means I can't. You are regrettably authorized to terminate them both."

That caught David's breath in his throat. There wasn't any mistaking the meaning of what Isaiah had just said. They were talking about killing Owen and Javier, and suddenly everything Monroe had warned them about the Templars returned to his mind. How ruthless and dangerous they were.

"Yes, sir," Cole said.

"They must be found," Isaiah said. "Keep me informed."

The director turned around and stalked away, while Cole and the other agents unloaded from the vehicles. David stayed down, sweating, holding so perfectly still his muscles and joints started to ache, but eventually the garage sounded quiet and empty.

It was still a long time after that before he dared to stick his head up and look around. When he was certain the room was clear, he climbed out of the car and scurried back through the double doors, down the hall, back to the walkway that hugged the side of the mountain. When he reached the second building, he found it once again secured by the same electronic lock, only this time he didn't hear anyone coming. He had to wait, and wait, hiding in the shadow of a nearby door's alcove, the handle digging into his back, for another guard to come by. Eventually, one did, and after he'd passed by, David dodged through the opening just before it shut behind him.

From there, he crossed the walkway, back through the trees, and returned to his building. He didn't know whether to wake Grace right then, or wait a few more hours until morning, but either way they had to call their dad and get out of there.

He was walking toward his room, thinking about what to say, when a voice behind him called, "Hey, what are you doing?"

David panicked and acted on an impulsive idea. He turned sharply to the right and walked straight into the wall, then did it again, and again, like a fly bumping its head against a window.

"Hey," the guard said. "Hey, are you okay?"

David walked into the wall one more time before he felt the guard grab his shoulders and spin him around.

That's when David pretended to wake up. "Huh?" He acted as confused and frightened as he could, and rubbed his eyes. "Where . . . ?"

"Were you sleepwalking?" the guard asked.

"I guess so." David blinked and rubbed his head. "I haven't done that in a long time. Do you think it's the Animus?"

"I don't know." The guard's mustache sat at the angle of his frown. "But you should go back to your room, and I'll let Dr. Bibeau know about this."

"Okay," David said, yawning again. "Thanks for waking me up."

He turned and walked straight toward his door. The guard followed him the entire way, and nodded when David reached it and went inside. The small room, which until then had felt bigger than his own bedroom back home, suddenly felt instead like a prison.

He never did get back to sleep. He lay there trying to figure out what to say to the others, and worried that as soon as that guard mentioned the sleepwalking to Victoria, she'd pull up the security footage to see what he'd been up to. If Isaiah was willing to kill Owen and Javier, he was probably willing to kill any of them.

When his alarm finally went off, he hurried through his shower and got dressed quickly, and then went to the lounge to meet up with the others for breakfast.

Natalya was already there, eating a yogurt. David sat down next to her, bouncing his leg.

A few minutes passed.

"What?" Natalya asked.

David frowned. "What do you mean?"

"You look like you have something to say."

"I do," David said. "But let's wait until Grace and Sean are here."

Natalya went back to her yogurt. "Oh-kay."

His sister took a long time to show up, but when she finally came in, Sean wasn't too far behind her. They got their food and sat down, and then David leaned in toward them.

"We have to get out of here," he said.

"Why you whispering?" Grace asked.

"Because I don't want them to hear me," David said. "Obviously. And I'm serious. We have to go."

"Go where?" Sean asked.

"Home," David said. "But that probably isn't safe, either."

"What are you talking about?" Grace asked.

So David told them everything. How he had left his room and gone to explore, how he'd found the black jet-car, and everything Isaiah had said. He told them how he'd fooled the guard on the way back. They listened to him with frowns and scowls, and when he finished, Sean shook his head.

"You're making this up."

"No, I'm not," David said.

"Then you were dreaming," Sean said. "Maybe you really were sleepwalking."

"I wasn't," David said.

The three of them looked at one another.

"I didn't dream it," David said, his frustration rising.

"Think about it," Sean said. "We've been here for weeks, and we could have left at any time. They've treated us really well, and now you say they're trying to kill Owen and Javier? I don't buy it. The Templars are not what Monroe said they are. They're trying to improve the world. That's what I've been working on with Isaiah—"

"That's just what he wants you to think." David turned to his sister. "We need to call Dad."

"And tell him what?" she asked. "That Abstergo is really a front for a secret society that murders kids?"

"Yes," David said.

"You know what I think?" She raised an eyebrow and fixed him with her older-sister glare. "I think you've been playing your World War video game for too long."

"I'm not making this up!" David said. "You're my sister. Why can't you have my back?"

"I always have your back," she said. "Why can't you have my back for once?"

"You don't think I have your back?"

"No, I don't. I'm trying to keep us both here, and what do you do? You go sneaking around at night. You're going to get us kicked out!"

David leaned away from them. The only one who hadn't spoken up was Natalya, so he turned toward her. "What do you think?"

She pushed her empty yogurt cup away. "I certainly don't trust Abstergo. But I'm not sure they would murder Owen and Javier."

David couldn't believe this. All three of them were idiots.

"Hey." Natalya reached her hand along the table toward him. "I don't think you're lying. I just don't know if you heard what you think you heard."

David knew what he'd seen and heard. He just couldn't make them believe him.

"Do you know what we're giving up if we leave?" Sean asked.

"Are you talking about the money?" David asked.

"That's a part of it," Natalya said.

"But that's not all of it," Sean added. "If we leave, we're giving up an opportunity we won't find anywhere else. I'm not ready to throw it away."

"Neither am I," Grace said.

So this was hopeless. David wanted to leave, but he wasn't ready to leave his sister behind, and without Grace on his side, he wouldn't be able to convince their dad to come get them. So he sat back in his chair, feeling as though he had just slipped sideways into some alternate world where he had to just forget about the fact that Isaiah wanted two of his friends dead, and go on with the Animus simulations like nothing was wrong.

"I'm heading out," Sean said, wheeling away from the table. "See you all later."

"I'm going, too," Grace said, rising to her feet.

David looked up at her, and she waited a moment. Normally, they went to the Animus corridor together, but this time he just folded his arms. She rolled her eyes and walked away, leaving him alone with Natalya.

"You said you don't trust Abstergo," he said.

"I don't."

"Why?"

"Because I know they have a hidden agenda. There are things they don't tell us. But that's a long way from killing someone."

"But Monroe said—"

"Monroe had his own hidden agenda. I wouldn't trust him any further than Abstergo. So let's just wait and see what happens. Okay?"

David refused to answer that.

Natalya rose from the table. "You coming?"

"I'll be along."

"Okay." Then she threw away her garbage and left the lounge.

David sat for a few moments longer, and then, because there didn't seem to be anything else he could do, he got up and followed the others toward the Animus corridor. When he reached his room, Victoria was there.

"David," she said. "Good to see you. I understand you had a little adventure last night."

"Yeah," he said, his body suddenly flush with cold panic. How much did she know?

"The security guard told me he found you walking into a wall. I'm concerned, because somnambulism and other sleep disturbances might be Bleeding Effects."

"Oh, really?"

"Yes. We will have to watch you closely. It may even be necessary to lock the door on your room at night until we can be sure you're safe."

That sounded very sinister to David, but Grace and Sean would probably say it was for his own good. "I don't know if I want my door locked."

"Only temporarily," Victoria said. "I've also ordered the security footage pulled from last night, just so I can see what was going on for myself."

David's panic escalated, raising his heartbeat with his alarm. "Really?"

"Nothing to be embarrassed about," she said. "I just don't want anything bad to happen to you."

CHAPTER ELEVEN

Once again, it was all about Owen, and Javier had to sit back and watch as Griffin monitored his friend in a shiny new Animus. But that was fine. That's how it was, which was why he had needed a break from Owen. Javier just had too much of his own stuff going on to deal with Owen's stuff as well. But in this situation, that didn't really matter. It just was what it was. He couldn't stay mad at Owen anyway. Javier felt as if he owed him.

But that didn't mean he wasn't bored out of his mind, just sitting there, waiting.

Rebecca had left a few hours ago. There were apparently a couple of cars in the nearly collapsing barn outside, and she had taken one of them, probably heading off on another Assassin mission of some kind. That left another car, and Javier was seriously tempted to take it and go for a ride.

But where?

They were hiding out in the middle of nowhere for a reason. The Templars were after them, and they were seriously outnumbered. Javier had begun to think that's basically what it meant to be an Assassin; always on the run, always in hiding, often alone.

In a way, that was how Javier had felt for most of his life. In third grade he'd realized he was different. By seventh grade he'd given it a name. A lot of the time between and since had been spent hiding the fact that he was gay from almost everyone, and feeling very, very alone. Things had gotten better after he'd come out to his parents and his brother, and now that he'd come out to Owen, a bit more of that aloneness had gone away. But he didn't think he would ever be fully rid of it. There would always be a kid inside him who felt as if he was faking it. Just pretending to be like everyone else.

"You hungry?" Griffin sat at the computer console where he monitored Owen's simulation.

"Yeah," Javier said.

"There's a mini fridge in that corner over there. Rebecca probably stocked it."

Javier got up from the crate he'd been sitting on and walked over to check. He opened the door, letting out the cold and the hum of its fan, and inside found a supply of vegetables, along with some tofu products boldly claiming to taste like turkey and cheese.

"Rebecca a vegetarian, by chance?" Javier asked.

"Yeah, why?" Griffin said, turning around.

Javier just nodded toward the fridge.

"Ah, crap," Griffin said.

A box of groceries on top of the fridge held a loaf of sprouted wheat bread, so Javier made himself a not-turkey-and-cheese sandwich.

"You want one?" he asked Griffin.

The Assassin seemed to think about it a moment, and finally nodded with a bit of a scowl, so Javier made a second sandwich and brought it over.

"He's in the Mongol war camp," Griffin said, pointing at the code scrolling across the screen, and the image of Javier's ancestor sneaking around the tents. "Want to pull up a chair and watch?"

"I'm good," Javier said, returning to his crate. He didn't want to watch. He wanted to *do*. Something real, not a reenactment of an ancient memory in the Animus. "How much longer do you think he'll be in there?"

"No idea," Griffin said, his sandwich already half gone. "Your friend Monroe didn't exactly leave us a road map."

A map would've helped *before* Monroe dragged them into this secret underworld. Javier thought back to that first time in the Animus, back when Owen had hoped he could use his genetic memory to prove his father's innocence. That kind of proof wouldn't exactly be admissible in court, so it wouldn't do any good legally. But then, Javier didn't think it had ever really been about the courts. Owen had something to prove to himself.

That gave Javier an idea for something he could actually do. Something that would really help Owen, while giving Javier a chance to do something important. He still had a lot of gear in his leather jacket from their escape earlier that night.

"I need to go for a walk," he said.

Griffin barely glanced over his shoulder. "Not a good idea."

"I'm going crazy, man. I just need some air."

Griffin grunted.

"There's nothing out here for miles." Javier got up from the crate. "I won't go far."

Griffin finally turned around to face him, looked him in the eye, and said, "Fine. Be back in twenty. Don't make me come looking for you. I have a simulation to run."

Javier nodded and walked up the stairs, leaving the high-tech Assassin hideout for the haunted house above. He had no intention of returning in twenty minutes, but there wasn't anything Griffin would be able to do about that without leaving Owen stranded in the Animus. Griffin would probably be furious, but right now Javier wasn't really concerned about that. This whole deal had always been more Owen's than his.

Upstairs, it was still pretty dark out, the house a creaking framework of rusty nails, splinters, and dust. Javier left through the front door, careful to close it behind him so the electronic lock engaged, and then marched straight for the barn.

A wind had picked up, stirring the trees and tall grass. Javier pulled up his cowl, dug his hands into his pockets, keeping his elbows tight against his torso and his head down. When he reached the barn, its wide doors groaned open, revealing the plain sedan inside. The next issue would be the keys. Javier had no idea how to hotwire a car, so he hoped Assassin getaway protocol meant the keys would already be in the car.

They were, right under the mat at his feet.

He climbed in and turned the ignition, then pulled out of the barn, keeping the headlights off as he passed the house. He almost expected Griffin to come charging out the front door at any moment, but the Assassin didn't show, and Javier eased down the long dirt drive. A hundred feet away from the house, he switched on the headlights, gave the car some gas, and drove back toward the city.

The police warehouse wasn't even really guarded. A couple of blue uniforms stood on duty at the doors, but Javier didn't plan on going in through the front. He wasn't even sure this wouldn't be a complete waste of time, but he wanted to do something for Owen to make up for the years he'd more or less abandoned him without any explanation.

A chain-link fence topped with razor wire surrounded the warehouse, while security cameras at the corners of the building and fence swept the area. Javier used his crossbow pistol to take out the nearest cameras. Then he scaled the fence and vaulted himself over the razor wire, landing easily on his feet.

From there he raced up to the wall of the warehouse and climbed. At first, the experience felt like it had in the memories of Cudgel Cormac, scaling the buildings of New York City. But now, in the real world, and only a dozen feet up, things got hard. Javier's fingers grew tired, and his muscles quivered. He froze, clinging to the vertical face, and looked up, the nearest window still another twenty feet above him. He wasn't going to make that.

A moment later, his grip slipped, and he fell hard to the ground. It seemed the Bleeding Effects had limits, and now his right ankle hurt.

Javier wasn't going to give up, though, so he scouted around the walls of the warehouse until he found a loading dock and a back door behind the building. An older electronic keypad secured the lock on the door, but Javier smacked it with one of the EMP grenades, and it clicked open.

Inside the warehouse, rows and rows of shelving towered over him, each filled with boxes of different sizes and shapes. A quick glance at some of the labels on the shelves and Javier learned they were organized by date and case number. He knew the rough date of the trial for Owen's dad, but not the case number.

So he got as close as he could, using the information he had, and checked the labels on each of the boxes, climbing up and down the shelving units. It took about forty-five minutes before he located the right one and pulled it from its stack on the shelf.

Back on the ground, he set the box on the floor and opened it. Inside, he found orange evidence bags containing DVDs of security footage, shell casings, and more than six inches of reports and files. He hoped there was something in there to bring Owen some closure, one way or another.

"I'll check this way," a woman said from a far corner of the room.

Then footsteps.

Javier snatched up the box and rushed in the opposite direction as quietly as he could, ducking and dodging among the rows toward the loading dock. When he got there, a uniformed cop was standing in his way. Before he could react, Javier rushed him and rammed him with his shoulder, and they both went down on the ground. The cardboard box of evidence crumpled, but Javier held on to it and leapt to his feet, racing out the door and toward the fence.

"Over here!" the policeman shouted behind him. Javier glanced back, and saw the man in pursuit, his hand on his sidearm.

Javier reached into his pocket and pulled out a smoke grenade, which he hurled to the ground behind him. The explosion choked the air for fifteen feet, giving Javier the chance to stop and load his crossbow with some sleep darts. As soon as the cop appeared, Javier shot him, and a few seconds later the officer went down.

The fence lay another ten yards away, but Javier wouldn't be able to climb it with the box under his arm. He had to get through it.

More voices shouted behind him, the other police officers catching up.

Javier had one explosive grenade he'd never used before, and he had no idea if it would do the job or blow him up in the process. But he pulled it out of his pocket, threw it at the fence from as far away as he could, and then dove to the ground.

The explosion rang in his ears and threw gravel and dust over him, and a few tiny fragments struck the back of his head. They stung, but didn't do any damage, and he climbed to his feet as the smoke finished clearing away.

A narrow opening flared outward in the fence, possibly big enough for him, but possibly not. He ran for it, his only shot, pushing the box through ahead of him, and then wriggled through.

His jacket caught on the mangled wire, but he ripped it free and raced toward the car. A short distance from it, he tossed another smoke grenade, just in case any of the police in pursuit could spot him, and then he charged the rest of the way.

When he reached the vehicle, he threw the door open, heaved the box across into the front passenger seat, and then jumped in. A moment later, he raced away, checking his rear-view mirror for flashing lights. Sirens wailed from some distance behind, no doubt heading for the warehouse. None of them seemed to be chasing him.

Even so, his heartbeat didn't slow, and his breathing didn't settle down, until he'd reached the highway heading out of town. As he drove, the sky to the east bloomed with the first light of dawn. By the time he reached the haunted Assassin house, he'd been gone for just under three hours, and the sun was up.

As he parked the car in the barn, he wondered what Griffin would do to him when he got inside, but he grabbed the box of evidence and went to find out.

It turned out Griffin was already standing on the porch, arms folded, fury in his eyes.

"Have you been waiting there this whole time?" Javier asked.

Griffin looked ready to spontaneously combust. "I've been tracking you since you left, you little punk. You think you can steal my car without my knowing it?"

It occurred to Javier that this was a man who regularly killed people, and that it might be smart to adopt a more conciliatory tone. "Sorry," he said as he approached the Assassin. "I didn't—"

Griffin grabbed him hard by the collar of his jacket and wrenched him in close. "You don't know how thin the ice is beneath you. Do you want to tell me what you were doing at a police warehouse?"

"I went for Owen." Javier jostled the battered box. "This is the evidence they used against his dad."

That seemed to cool some of Griffin's anger, and he let go of Javier. "Get inside. We'll deal with this later."

Javier followed the Assassin back inside, down the stairs, into the basement. Owen still lay in the Animus chair, and Griffin went back to the computer console without saying any more. Javier took the box over to the table and sat down to look more closely at what was inside it.

He took everything out and spread it over the surface of the glass. The evidence bags were easy, but the files took some reading and organizing. There were crime scene reports and photos. There was an autopsy report on the bank security guard. There were witness statements, and transcripts of interviews and interrogations. Financial statements. Javier laid it all out and stepped back, rubbing his chin.

"Doing the wrong thing for the right reasons is still the wrong thing," Griffin said behind him.

"I'm not sure how to take that, coming from a guy who kills people. And the truth is that I'd do it again."

Griffin nodded. "I know you would. That's the problem. What if you'd been caught? Arrested? What if they followed you back here?"

"They didn't."

"You're smart enough to know that's not the point."

"And I'm smart enough to not get caught."

Griffin stepped up to the table and scanned all the evidence. "The Assassins have a Creed," he said quietly.

They were a secret society. Of *course* they would have a creed. But Javier refrained from offering a sarcastic response, because he could sense how seriously Griffin took what he was saying.

"Three Tenets," the Assassin continued. "Stay your blade from the flesh of an innocent. Hide in plain sight. Never compromise the Brotherhood."

"Okay," Javier said. "Sounds . . . simple."

"Not so simple you didn't violate the third Tenet tonight."

"I'm not a member of the Brotherhood."

Griffin nodded. "Not yet. But you've become a part of this war whether you like it or not, and eventually you'll have to choose a side. I'd like to think you'd choose ours."

"You know," Javier said. "Monroe warned us all about this."

"About what?"

"They said that you guys and the Templars would try to recruit us."

"He was right."

"He also told us not to choose a side."

"Well, you may not have that choice."

Javier smirked. "Thought the Assassins were supposed to be all about free will."

"I'm aware of the irony. But you're not ready for that yet."

"Ready for what?" Javier asked.

Griffin ignored him and returned to the computer console. Javier shook his head and went back to studying the evidence. Owen had always maintained that his father had been set up somehow. Framed or something. But it was hard to argue with the gun they found in his dad's car that matched the bullet that killed the guard. It was hard to argue with the fingerprints at the scene. It was hard to argue with the gambling debts that gave his dad one hundred and sixty-seven thousand dollars of motive. Javier didn't want to believe it, and he would never say this to Owen, but the truth was that he probably would have voted guilty, too.

But he shook that thought out of his mind, assessed the table again, and nodded to himself, feeling pleased. When Owen finished the simulation, he could take a look at all this for himself. There had to be something here that Javier was missing, just like the jury had.

He grabbed a kombucha from Rebecca's mini fridge and took his seat back on the crate, watching the back of Griffin's head.

A few minutes later, that shaved head leaned closer to the monitors. "Your boy's in trouble," the Assassin said.

Javier got up. "He is?"

"His ancestor is."

Javier crossed the room and looked over Griffin's shoulder. Javier saw Owen's ancestor, that Chinese Assassin, racing through a camp of large tents, an actual army of Mongol warriors chasing after her.

"Any sign of the prong?"

Griffin clenched his jaw. "Yes."

CHAPTER TWELVE

Natalya had to admit that David had unsettled her. She'd never been completely comfortable with Abstergo and the Templars, but she hadn't even suspected they would kill anyone, especially not kids. Maybe in the past, but in the modern world that sounded too much like wild conspiracy theory talk. What David claimed to have heard seemed unbelievable, but it did strengthen some of Natalya's own private doubts. Those doubts lingered as she waited in her Animus room.

Victoria seemed quite distracted when she came in, with tired, red eyes. "Okay . . . Natalya," she said, as if reminding herself of something. She stared at her tablet for a moment. "Where were we? Oh, right. Okay."

"Is everything all right?" Natalya asked.

"Of course," Victoria said. "Are you ready to enter the simulation?"

"Sure." Natalya stepped into the ring and climbed into the harness. Victoria went about hooking her up, and the woman's distractedness only added to Natalya's unease. She decided to test the water a little bit. "Have you found Owen and Javier?" she asked.

Victoria stopped moving. She looked at Natalya. "Why do you ask about them?"

The mood in the room shifted, and it felt to Natalya as it did when Bayan crossed onto enemy ground. It seemed she'd made a mistake. "I was just wondering. I worry about them."

Victoria closed her eyes and nodded. "I worry about them, too. I know about the Assassins." She resumed connecting Natalya to the Animus. "Believe it or not, there was once a time I even assisted them, though I never became one. The Templars still gave me another chance and showed me a better way. We'll help your friends, too. But right now, we must concentrate on the mission at hand." She crossed to the controls.

"Okay," Natalya said, glad to step back from the subject, at least for now.

"Are you ready?"

"Yeah."

"Let's get your helmet on."

Bayan stood at the edge of the encampment, mourning the loss of Wang Dechen. The morale of the Horde had fallen in the days since the death of their general. All wondered what it meant, as even the Great Khan had become sullen and withdrawn to his tent where it was said he mostly slept.

The night assault on the gate had been flawlessly executed, given what had been known of Fishing Town. Thus far, no Song force had left the safety of the fortress to engage them directly, and yet this time, enemies had appeared out of the forest like spirits. That meant a secret entrance existed somewhere, a cave perhaps. There could be no other explanation, and Bayan decided he had to find it.

He went to the commander of his Mingghan, explained his theory, and requested permission to scout around the wall that night, which was then granted. Bayan spent the rest of that day resting and preparing. He had been up the entire night previous, and would be up again tonight. He thought about taking one or two of his men, but decided he would be more likely to escape detection alone.

After the sun had fallen and pulled the train of its sunset robes with it, Bayan put on his armor and took up his sword and bow. He said a prayer to the Sky-Father and left the encampment behind, but did not feel truly endangered until he stepped out from behind the safety of the bulwarks to the northwest, near the mountain. The forest offered him shadows and cover, through which he crept as silently as he could, returning to the Hu Guo Gate. His movement through the underbrush stirred mosquitoes that attacked his fingers, ears, and neck as bravely as any warriors of the steppes.

When he reached the battleground, he found it still smelled of scorch, the fallen trees reduced to black charcoal. The scent of it scattered the insects, offering relief from their stings, and

Bayan took in the land before him with greater calm and calculation than he had brought to bear during the assault.

The stone arch of the gate looked down on the steep mountain slope, the steps and walls rising nearly fifty feet. Torches burned along the top of the wall, and Bayan observed the watchmen for some time, so certain of their defenses, so arrogant in their defiance. His anger at them turned to hatred over the death of Wang Dechen, but Natalya knew the deeper reason for Bayan's animosity. The Song had caused him to doubt.

Bayan retraced his movements from that night as best he could, heading west into the forest. Memories of that night rose up like mist from the ground. The sounds of combat, the smell of blood. Bayan's body responded to it all as if it were happening again, his blood raging in his ears.

He found the spot where he had fought the soldier missing his ear. The one who had nearly killed him, and likely would have without the distraction of the artillery fire. The body was gone, of course. But Bayan stood where it had lain, and he peered off into the trees around him. This would be the point from which to begin searching for the entrance to the secret cave. In his silence, he detected the gentle trickle of a stream some distance on, which had to be falling from above. It was possible the water came from a cave, and thus presented a possible location for the passage.

Bayan moved toward it, crouching down now, keeping close to the tree trunks, for if there was a secret entrance, it was likely guarded, and the discovery of it would do no good if Bayan was captured before he could report it.

The water sounds grew louder, getting closer, but then he

heard a different sound over the top of the rill. A little *splash*, and the light patter of footsteps.

Bayan went almost all the way to ground, lying in the darkness. He didn't see exactly where the enemy came from, but he did see her moving away through the forest, down the hill, dressed all in black. She didn't seem to have noticed him, and he decided to abandon his search for the passage in favor of capturing her. Under torture, a Song scout would have much to reveal.

Bayan rushed after her, but it proved impossible to keep up. She flew along the terrain as though it knew her as well as she knew it, and it welcomed her, while it treated Bayan as the enemy. The mountain tripped him, mired him, whipped him, and stung him, until he lost the scout completely.

His failure represented everything wrong with this campaign to begin with. Bayan knew with absolute certainty that if this chase had taken place on the open steppes, the scout would already be bound over his horse. But here in this foreign land, beset with plague and heat, the Horde had failed to capture this elusive fortress.

Bayan returned to the mission that had brought him to the mountain. Perhaps he could locate the passage. He found his way back to the place he had been when the scout appeared, and began his search, following the sound of the stream.

He eventually found its source, but that did not help him. The water gurgled from a small crack in the rock wide enough for a rodent, and nothing more. Bayan cursed and stooped to drink, and found the water sweet and cold. Another reason the taking of Fishing Town had proved so difficult. If the Song could afford to let all this water run down the mountain, that meant they had more than enough for themselves within their walls. A few weeks ago they had likewise dropped two enormous fish down the hill, freshly caught, along with a hundred steamed buns, to demonstrate their food reserves.

Bayan took another drink, wet the back of his neck, and then returned to his exploration. The scout had confirmed there had to be an entrance somewhere nearby. He swept back and forth along the slope, up and down, methodically, but after two hours, found no cave entrance.

At last, he decided that the best way to find it might be to wait for the scout to return, so he found a tall tree, located near the spring and the place he thought likeliest, and he climbed up into its branches, where he settled and watched.

Natalya was glad for the reprieve, glad the scout had escaped Bayan before, and hoped she would again. From the way the woman had moved, Natalya assumed she was an Assassin, perhaps even on her way to kill the Khan. Killing to stop the killing. It was like the Ouroboros to her, the snake eating its own tail.

Bayan's mind saw things very differently. He looked up at the sky overhead, and the earth beneath him, and believed that heaven had sent them to this country to deliver the punishment of the gods. If the Song would have simply submitted, they would have been spared.

Movement below caught Bayan's eye.

The scout had returned.

Her movements were now much more frantic. He could hear her grunting and breathing as she passed beneath him.

Bayan realized she might soon be lost in the trees again, taking with her the location of the passage, but it also seemed unlikely he could capture her alive. He didn't have to kill her instantly. He could wound her, and then make her talk. She might scream, which would draw attention from the wall, but he would be quick.

He nocked an arrow and drew his bow, the horn and wood and sinew flexing as he aimed for her thigh. Natalya wanted to scream a warning, but Bayan released the string, and with a snap, the arrow flew and struck its mark. She went down without a sound.

Bayan scrambled from his perch and raced toward her, his sword drawn. When he reached her, she was somehow already on her feet, a knife in one hand, a small crossbow mounted to the opposite wrist, but he figured she had no bolts, or she would have already shot him.

His own arrow had missed her thigh, but impaled her knee instead. The pain had to be excruciating, but she growled and stared at him with eyes much like the Song warrior he had fought the other night.

"Where is the passage?" he asked in the Song language.

She spat and tried to move into a defensive stance, but she stumbled, and Bayan could see she was completely hobbled. He also noted that the knife in her hand was actually mounted to her wrist, like her crossbow.

"If you tell me," he said, "I'll kill you quickly. You don't need to suffer."

She retreated a few paces, the blood from her knee a heavy flow down her leg. It wouldn't do him any good if she passed out from it.

He stepped toward her. "Be at peace. Your work is done. The time of defending your city is over. The Sky-Father brought you to me."

She blinked and shook her head.

He would have to do more injury to her, the thought of which horrified Natalya, but she could do nothing as Bayan circled to the Assassin's right. She shifted her weight, grimacing as she rotated to face him, while he took his time, planning his attack, watching that wrist-blade. She was injured, but possibly still very dangerous. He wondered why she hadn't called for help.

When he lunged, something slammed his right shoulder, and then an explosive pain shot through his arm, causing him to drop his sword as he stumbled forward. The scout lowered her crossbow as he collided with her, and he realized she'd kept her last bolt hidden. Before he could recover his footing, she stabbed him in the side.

He snarled through the pain and kicked the arrow protruding from her knee. The head snapped off, and she screamed, falling away from him.

He backed away, too. He didn't think her wrist-blade had made a fatal thrust, but the bolt sticking out of his shoulder was clearly poisoned, and he'd lost the use of his arm. He had to retreat, now, while he was still conscious.

He turned and stumbled down the mountain, finding it hard to keep his balance. The wound in his side robbed him of breath, and the dead weight of his arm dragged him downward. Several yards on, a dizziness set in, and he fell forward in a hard roll. The impact drove the bolt deeper into his shoulder, but it didn't hurt as badly as it should have. He slid, staggered, and fell the rest of the way, until he reached the base of the mountain.

From there, he lurched forward and eventually ended up in a crawl toward the bulwarks an impossible distance away. Natalya felt it all, at a remove, and through the torture of it, she finally admitted some admiration for Bayan. His will and determination carried him over the rocks and mud until he reached the Mongol line.

Friendly warriors ran toward him, shouting, and he rolled onto his back, at last allowing himself to either die or fall unconscious, whichever destiny the Sky-Father had apportioned him.

"Is he dead?" Natalya asked, feeling as though even her thoughts were out of breath.

He can't be dead, Victoria said. *He lived to pass on this memory. Otherwise, you wouldn't be able to experience it.*

"Right," Natalya said. She'd forgotten about that.

He is unconscious, but we know he will live.

"That was . . ."

Terrible. How are you doing?

"I'm not sure," Natalya said. "Not good."

Do you want to come out?

Natalya thought about it, but now that the fight was over, she was actually curious to see what would become of Bayan. She wasn't worried, exactly, but she felt involved, and the gray void of his unconsciousness gave her some breathing room to recover.

"I'll stay," she said.

Very well, Victoria said. *If you're sure you're ready to go on, I'll speed up the simulation a bit.*

Natalya sighed and let herself drift, appreciating the form-lessness that enveloped her. She knew that time was relative in the Animus, and she wouldn't be here for long, but she took advantage of what she could, thinking about everything that had just happened.

As strong as Bayan had been, that Assassin had perhaps been stronger. She'd beaten Bayan in a fight with an arrow through her knee. Natalya could only guess at what it would take to drive someone that far. She wondered if the Assassin had made it back into the city.

I'm seeing memory activity, Victoria said.

The void took on half-made shapes that faded in and out of view; faces, fire, the ribs of a ger, the mask of a shaman all passed across the stage of her mind. Natalya knew right away that Bayan was being attended to, only partially aware of what was happening to him. When he finally came fully to, the Great Khan's teenage son stood over his bed in his robes of silk and gold, holding a short crossbow bolt.

Bayan tried to get up, a white storm of pain in his eyes. His side ached and throbbed, but that discomfort was nothing compared his shoulder, which felt as though someone had rammed a burning stick deep into the wound.

"Be still," Asutai said. "You will open your wounds."

Bayan paused, then relented and laid back down, breathing hard, mostly averting his eyes from the young prince.

"They pulled this from you," Asutai said, rolling the bolt between his fingers.

"I was careless," Bayan said, his voice the sound of a woman scraping a new hide. "She hid it well."

"You fought her?"

Bayan nodded. "But she'll never fight again. I shot her through the knee."

"You did more than any other warrior." Asutai tapped the bolt against his palm. "My father is dead."

Bayan lifted his head. "What?"

"The woman you fought assassinated him while he slept."

"How . . . ?" *How could that be?* he wondered. The Great Khan was dead? Had the Sky-Father abandoned them completely, here in this accursed place?

"Not many know," Asutai continued. "With the death of Wang Dechen, the other generals fear it would be too much for the Horde's morale."

Bayan pushed his own doubts aside for the moment to deal with what needed to be done. "How will you keep it a secret?"

"We've let it be known that he is sick with the fever. In several days, we will report that he has died from it."

That plan made sense. The Khan's death would go hard with the Horde regardless, but harder still if it was a Song assassination. A fever could be accounted for fairly innocently, but a death at the enemy's hands, during a siege, in the middle of his own tent, meant the Great Khan and his entire rule had been overturned.

"Tomorrow," Asutai said, "we will raise the watchtower he'd planned, as though the battle will continue."

"But will it?"

Asutai sighed. "No. When word reaches my uncles, there will be a struggle for power. Possibly even war amongst the Great

Khan's three brothers. Hulagu will likely support Kublai against Ariq Boke. The Hordes will be summoned."

Bayan nodded, but felt something amiss. "Why do you tell me this, my lord?"

The prince was silent a moment, and then held up the crossbow bolt. "Every other warrior struck by one of these has died."

"I . . . am sad to hear it."

"I have been learning about you. Your heroics in past battles. Your actions at the Hu Guo Gate with Wang Dechen. Your attempt to locate a secret passage, after which you fought the assassin and then dragged yourself half-dead for miles to reach the camp."

Bayan frowned. "I failed to kill her, or find the passage, my lord."

Asutai slipped the crossbow bolt into a pouch at his waist. "That doesn't matter to me. I have seen what I need to see."

"My lord?"

"I will name you one of the Kheshig. You will join my personal guard."

Bayan's eyes widened. "You honor me, my lord. Greatly. But I am wounded—"

"They tell me you will heal. And I have need of men like you. After we announce my father's death, his body will be prepared, and then I will escort him to Burkhan Khaldun, to be buried alongside Genghis Khan and his ancestors. You will accompany me."

In his state of pain and exhaustion, Bayan could not fully comprehend this offer, nor did he know how to reply to it. But he nodded his head slowly, trying to effect a bow, and simply said, "It is more than I deserve."

"The Khans reward merit," Asutai said, turning to leave. "And you have shown it. I know I can rely on you. Now, you must rest."

With that, the prince was gone, and Bayan's mind fell, reeling, into sleep.

CHAPTER THIRTEEN

Sean made his way to his Animus room, excited to find out where he would be going that day. The experience in Ireland had been difficult for him. Maybe even a bit traumatic. He'd woken up in the middle of the night, worried the Aerie was burning down, and he still wanted to know what happened to Brandon and his family.

But Victoria and Isaiah had reminded him that those memories had all happened in the past, hundreds of years ago. They couldn't be changed. The only thing that could be changed was the future, and what kind of future did Sean want?

A future where violent rioters and chaos ruled? Where innocents suffered?

Or a world of peace and order?

Sean didn't even have to think about the answer to that question.

When he reached his Animus room, he found the computers mostly darkened. A tech knelt over an open panel in the floor at the base of the ring, rooting around in its innards.

"Where's Victoria?" Sean asked.

The tech looked up. "Oh, they want you in the corporate conference room."

"Where is that?"

"In the main building," the tech said. "Want me to wheel you there?"

"No need," Sean said. "I know the way."

He reversed out of the room and pushed himself in the direction of the main building, the first one they'd entered when Abstergo had brought them to the Aerie. It was a quick ride through the corridors to the glass walkway, and then just a roll through the trees, the air in the tunnel warmed by the sun, the tree shadows strobing him until he reached the far side. From there, he entered the main building, with its shiny floor and its central atrium rising several stories above.

He wheeled across the open floor, activity bustling all around him, toward the big, main conference room. Victoria and Isaiah were in there, talking, and it looked like a fairly heated conversation. Sean wondered what it was about. Victoria's voice was raised, Sean could hear it muffled through the glass, and Isaiah looked down at her with an implacable expression. Neither of them seemed to have noticed Sean, so he eased the door open.

". . . isn't fair to him!" Victoria said. "I don't like the way you're using him—"

"Using him?" Isaiah said. "Aren't we using them all?"

"But you're getting his hopes up with this prosthetic research. And he's becoming too dependent on the Animus. I don't like it."

"Are you talking about me?" Sean asked, though he knew the answer.

They both spun toward him. Victoria looked embarrassed, casting her gaze at the table, the wall, anywhere but Sean. Isaiah looked directly at him.

"Yes, we were," the director said. "Why don't you join the conversation."

"Are you serious?" Victoria asked Isaiah. "After everything I just told you—"

"He's certainly both smart enough and mature enough." Isaiah motioned for Sean to come closer. "Victoria thinks I'm placing too heavy a burden on you."

"I can take it," Sean said.

"I know he thinks that," Victoria said. "But he's a—"

"I'm right here," Sean said. "You don't have to talk about me in the third person."

Victoria pursed her lips. "Sean, at your age, you probably don't think you're at any kind of risk using the Animus. That life is limitless—"

"I'm sorry." Sean held up his hand. "I'm going to stop you right there." He pointed at his wheelchair. "I've spent the last few years learning exactly what my limitations are. I'm still trying to figure out what kind of life I can have—"

"Oh, but Sean." Victoria walked toward him and crouched down. "Regardless of your wheelchair, or your legs, you are a whole, capable person. You can have whatever life you choose."

"I've heard this before," Sean said. "Grace tried to tell me something similar the other day. I get it, I do. And I appreciate it. But if Abstergo is making a prosthetic that will give me back my legs, then I want in. And if the Animus will help with that research, while also giving me a chance to walk in someone else's memories, I'll take that, too. You don't need to worry about me."

Victoria covered her mouth a moment, and then she got to her feet and turned away.

"Well said." Isaiah gave Sean an approving nod. "And just what I would have expected from you."

Sean appreciated the director's confidence in him. "The tech said you wanted to see me?"

"Yes," Isaiah said. "I thought you might want to be here for this."

"For what?"

"We're about to have a meeting with one of the lead research-ers from our bioengineering department."

"Is he working on the prosthetic?"

"He is," Isaiah said. "He should be here momentarily with some others from his team. I wanted them to meet you, to have a face to put with the data."

Isaiah took a seat at the head of the table, and Victoria sat down near him, but Sean could sense an icy barrier growing between them. A few minutes later, five people entered the room, two men and three women, all wearing the cliché white lab coats Sean would have expected. One of the men, with reddish hair and a thick beard to match, nodded toward Isaiah.

"Director, Dr. Bibeau," he said. "Good to see you."

"Good to see you, too, Thomas." Isaiah smiled. "Welcome to you and your team."

Thomas turned to Sean. "And is this the young man whose brain I know so well?"

"It is," Isaiah said. "Sean, this is Dr. Thomas Marshall."

Thomas walked over and shook Sean's hand. "Pleasure."

"Same," Sean said.

"I can't tell you how exciting this is," Thomas said. "The results so far are—"

"Why don't you show us," Isaiah said.

Thomas nodded and went to the head of the table, where he inserted some kind of data stick into a console. The lights in the room dimmed, and the glass walls of the room frosted over, some of them becoming a giant screen.

A three-dimensional image of a brain appeared, with thousands, perhaps millions, of little electrical impulses traveling through its network of cells and brain wiring.

"This is you," Thomas said. "Every time you enter the Animus, our map of your brain gains detail. Accuracy. The millions of varied motions your legs can make will all be coded, and then programmed into a customized robotic brace for your legs."

"What is the time frame until we have a working prototype?" Sean questioned.

"Faster than I first estimated," Thomas said. "With the Parietal Suppressors, we're getting data of greater purity than I expected. We might be able to have something to test in six months to a year."

"Really?" Sean asked.

Thomas nodded. "Yes, really. If the data keep rolling in, we'll be on track."

"Then what are we waiting for?" Sean said. "Let's get me into the Animus."

A chuckle rolled around the table.

"Have you ever had such a willing research participant, Thomas?" Isaiah asked.

"Not that I can recall," Thomas said. "But don't you worry, Sean. Give us time, and we'll help you."

Sean looked down at his wheelchair, his scrawny legs, the ones that used to drive him down the football field, people cheering from the sidelines. He doubted the prosthetic would be good enough to bring all of that back, but he would take anything they could give him.

"Excellent," Isaiah said. "From here, we'll dive into some budgetary and technical concerns. I think you'd probably be happier in a simulation, Sean."

"I'm ready to go," Sean said.

Isaiah turned to Victoria. "Could you see to that?"

Victoria, who Sean realized hadn't said a word for some time, simply nodded and rose from her chair.

Sean looked at Thomas. "Thank you."

"My pleasure," Thomas said. "Truly. This is what I love to do."

Sean nodded, thanked Isaiah, and then rolled through the door Victoria held open for him, back into the main atrium. Victoria walked up alongside him, clutching her tablet to her chest. She said nothing, but looked as if she had more thoughts than she knew what to do with. He did appreciate her concern, even if he didn't think it was necessary.

"I really will be okay," he said, trying to reassure her.

"Define okay," she said.

"Oh-kay," he said. "You know, fine. No problems."

"No problems?" she said. "We all have problems, Sean. That's normal."

"Fine, then normal problems. Just not . . . whatever problems you're worried about."

She sighed and shook her head. "I hope you're right."

They traveled the rest of the way, through the glass tunnel, to the Animus corridor in silence. When they reached it, Victoria switched everything on and waited for Sean to lift himself into the ring. Once he'd climbed into the harness, she went about hooking him up, her forehead creased down the middle. He didn't know what more he could say to relieve her of her concern.

"We're going to go back a little farther," she said. "Mitochondrial DNA puts some of your ancestors in tenth century Scandinavia."

"Scandinavia? You mean, like Vikings?"

"Yes."

"Uh, yeah," Sean said. "Let's definitely do Vikings."

"Very well." She returned to her computer. "It will take a few minutes to load the simulation from that segment of your genetic memory."

"I can wait," he said.

Some of those minutes went by, and then Victoria spun around in her chair. "Thomas was wrong. He can't fix you, because you're not broken."

"Tell that to the X-ray of my back."

"But you aren't your back or your bones."

"Maybe not, but I was a football player, and now that's gone. With a lot of stuff."

Victoria's head drooped a bit. "What happened to you wasn't fair."

"Nope. It was just a guy using his free will to get hammered and run me over." Even though it had been a couple of years, he could still hear the anger in his voice over it.

Victoria laid a hand on his shoulder the way his mom did. "I hope you know I truly do want what is best for you."

"I know you do," Sean said.

She nodded, and then spun back to her computer. "The simulation is loaded."

"I've heard Vikings didn't really wear those horned helmets."

Victoria laughed. "No, I don't think they did. Are you ready?"

"Ready. Let's go meet Thor."

The pale void of the Memory Corridor didn't seem to clear, at first, but then Sean realized he was surrounded by actual fog. He now stood at the bow of a longship, a *drakkar*, a ship of war. The snarling serpent carved into the wooden prow slithered ahead of them over the ocean, spraying salty mist into the air. Behind them, thirty benches of oarsmen heaved them over the water.

The thump of the waves beneath his feet flexed the ship's sinews and spine. His men rowed to the beat of the drum, and the wind stretched the wide sail as tautly as it could. Gulls and cormorants and ospreys flew overhead, heard but not seen. Sean felt more alive, more free, and more powerful than he had in any simulation thus far, including that of the towering Tommy Grayling.

"How far?" his sister asked as she stepped up beside him. She'd wrapped herself in a gray-and-silver fur, her blond hair pulled back with a leather cord, her blue eyes still a bit sunken.

"You should be out of the wind, Gyrid," he said. "Until you have your strength back."

"I want to see it," she said.

Within the simulation, Sean knew what she meant, because the current of his ancestor's mind carried him to that knowledge. She wanted to see the harbor gates of Jomsborg, the fortress of the Jomsvikings. She wanted to catch the first glimpse of their destiny.

"Is it far, Bjorn?" she asked.

"Call me Styrbjörn," he said, his voice low.

"Why do you insist on that? It was meant to be an insult."

"That is exactly why I claim it. So it has no power."

She shook her head, some of her hair falling loose in the wind, her skin pale. If he had known she was sick, he might not have taken her with him, for her own sake. But he also knew she would have fought him on that, and probably come with him anyway. She had no more love for Eric than he did, and possibly more hate, even though the crown upon their uncle's head rightfully belonged to Styrbjörn.

"It isn't far." He put his arm around her to keep her warm. "Keep your eyes open."

"I see more than you," she said, and gently elbowed him in the side.

The fog rolled, and the waves marched, and the ship dug in, until at last something moved in the gray. Gyrid stepped forward, letting the fur slip a bit. Styrbjörn held up his hand, and his *skipari* called the oarsmen to halt. The ship slowed, and Styrbjörn studied the shadows taking shape.

At last the gates emerged from the emptiness, as though from the dark realm of Niflheim itself. The timber of the gates, cut from the largest trees and banded with rust-red iron, guarded the entrance to the harbor. The stone arch from which the gates were hung boasted proudly of its tower and its catapults.

Styrbjörn stepped up to the prow of his ship.

"I am the son of Olof!" he bellowed, his voice echoing off the rocks. "Once called Bjorn, rightful king of Sweden! I seek an audience with the chieftain Palnatoke!"

No reply came from the tower, as Styrbjörn's ship careened toward the gates under wind power.

Gyrid looked at him, unafraid, and impatient.

"I ask that you open the gates of your harbor!" Styrbjörn shouted. "Or risk my wrath if you dishonor me!"

Another moment passed, and then the distant squeal of metal and chain could be heard, and after that, the gates groaned open, wide enough for a ship to enter. Styrbjörn ordered the sail lowered, and the men resumed rowing. They glided through the gate and entered the Jomsborg harbor, a natural anchorage large enough for a dozen longships. The city itself, fortified with a wall of stone and wooden palisade, stood at the end of the inlet. Styrbjörn's *skipari* ordered the helmsman toward it, and the oarsmen to row.

"How will you explain me?" Gyrid asked.

"I won't have to."

"But the Jomsvikings allow no women in their stronghold."

"Until now," Styrbjörn said. If successful in his purpose for coming here, there would be many things about this order of warriors that he would change.

When his *drakkar* reached the pier, Styrbjörn found a delegation of men waiting for him, all of them giants, though smaller than him, and all of them well forged in battle, as was required of any Jomsviking. Seeing them, Sean was reminded of the famed Broadway Squad of the New York police department, to which Tommy Grayling had belonged.

"Why have you come?" one of the men asked from the dock.

Styrbjörn climbed out of his ship as his men tied it securely to the moorings. "I seek an audience with Palnatoke."

"So you said. Why?"

"That is between me and him."

"Why have you brought a woman into Jomsborg?" asked another of the giants, staring toward Gyrid at the prow of the ship.

"She is my sister," Styrbjörn said. "The daughter of a king."

The giants looked at one another, and then the first of them said, "Palnatoke will decide her fate."

Styrbjörn nodded, and he returned to help Gyrid climb out of the boat. Together, arm in arm, they followed the delegation from the pier, through the city defenses, and then through the city itself, which was not a town so much as a permanent barracks. Blacksmiths worked, warriors trained, carpenters sawed and sanded. Everything about this place spoke of war, and raiding, and strength, and glory.

At last the delegation reached the great hall, and the doors opened to admit Styrbjörn and his sister. They entered into a long, dim room, the hearth a channel of red coals down the middle, benches to either side among the carved wooden columns, and banners hanging from the rafters. At the far end stood a man of Styrbjörn's size, with dark hair and a dark complexion, draped in the skin of a black bear.

"Come forward!" the man called.

Styrbjörn and Gyrid marched toward him.

"What brings you to my hall, Bjorn?"

"Palnatoke," Styrbjörn said, arriving to stand before the chieftain. "I expect you've heard about my uncle's treachery."

"I heard he poisoned your father and denied you the crown."

"That is true," Gyrid said.

Palnatoke ignored her, and had so far refused to even look at her. "I ask you again. Why have you come, Bjorn?"

Styrbjörn stared hard at the chieftain. "I've come to take your army," he said.

CHAPTER FOURTEEN

Zhi waited until the Mongol warrior had truly fled before she allowed herself to collapse. Without that last bolt, saved for the right moment, she had no doubt she would be dead. She only wished that she had killed him, but with the pain in her knee robbing her of balance and clear thought, her blade had missed anything vital. Perhaps he would make it back to his camp, perhaps not. Zhi now had to make it back to hers.

The arrow had entered her knee through the side, at an angle, so that her kneecap had been shoved aside by the shaft. But after the Mongol had kicked the arrowhead, her bones had broken further. She couldn't think about the damage yet. She had to climb.

Every movement brought tears to her eyes. She clamped her jaw shut, grinding her teeth so hard she feared they would shatter, and kept silent. Within her thoughts, Owen could hear her screaming, her mind overwhelmed with agony.

She tried hopping toward the cave, pulling the leg behind her, until she couldn't do that anymore, and she dropped to the ground. But crawling was impossible. Her only option was to drag herself, whimpering every time the arrow shaft snagged on a rock or a root, stirring her bones like a bloody stew.

Eventually, blinking sweat and tears from her eyes, she reached the cave entrance. She did her best to look behind her, searching the trees for any signs of scouts or spies, and when she was as satisfied as she could be, she wiggled inside.

The cool water from the stream felt good in her hands, and she splashed it on her face and drank. She felt safe here, and if she held still, the pain settled to the dull strike of a hammer. It occurred to her that she could hide there, as a wounded animal seeks a burrow in which to die. She could close her eyes, lie down, and let herself drift away.

But her father wouldn't allow it. She could feel his spirit, as if it resided in the gauntlet on her wrist, and it praised her and urged her forward.

She resumed her climb, up through the cave, listening to the haunting echoes of her own moans as the hammer strike of pain became the heart of the blacksmith's furnace, burning everything else away. The broken shaft of the arrow scraped the stone, and the abrasion rattled every bone of her spine.

She stopped many times to rest, letting the darkness receive her, only to pull herself back before she became utterly lost in it, and resume her journey.

After what felt not like hours, but many nights, she caught a glimpse of light above, and she strained toward it, the final distance the most arduous, until she emerged from the cave into the harsh, predawn world.

No one saw her as she crawled to the Fishing Terrace, and then over it, coming to a blissful rest before Kang's hut. There she waited, tossed on the waves of pain, until she heard the door open behind her, heard the thump of a staff, and then saw Kang standing over her.

"Am I late?" she whispered.

"No," he said. "You are here on—"

Owen floated in the void of Zhi's unconsciousness, awed by the strength and will she had just shown, the distance she had gone to honor her father's memory. He admired her, and only wished he could be more like her.

You doing okay? Griffin asked.

His voice, from outside the simulation, was very different than Monroe's had been. Griffin came across like a 911 dispatcher, all calm professionalism. Monroe had been more like Gandalf, a kindly voice of reason and wisdom, with the occasional, frustrating riddle of an answer, but Owen almost missed that.

"I'm doing okay," he said.

That was intense.

"Doesn't get much worse."

Need a break?

"No. I'll keep going."

Good man.

So Owen waited, until Zhi awoke in her bed to the smell of fish. She opened her eyes and found Kang seated nearby, sitting upright against the wall, dozing. She looked up at the ceiling, and when she tried to move, her knee reminded her of everything she'd done. But when she lifted her head and looked down at her leg, she noted only the bandages with a small red bloom, the arrow gone.

Her head slumped back onto her pillow, and the sound awoke Kang.

He snorted and rubbed his eyes. "Ah, welcome back."

"How long?" she asked, and the words burned her throat.

"Nearly three days," he said. "I kept you sedated. You probably have no memory of any of it."

She searched backward, and found the scroll of her mind blank after the fight outside the cave. "None."

Kang nodded. "Just as well."

"I killed him," Zhi said. "Möngke Khan is dead."

"I wondered," Kang said. "The Mongol army hasn't left yet, though."

"It will."

The old man smiled. "When I asked you to show me you were ready, this was not exactly what I intended."

"I know," Zhi said. "But now you know I am my father's daughter."

"You are, indeed. Headstrong, just as he was."

"I used his blade to kill the Khan." She lifted her wrist, but, of course, the gauntlet wasn't there. "Where did you put it?"

Kang's smile vanished, and his eyebrows bent in sadness. "I took it."

"Where?"

"Away."

He seemed to be grieving over something, and Owen felt a powerful dread pressing down on his shoulders. "What do you mean?" Zhi asked.

"You are not to have it."

"What?" Zhi raised her head and her voice. "Why?"

"Because you will not be taking your father's place in the Brotherhood. You will not be an Assassin, so the gauntlet does not belong with you."

"Why will I not be an Assassin?" The pain in her knee had begun to rise with the heat of her anger and confusion. "Because I went without permission? I killed the Khan! Have I not proven myself worthy? Are you so bitter and vindictive you would—"

"No." He held up his hand and shook his head. "No, it is none of those things."

"Then what is it?"

"It is your knee," he said. "It will . . . never be what it was."

Zhi glanced down again at her injury. She had known it was bad. The crawl back to the fortress could not have been good for it, but surely it would heal. "It will be fine," she said.

Kang's shoulders slumped. "No, Zhi, it will not. You will walk again, with time. But you will not *run*. You will not climb, jump, or kick."

Zhi shook her head, overcome by a new pain, one Owen felt with her. "I don't believe you—"

"I set the bones myself," Kang said. "I have tended many, many injuries, and I know of what I speak."

Her life and honor were being taken from her. The spirit of her father was being taken from her. What would she be? Who would she be without it? Owen could not help but rage at the injustice of it, not only the injury, but this old man who seemed to have already cast her aside. He looked at Kang through Zhi's eyes, and wondered, *what of his leg?* He walked with a staff.

"But you are a crippled old man," Zhi said, and Owen wondered whose thought he had just had, his or hers.

"I am now," he said. "But I served the Brotherhood for years before old age found me and dragged me out of the fight."

Zhi looked back up at the ceiling, the house now a prison.

"For what you have done, for our people and for the Brotherhood, I honor you." Kang heaved himself to his feet, his staff thumping the floor to find his balance. "The Brotherhood shall see to your needs for as long as you live."

"Because I am now worthless," Zhi said.

"No," Kang said. "But you are no longer useful. To the Brotherhood. As a hero, you are invaluable, even though others may not ever know what you have done."

His words did nothing to comfort her. Nothing to fill the emptiness he had just carved out of her. But after he had said good-bye and left her alone, she lay there and realized that Kang hadn't made that hollow in her. She had felt it in her soul since the night her father had died, like an open tomb inside her. She had filled that chamber with vengeance and purpose and hate. But the emptiness inevitably ate such things, and then demanded more.

Owen knew exactly what she felt. He carried that emptiness around, too. He had managed to fill it and ignore it, but under the burden of Zhi's grief, his defenses buckled, like a popping in his chest.

"Griffin," he said. "I need out."

Out?

"Out." He didn't want to answer why, but Griffin didn't ask.

Give me a minute, here.

Owen waited. Zhi began to sob.

Okay, terminating simulation. Now.

For once, the mental stress of leaving the simulation felt preferable to the pain of staying in it. Owen closed his eyes, and then opened them in the Memory Corridor, where he tried to remind himself of who he was. But it was hard to shake off Zhi's grief, or the wound it had reopened inside him.

Ready to come out?

"Ready," Owen said.

Another reality-smashing earthquake, and then he was back in the Assassin's lair, in the basement of the old firetrap of a house. The helmet lifted away, and Griffin disconnected him. Javier stood nearby, watching him.

"You okay?" his friend asked.

"I don't know," Owen said.

"We were watching. That was brutal, man."

Griffin stepped away, and Owen sat up, feeling very heavy. "Yeah, it was."

"And no further sign of the Piece of Eden," Griffin said. "So far."

"Do you think it's worth going back in?" Owen asked, but he didn't want to. "Seems like Zhi saw it in the tent, and that was it for her."

"I think you're probably right," Griffin said. "We need a new approach."

Owen needed a new approach, too. Something. Anything. All he could think about now was his dad, and he missed him so desperately he felt as though he could just implode right there, becoming a human black hole, endlessly collapsing on himself. Nothing anyone had told him, not his mom, or his grandparents, or that grief counselor they'd taken him to see, none of it could stop the process from taking place. Monroe had failed to warn him about this Bleeding Effect.

"You hungry?" Griffin asked.

"No," Owen said out of breath, or maybe he hadn't taken one.

"Come here." Javier walked away, toward the conference table. "I want to show you something."

"What?" Owen asked, his feet rooted to the floor.

"Just come look," Javier said.

So Owen forced himself across the basement to where Javier stood. He looked down at the stuff on the table. Files and papers and what looked like police evidence bags. But the name written on the bags, in Sharpie, caught Owen's eye. It was his dad's name. He looked back at the files, and found they all had his dad's name on them, too.

"What is this?" Owen asked.

"It's the evidence from your dad's trial," Javier said. "Thought you could look through it. See if they missed anything."

"How—?"

"Javier went rogue," Griffin said, and Owen could tell the Assassin wasn't happy about it. "He broke into the police warehouse and stole it."

Owen turned to his friend. "You did?"

Javier nodded. "But you don't know how boring it was out here. I had to do something."

Owen couldn't believe it. He looked back down at everything, and noticed a smaller evidence bag tucked behind one of the others. It had a cotton swab in it.

"What . . .?" But then Owen realized exactly what it was. "This is DNA."

"Looks like it," Griffin said. "A spit sample."

"But it's from *after* the robbery," Owen said.

Javier grinned. "So it would have the memory of the robbery."

"I could go into a simulation," Owen said.

"Hold on." Griffin looked back and forth between them. "Yes, with the right equipment, you could. But the Animus we have doesn't do that. This one needs a live subject participating in a simulation of their own memories."

"But there is an Animus that could," Owen said.

Griffin gave him a nod that seemed reluctant. "Yes. That tech exists. It's called Helix. Abstergo developed it after the Animus. But to use it we would need to upload your father's decoded DNA to Abstergo's database—"

"The Assassins don't have their own Helix?" Owen asked.

Griffin pointed across the room. "I don't think you realize just how rare that Animus over there really is. It's not like the Brotherhood issues them with your hidden blade."

But Owen felt hope again, and that filled the emptiness inside him better than Zhi's revenge and hate had filled hers. The emotional effects of the simulation faded. Owen now believed he had another chance to finally make things right. To prove to his grandparents, and the world, and even his own mom, that his dad was innocent. He just had to find the type of Animus that would let him do it.

He turned to Javier. For the last few years, Owen had thought his friend just didn't care anymore. But Javier had risked himself to find the exact thing Owen had been searching for. He held up the evidence bag, and with a little catch in his throat, he said, "Thanks."

Javier shrugged. "Don't worry about it. Like I said, I was bored."

"Doesn't change the fact that you could have been caught," Griffin said. "And it's not the most pressing issue we face."

Owen tucked the evidence bag into his pocket. "Right. The Piece of Eden."

"Exactly. I need to report to Gavin that this simulation was a bust. Maybe Rothenberg has a new lead for us."

"Who is Rothenberg?" Owen asked. "Do you know?"

Griffin walked over to a different computer terminal than the one he'd been using to run the Animus. He clicked on a few folders, and selected a file. The picture was of a generic avatar silhouette, not even a man or a woman. Griffin pointed at the screen.

"That's what we know."

"But you trust him?" Owen asked.

"Or her?" Javier added.

"Yes," Griffin said. "Rothenberg's intel has always been solid."

"But could this person be, like, a double agent or something?" Owen asked.

"No," Griffin said. "Rothenberg has never asked for anything in return. If that were to ever happen, Gavin would terminate the operation."

"So what if Rothenberg doesn't have a new lead for us?"

Griffin turned back to the computer terminal. "For now, we wait and see. Both of you stay quiet. I'm going to contact Gavin."

Owen and Javier slipped away, back to the evidence table. Owen flipped through some of the files and reports. This looked like everything, down to the bullet casings and the footage from the security cameras. This was the whole case against his dad, right here, and Owen couldn't wait to start poking holes in it.

"So was this hard to get?" he asked.

"Nothing I couldn't handle," Javier said. "I did get to drive a car. And now I know what a grenade does to a chain-link fence."

"So it was worth it, then."

"Totally."

"So really, you should be thanking me," Owen said.

"Probably."

Griffin's lowered voice reached them, and over the Assassin's shoulder, Owen saw the face of Gavin on the screen. He tried to listen in, but couldn't hear what they were saying. Several minutes went by this way, before the screen went black. Griffin left the computer and walked over toward them.

"Rothenberg has been silent," he said. "No new intelligence."

"So where does that leave us?" Javier asked.

Griffin leaned on the conference table with his fists. "We have to assume the Templars still have someone, one of your friends, with access to the right genetic memories. Yours didn't pan out, Owen, but theirs might."

Owen had already realized that. The Assassins needed someone with the right DNA if they were going to beat Abstergo to the prong. But who had the right DNA?

CHAPTER FIFTEEN

D avid expected that, at any moment, Isaiah and that paramilitary lady, Cole, would come for him. If Owen and Javier could be *terminated*, then what about him?

The fear had kept him up at night, and followed him around during the day. Sometimes, he was almost able to convince himself that he had misunderstood, grabbing on to the sound bite without the context. The conversation was probably about something else, and if David had the missing piece, it would all make sense. But that didn't mean he wasn't worried about what would happen when Victoria pulled the security footage and saw where David had gone that night.

But fortunately, she hadn't done that yet. Apparently, Natalya was getting closer to the Piece of Eden in her simulation, and

Sean was involved in some new brain research, both of which kept Victoria busy and bought David time.

And today, his dad was coming to visit.

David had to decide if he was going to stay here. He could ask his dad to take him home. He didn't even have to tell what he had overheard. His dad probably wouldn't believe him anyway, just like the others. David could just say he was done.

But would Grace leave with him?

That was the hard part. Grace would probably want to stay, and David didn't know if he was willing to leave her behind.

She was already eating breakfast when David entered the lounge, and he took a seat next to her. Sean was there, and Natalya, too.

"So you've seen it?" Grace asked.

Natalya ate a spoonful of berry yogurt and nodded.

"You're sure it's the Piece of Eden?" Sean asked, with a bit of a frown, like he was envious.

"Yeah," Natalya said. "It's a dagger, just like the one in New York."

David didn't think she seemed too happy about finding it, especially considering that's the entire reason they were there in the first place.

"So that's two of the prongs," Grace said.

"Just one more to go," Sean said.

David looked back and forth between them. They were talking like it was a race, and they were neck and neck at the finish line. He knew right then there was no way Grace would leave with him. She never backed away from a competition.

"We still don't know where the first one is, remember?" Natalya said. "Maybe Monroe got it, maybe he didn't. And I don't actually know where this second one is going to end up."

"Where is it now?" Sean asked.

"My ancestor and a bunch of bodyguards are escorting the Khan's body back to Mongolia for his burial. It's, like, thirteen hundred miles away. But I've seen the dagger with the Khan's armor in a big wagon."

"Are they going to bury it with his body?" Sean asked.

Natalya shrugged. "Probably."

"That's how we'll find it," Grace said.

"That's how *Isaiah* will find it," Natalya added.

Grace turned to Sean. "What simulation are you doing now?"

"I'm a Viking." Sean leaned back in his wheelchair, sitting up straighter, like he felt taller just talking about it. "I just challenged this other guy to single combat for the right to lead the Jomsvikings."

"The what-Vikings?" David asked.

"Jomsvikings," Sean said. "The best of the best."

"Does Isaiah think there's a Piece of Eden there?" Grace asked.

"Not sure yet," Sean said. "But the—"

Victoria entered the room then, and smiled at them all. "Visiting day," she said. "Grace, David, your father is here."

They both rose from the table at the same time and made their way toward the door. David still hadn't figured out what he was going to say. They left their building and proceeded along the glass walkway. The day was overcast, and up here in the mountains, the clouds seemed closer and heavier.

Before they'd reached the far end, Grace stopped and tugged on David's arm. "You're not gonna to go saying anything stupid, are you?"

He turned back to face her. "What do you mean?"

"I mean that whole crazy story."

"It wasn't a story. It happened."

"Would you cut it out? Listen to yourself. Look around you. You really think these people are out there killing kids?"

"Remember Boss Tweed? Back in New York?" David folded his arms. "That's what *these people* do."

"Used to," she said. "That was a hundred and fifty years ago. Lots of people killed people back then. Our people. Remember?"

Her question hit him with the sharp end, and a tight pain squeezed his chest. His ancestor, Abraham, had been murdered in the Draft Riots by a bunch of racist Irish thugs. He tried not to think about that too often. The memory of it made him feel sick, and angry, and helpless, and he didn't like feeling any of those things.

"Don't take it there, Grace."

"I'm sorry. I'm just trying to help you see things the right way."

He turned away from her and kept walking. "I do see things the right way."

She hurried to catch up to him. "But you're not going to say anything to Dad. Right?"

"I don't know yet," he said.

"David—"

"I said I don't know." He pushed through the doors, and entered the big atrium in the main building of the Aerie. This space was big and open enough to eat all the echoes. David walked past the plants and the wide stairs toward the main lounge. Grace followed him, and he could tell she wanted to keep arguing, but she wouldn't, because she didn't want to be in the middle of it when they walked through the door, or else their dad would ask them what it was all about.

They entered the lounge and their dad got up from one of the armchairs, smiling. He'd dressed up in his dark, navy blue suit, a white button-down shirt, and no tie. "Good to see you two," he said in his slow and even way, walking toward them with his long arms outstretched.

David and Grace each got a hug, and the three of them went to sit together at one of the tables.

"So how have you both been?" Their dad propped his elbows on the table, his rugged welder's hands clasped together. "David?"

Grace gave David a glare, which he tried to ignore. "I'm good."

"And you, Grace?" his dad asked.

"I'm good," she said. "You shaved your beard."

"I did." He rubbed his cheek and jaw. "Are you still in the simulation of our Wangaran ancestor?"

"Not anymore," she said.

His dad's mouth settled into that disapproving frown he wore a lot of the time without realizing it. "That's a shame. I thought that would be a good experience for you. The education system today treats our history as though it began with slavery. Before that, the empires and kingdoms of Africa were—"

"I know, Dad," Grace said.

He turned toward David. "And how is your great-grandfather?"

"He's an ace pilot," David said.

"Yes, he was. He earned the respect of every commanding officer he ever served under. He let me try on his old flight jacket once. It was so big on me."

"Fits me perfectly," David said.

His dad laughed. "You know, his father flew with the Harlem Hellfighters before him, during the First World War. Maybe they'd let you experience those memories, too."

"Maybe," David said.

Then their father fell back into seriousness. "I've always told you how important it is to know where you come from. Who your people are. Who your family is. What it took to get you where you are. But this opportunity is better than anything I could've ever done to teach you on my own. You're . . . you're living it." He paused, and the frown deepened. "I just wish you could have begun this journey with Abstergo from the beginning. I understand they still haven't caught Monroe."

"No," David said.

"It really is criminal how he took advantage of you and the others. I would never have allowed you to go back to the Draft Riots. There are some things you shouldn't ever experience, even in a simulation. I've made that clear to the director and Dr. Bibeau."

"We're fine, Dad," Grace said.

David said nothing.

"Are you still happy here?" his dad asked. "Grace, you're looking out for your brother?"

"I'm trying," Grace said, with an edge that only David could detect.

"I knew I could count on you." Their dad brought his smile back. "That's why I agreed to this, and I'm happy with this arrangement."

David felt as though this would be the ideal time to ask if he could leave. His dad had basically brought the issue up, and sounded open to the possibility that maybe this wasn't the right place for them. But Grace would be furious, and she'd probably refuse to leave. David still hadn't come up with a good reason to give his dad, other than telling him about Isaiah's murderous statements, which he knew would seem as unbelievable as Grace made them sound.

"Let's go get some lunch," his dad said.

"Where should we go?" Grace asked.

And the moment passed, the window closed, and David knew he was stuck there at the Aerie. For now.

He and Grace spent the next few hours with their dad. The heavy clouds made good on their promise of rain, which fell more like a mist through the trees and filled the air with the scent of wet leaves and pine needles. They drove down the mountain to a Chinese restaurant, and then drove back up, where their dad dropped them off and said good-bye.

After that, they had the rest of the day to themselves. The weekends, when parents usually came, were a time away from the Animus. That had been entirely Victoria's idea. David had recently gotten the impression that if Isaiah had his way, they'd be in simulations 24/7.

So David and Grace watched a movie in the lounge. A little while later, Sean came back, and then Natalya, and then they all ate dinner. No one talked about the Pieces of Eden that had come up earlier that day. Tonight, the chefs at the Aerie had cooked up a perfect rainy-day soup with potatoes and sausage. David had two bowls, and he was thinking about a third when Isaiah stalked in, Victoria behind him.

Right away, something seemed off. Isaiah looked mad, and the way David's stomach suddenly lurched, he wished he hadn't eaten anything.

"I trust you all had an enjoyable afternoon with your parents," Isaiah said without a hint of genuine care. He didn't even wait for their acknowledgment. "But now we must turn to a more serious business."

"What business?" Sean asked.

Isaiah looked right at David. "Youthful curiosity."

Now Grace and Sean and Natalya were looking at David, too.

"I think David knows what this is about," Isaiah said. "Perhaps he even told you all about it."

No sense hiding it or denying it. They had the security footage, obviously. So David leaned forward, put his elbows on the table, and clasped his hands together. "I did tell them."

"What did you tell them?" Victoria asked.

"It doesn't matter," Isaiah said. "The point is, David, you left your room in the middle of the night and covertly entered restricted areas. That was extremely unsafe. The garage is often dark and we have vehicles coming and going at all times. What if you'd been hit? What if you'd been locked out somewhere? The rules are not in place to keep anything from you, but to keep you all safe. That's our chief concern."

David wasn't sure yet what to make of the situation. So far, this felt like any normal lecture for breaking the rules, not a termination order. He relaxed, just a little, and wondered if he really had misunderstood the conversation he'd overheard.

"So what are we to do?" Isaiah said. "You know how important you all are to what we are trying to achieve. We haven't found the final resting places of the other Pieces of Eden yet, and we still don't know exactly what else Monroe found in your DNA. But at the same time, I won't have you violating the security of this facility. Ordinarily, such actions would be grounds for dismissal. For all of you."

"What?" The glare Sean fired at David was worse than Grace's. "But we didn't have anything to do with him running off."

"I know that," Isaiah said. "And I don't think David actually meant any harm. As I said, youthful curiosity."

"So you're not going to send us home?" Grace said.

"I do not want to if it can be avoided. So let's call this a probation."

"Meaning what?" Natalya said.

"Your rooms will now be locked at night. In the unlikely event of an emergency, they will automatically open. But otherwise, you will be confined there during the off-hours."

"Like house arrest," David said.

Isaiah raised his eyebrows and nodded. "You can think of it that way, I suppose. A natural consequence."

"So we're prisoners," Natalya said.

"Not at all," Isaiah said. "If you would rather, you can call your parents and have them come get you. But if you would like to stay to be a part of this important work, these are my terms."

Isaiah made eye contact with each of them. Victoria stood behind him, and David couldn't read her expression. Sean's glare at David had lessened, but not by much. Natalya didn't seem angry with him, but Grace did. He knew what she was thinking. In her head she was yelling at him for getting her in trouble again. Well, it wasn't David's fault that their dad always made Grace feel as though she was responsible for him. David hadn't ever asked for that.

"What do you say?" Isaiah asked. "Shall I call any of your parents? They might be able to come back and pick you up tonight."

"I'm staying," Sean said. "I wasn't planning to leave my room at night anyway."

"I'm staying, too," Grace said. "And I apologize for my brother."

David rolled his eyes.

Victoria looked at Natalya. "What about you?"

"I'll stay," Natalya said. "But I still feel like a prisoner."

"I hope that will change," Isaiah said. He turned to David. "And you? Our automotive enthusiast?"

That confirmed what David suspected, that they'd seen him climb into the jet-car on the security footage. But maybe Isaiah didn't think David could have heard his conversation with Cole from inside the vehicle, and that's why he hadn't done anything more drastic than lock their doors at night. If David wanted to keep Isaiah believing that, he had to pretend that he wasn't afraid, and didn't want to leave.

"That's fine," David said.

"No more late night excursions?" Isaiah said.

"Not if my door is locked," David said.

Isaiah nodded. "I'm pleased we were all able to come to an understanding. And now, I'll leave you to the rest of your meal."

He turned and strode from the room.

Victoria smiled. "I'll see you all tomorrow morning for your simulations."

Then she left as well, and the moment the door closed, Grace was on her feet. "When are you going to grow up?"

"When are you going to back off?" David said.

"When you stop acting like a child!"

"Hey, listen up," Sean said. "I don't care if you grow up or not, David. But you will not mess this up for the rest of us. Do you understand? Some of us actually take this seriously. I take this seriously."

"So do I," Grace said.

David shook his head. He could feel his ears getting hot, and his mouth drying up. "Whatever," he said.

"Whatever?" Grace said. "You did not just *whatever* me."

"Actually," David said. "I think—"

"I am getting sick of this sibling rivalry thing you two have going on," Sean said. "All I want to know is that you're not gonna cause any more trouble for me. Or the rest of us. Right?"

David pushed his glasses up and glowered at the table.

"Right?" Grace said.

David nodded. Barely.

"Good," Sean said. "Then I'm going to my room for the night. I'll see you all in the morning." Then he left the lounge.

"I'm going to bed, too," Grace said. "I can't take any more of this right now."

Then she was also gone, leaving David alone with Natalya. He sat there for a few minutes, and after he'd calmed down a bit, he said to her, "You've been quiet."

"I've been thinking."

"About what?"

"My simulation."

"What about it?"

She hesitated. "I think I've decided that I don't want Isaiah to find the Piece of Eden."

CHAPTER SIXTEEN

Javier liked the idea of a rescue mission, but not the idea of being left behind, doing nothing, and right now Griffin didn't sound as though he planned to take them with him.

"You need us," Javier said.

"Oh, really?" Griffin asked. "How so?"

"Our friends don't know you," Javier said. "What makes you think they'll go with you? What if the Templars have convinced them that the Assassins are the bad guys?"

Griffin's grin had a bit of smirk in it. "Believe me. I can take people against their will."

"Four teenagers?" Owen asked. "How easy will that be?"

"It's doable," Griffin said.

"But easier with us," Javier said. "They'll come with us."

"Oh, you think so?" Griffin said.

"Yes," Javier and Owen said at the same time.

The Assassin shook his head. "This isn't like that police warehouse you broke into. This is an Abstergo facility. They've got better security than some heads of state."

"All the more reason to take us," Javier said. "Just how are you going to get four people out of there if those people don't trust you?"

"You're not fully trained." Griffin turned away and walked over to a worktable beneath the wall with all the weapons. "You'd be a liability."

"You took us to Mount McGregor," Owen said.

"That was because I needed you to recognize the Piece of Eden."

"And now you need our friends to recognize *us*." Javier said.

Griffin pulled a cartridge of some kind out of his gauntlet and swapped it for another one. Javier figured it was his electrical blade's power supply. Then the Assassin started mounting other attachments to the gauntlet, some kind of dart gun, and pieces of electronics with antennas and touch screens. "Last time I took you with me, you disobeyed a direct order," he said.

"I won't do that again," Owen said.

"Besides," Javier said. "I think you do need us. You were mad when Rebecca left, because I think you were worried. I don't think you're excited about the idea of doing this alone."

Griffin nodded. "Maybe you're right about that."

"So let us help," Javier said. "You've been training us. Let us use it."

Griffin shoved a few more weapons and gadgets into the

pockets of his leather coat, and then he leaned forward against the worktable. "Okay."

"Okay?" Owen asked.

"Yes," Griffin said. "Suit up."

Javier and Owen looked at each other, and they joined Griffin at the worktable. Javier grabbed his usual equipment and weaponry. He'd become really partial to the crossbow pistol, but this time, Owen grabbed one, too.

"Zhi used something like this," he said. "I got kinda used to it. It saved her life."

"Better take it," Javier said. Then he grabbed some of the usual grenades he'd used before. But the worktable and wall contained other pieces of gear that Javier hadn't seen back in Griffin's storage unit. He picked up a canister about the size of a slim can of soda. "What's this?"

"Pain grenade," Griffin said. "Emits a blast of energy a bit like a microwave. Cooks the top layer of skin. Hurts like a bed of nails, but it's nonlethal, even if you wish you could die."

Javier slipped one of those into a pocket.

"What about this?" Owen asked, holding up another pistol-like device.

"Laser array," Griffin said. "Point it at a target's face and it causes temporary blindness."

"Most of this stuff seems to be about disruption and distraction," Javier said.

"That's because the Assassin is the true weapon," Griffin said. "Governments kill indiscriminately with their drones and bombs. The Templars accept faceless, collateral deaths in pursuit of their agenda. But we're different. The Assassins kill only who we intend to kill, and according to our Creed. We face our target without any denial or cowardice over what we do. The minute we let something or someone else do the killing for us, we're no better than the others."

Javier found a kind of honor in that.

"Finish loading up what you want," Griffin said. "And let's move out."

Javier grabbed a few more grenades and bolts for his crossbow, then he noticed Owen standing by the evidence table, looking down at it all.

"Hey," Javier said. "We'll dive into all that when we get back. Okay?"

"Right." Owen nodded. "Okay, let's go."

They followed Griffin up the stairs out of the house, across the overgrown lawn, toward the barn where Javier had parked the car.

"You probably didn't fill it up, did you?" Griffin said.

Javier didn't say anything to that, and got an elbow from Owen over it.

"Get in," Griffin said.

Owen climbed into the front passenger seat, and Javier got in the back. They both waited as Griffin brought out a large gas can from one side of the barn and filled the car. When that was done, the Assassin got in, started the engine, and they rolled out.

It was already late afternoon, and Griffin estimated it would take a few hours to reach the Abstergo facility.

"It's called the Aerie," he said.

"Like an eagle's nest?" Javier asked. "Isn't the eagle kinda you guys' thing? You know, like Eagle Vision?"

"I'm sure the Templars were very aware of that when they named it," Griffin said.

They reached the highway and turned north, skirting the foothills for a little while before turning east again, heading up through the hills toward the mountains beyond. As they climbed, the trees grew taller and thicker, and the sky darkened with clouds. Before long, rain slapped the windshield, and evening fell.

When they reached an elevation where Javier's ears popped, Griffin pulled the car over to the side of the road. "We're going to have to make our way by foot from here to try and bypass Abstergo security."

Javier looked out his window. Water ran downhill along the edges of the asphalt mountain road. "I hope these hoods are waterproof."

"They are," Griffin said. "But apparently they're not whiner-proof."

"Good one," Owen said, his voice flat.

"Listen up." Griffin cleared his throat. "From here on out, you pay attention to me, and you do exactly what I tell you to do. We're a few miles away, but before long there'll be cameras and electronic sentries. We can't be seen by any of it."

"How do we do that?" Owen asked.

"Eagle Vision," Griffin said. "It seems you both have it. Try using it to find the surveillance and avoid it."

"Got it," Javier said, even though it made him nervous. His proficiency with Eagle Vision wasn't nearly as natural or advanced as Owen's.

"This facility is made up of five buildings. Your friends are housed in one of them. Let's go get 'em."

The three of them opened the car doors and stepped out into the rain. Griffin was right, Javier's coat and cowl kept him mostly dry, except for the drops that landed on his nose and cheeks.

"We have to move fast," Griffin said. "You've already seen the Assassin-hunting technology Abstergo uses, tracking our 'ghost signature.' We have to outrun that tech."

The air was more chilly up here, and more pure, uncontaminated by the exhaust and fumes of the city. Javier took a deep breath and felt cleaned out.

"Are you both ready?" Griffin asked.

"Ready," Owen said.

"Ready," Javier said.

"Let's move," Griffin said.

He raced off into the woods, and Owen and Javier followed behind him. The ground here was fairly even, with little undergrowth where the pine needles and leaves had formed a permanent shroud over the soil. The trees rose high and spread wide, their branches shielding them from some of the rain. Here and there, they climbed or leapt over large gray rocks, and crossed a few streams bloated with the downpour.

As they moved, Javier summoned his Eagle Vision. The ability wasn't something he could force directly, which he had learned early on. If anything, it was a relaxing of his intention, like playing soccer. In a penalty kick, Javier had to ignore the pressure and just let his body do what it knew how to do. It was the same way with Eagle Vision. His mind took in the sights, smells, sounds, and feel of his environment, gathering information Javier wasn't even consciously aware of.

When they reached the first infrared camera, Javier knew it was there. He thought maybe he could sense its range and its aim over the ground, and estimated where he needed to move to avoid it. All three of them did.

They glided through the trees, more quiet than the rain, and when Griffin pointed out a series of trip wires along the ground, Javier went up, climbing the trunk of a tree to the branches above, which proved easier than scaling the face of a building. From there they swung and leapt from branch to branch, and descended again when another camera came in range.

Before long, they had covered a couple of miles, and the storm had set the sun early. Griffin paused them at the base of a steep slope.

"You're both doing well," he said. "The Aerie is at the summit of this mountain."

Javier looked up, and couldn't see the top.

"Security will be more frequent, and not so easily avoided," Griffin continued. "From here, we take it slow. Stay sharp. In addition to unmanned surveillance, we might run into armed guards."

Javier and Owen both nodded, and then Griffin started up the hill. Javier found the wet ground slippery, and at times it was hard to keep his footing, forcing him to use his hands, climbing on all fours. Not far up the slope, they ran into their first obstacle, a series of cameras covering the forest in a coordinated sweep.

They took cover behind some trees and Griffin armed something on his gauntlet, tapping one of the touch screens. "Be ready to hustle," he whispered. Then he aimed his gauntlet at one of the cameras, and a thin razor of light pulsed from it.

"Now!" he hissed.

The three of them bolted, and Javier could see the gap. One of the cameras had stalled, and he dove through the narrow opening. Owen followed him, and then Griffin. Once they were safely beyond that point, Javier noticed the camera had resumed its patrol.

"What was that?" Owen asked.

"Laser interference," Griffin said. "These cameras are smart, programmed to track movement. I just sent it a signal that threw it off, glitching the software for a few seconds."

Griffin pushed ahead, and Javier whispered to Owen, "I gotta get me one of those gauntlets."

They climbed another dozen yards, evading more cameras and sensors. Javier noticed a few gun sentries mounted to the trees, ready to spring to life. The rain continued unabated, a steady drizzle, and as the hour grew later, Javier started to see wisps of his own breath.

"Our heat differential could be a problem," Griffin said. "These jackets hide a lot of our signature, but if it gets too cold out here, we'll stand out from the ambient temp."

"So what do we do?" Javier asked.

Griffin shook his head. "Try to keep yourself as calm as you can, to keep your blood pressure and temperature down. If we trip security this far out, we'll have a much harder time getting to your friends."

The slope soon declined by a few degrees, allowing for an easier climb, but the trees had also thinned, offering less shadows and places to hide from the more frequent cameras. Their progress became more a series of dashes, leaps, and rolls from location to location, slow and deliberate.

Eventually, they reached a fence twenty feet high, and not a chain-link fence like the one that had surrounded the police warehouse. The ground had been cleared of bushes and trees for at least thirty feet on both sides of it, and it appeared to be made of thick bars in a tightly packed grid. No cutting through them or blowing them up with a grenade. Besides, the whole thing was probably electrified and pressure-sensitive.

Griffin stared at it, chewing on the corner of his mouth, and raised his gauntlet. "Let me see if I can get some readings off that thing."

Javier and Owen waited.

Beyond the fence, away through the trees, Javier glimpsed a building that seemed made of glass. The whole thing glowed with internal light, the hallways and offices clearly visible. If they could get close enough, that might make it easier to find their friends.

"I can't get much," Griffin said. "But my guess is, if we try to climb that thing, they'll know. If we cut it, they'll know. If we disable it, they'll know. We have to get over it without touching it. Unless we want to just announce ourselves right here."

"That building isn't too far," Javier said.

"Yes, but this complex is big," Griffin said. "That's one of five."

"Can you jump that?" Owen asked.

Griffin squinted at the fence. "No. I'm going to have to run a zip line over it between the trees, but I'm pretty sure that will get us detected, too."

"Doesn't sound like we have a choice," Javier said.

Griffin looked up at the trees, glancing through the fence toward the far side, and finally seemed to settle on something.

He climbed up one of the nearest trunks into the branches, until he was higher than the top of the fence, and then he shot something into the trees across the gap, a thin line Javier could barely see in the darkness.

Griffin gave them a whistle, and Javier and Owen climbed up to join him. Javier looked down at the fence from above, and at the cable that disappeared into the trees fifty feet away. His Eagle Vision revealed several cameras, and once he was out on the line, there wouldn't be any way to move and avoid them.

"You have to get across fast." Griffin clipped a kind of pulley grip onto the line. "Take hold of this, and pull yourself across with your other hand. If you trip security, just keep going." He nodded toward Owen. "You're up."

Owen took a deep breath and grabbed on to the clip.

"See you on the other side," Javier said.

Owen nodded. "Right."

"Push off the tree," Griffin said.

Owen faced forward, bracing one foot against the trunk, coiling up. "Okay," he said. "Here goes—"

A siren blared, loud enough it jolted Javier and he almost slipped from his perch on the tree branch. Bright lights switched on up and down the fence, and distant shouts could be heard.

"Was that us?" Javier asked.

"I don't think so," Griffin said. "Cameras can't detect the cable, and Owen hadn't moved yet. Something else tripped their security. The Aerie will be in lockdown, and that's going to make things harder for us inside."

"So what do we do?" Owen asked.

"Get across. Hurry."

Owen nodded, got back in position, and heaved himself out into the open. The clip in his hand buzzed over the line, and Owen used his other hand to pull himself across. He covered the distance quickly, disappearing into the trees, and then Griffin attached a new clip.

"Now you," he said.

Javier gripped the clip and followed after Owen. The motion was harder than it looked, and the entire time, Javier felt exposed and vulnerable. Someone watching could have easily shot him right out of the air. He pulled and slid and pulled and slid his way across, until he reached the safety of the trees on the far side.

"Under different circumstances," Owen said, "that would have been fun."

The sirens went quiet then, but the lights remained on.

"I wonder what that means," Javier said.

Shouts rose up through the trees, and then a unit of Abstergo agents marched out of the forest into the open space before the fence, not too far from Javier and Owen. They wore the same black paramilitary uniforms, with Assassin-hunting helmets and weapons. There were eight of them, and before long, one of them pointed up at the cable, and they all looked in Griffin's direction.

"We have to get out of here," Javier said.

Owen had already pulled out an EMP grenade and chucked it at the agents. But when it landed, it had no effect.

"Griffin will have to find another way across," Javier said. "If we stay here, we'll get caught."

Owen nodded, and Javier moved as quickly and quietly as he could from their position to the next tree over, and then the next, free-running until they seemed to be safely away, and then they dropped to the ground.

The glass building stood a shorter distance off, and now Javier glimpsed two more structures some distance away, connected to one another by enclosed walkways.

They'd made it to the Aerie, but for now, they were on their own.

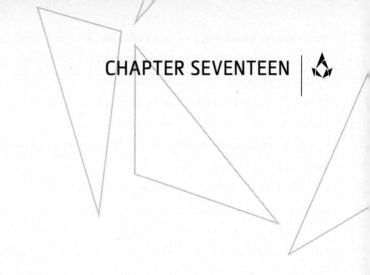

CHAPTER SEVENTEEN

G race lay on top of her bed, seething. She wasn't tired, at least, not in a sleepy way. She was tired of David. Not too long ago, she'd felt responsible for him, but more important, she hadn't really minded that. David was her little brother, and she was happy to look out for him.

But then Monroe had pulled them into this secret war, and after that, her sole purpose had been to get her brother and herself out of it safely. When they'd begun the simulation in New York City, her main concern had been for David, just like it was back home. But then the dynamics of the simulation had confused everything.

David had been in the memories of Abraham, while Grace had been in the memories of Abraham's daughter, Eliza. The role reversal had kind of messed with Grace's head, because David was suddenly the one looking out for her. The experience had done something to him, too, because ever since then, he hadn't listened to her like he used to. He was off doing his own thing.

Like going into restricted areas at night and getting them all in trouble.

She didn't know what to make of his story about that. Mostly, she figured his imagination had gotten the better of him. He was pretty immature about the Animus. It was all still a game to him, and a part of her didn't want to be the one responsible for him anymore. It was just so draining. Her experience in Masireh's memories had only made her wish she had a brother she could rely on.

It was still raining outside. Grace lay there listening to it, wondering where she would go next. Which ancestor's memories would she inhabit? Maybe this time, she would be the one to find the Piece of Eden. Not Sean and his Viking.

Her thoughts roamed, and before long, she did start to fall asleep, lulled by the sounds of the storm. And then the lock in her door clicked, automatically, startling her awake.

She looked over at it and sighed. She didn't like the idea of being locked in. She didn't think anyone would. But that was the way it was now, thanks to David.

She climbed off her bed to brush her teeth, the light in her small bathroom harsh and cold. Then she went to change into her pajamas, but before she'd undressed, an alarm went off.

It was loud. Like a siren throughout the whole facility.

An emergency?

She looked at the door, expecting it to open as Isaiah had promised, but it didn't. A moment passed, and then another, and still it hadn't opened, and meanwhile, the alarm continued to blare. Grace felt panic rising up her back and down her arms. She went to her window and looked out, but all she saw were some distant lights that had switched on and off in the trees.

Was it a fire? Was it an accident of some kind? Or maybe a drill?

She tried her door, just to be sure, but it wouldn't open. She paced her room, and then a few minutes later, the alarm simply ceased.

Grace stopped and listened, hearing nothing more, while the lights outside stayed on.

Whatever it was, it seemed as if it might have passed, and she thought that maybe it really had been some kind of drill. Next time, a warning from Isaiah or Victoria would be helpful.

She left the bathroom light on and lay back down in bed, but didn't change into her pajamas, just in case she had to get up again in the middle of the night for another alarm. It was some time before she managed to get anywhere close to falling asleep again.

Another click from the door awoke her.

She sat up.

Something was wrong. She looked around, listening, trying

to figure out what it was, and then she realized it was the bath-room. The light was off. In fact, all the lights in this part of the Aerie seemed to be off, even the ones outside.

The door to her room creaked a bit, and she jumped out of bed.

"Grace?"

"David?" she said.

Her door opened, and her brother stepped through.

"What's going on?" she asked him.

"I don't know," he said. "My door just unlocked and popped open."

"Mine too," Grace said. "The power's out."

"We should check on Sean and Natalya."

She agreed, so they left her room and crept down the hall-way, the corridor silent and dark, lit only by moonlight dripping in through glass still wet from the rain. But the storm had appar-ently moved on.

As they turned a corner, they actually ran into Natalya, who let out a little yelp and jumped back before she seemed to realize it was them.

"Are you okay?" David asked her.

"Fine," she said, touching her chest. "You guys?"

"We're fine," Grace said. "Did you hear that siren earlier?"

"Yeah," Natalya said.

"Have you seen Sean?" David asked.

"I assume he's still in his room."

So the three of them walked a little ways on, and found the door to Sean's room open a crack, as theirs had been.

"Sean?" Natalya whispered into the opening.

Nothing.

"Sean," David said, more loudly.

Grace heard the sound of tossed bedding from inside, and then a groggy, "Huh? Hello?"

"Sean," David said again. "It's us. The power's out."

"Hang on," Sean said.

Then came the familiar rattle of Sean's wheelchair, and a moment later, he opened the door. "What are you guys doing? You're not supposed to be out of your rooms."

"Power's out," David said.

"So?" he said.

"Didn't you hear that siren earlier?" Grace asked.

"What siren?" Sean said.

"Are you serious?" Grace said.

Sean rubbed his eyes and yawned. "I seriously have no idea what you're talking about."

Grace knew something was going on, even if Sean seemed completely oblivious to it, and even if she didn't know how someone could have possibly slept through it. She looked down the hallway in both directions, wondering what they should do.

"Should we stay here?" Natalya asked, apparently wondering the same thing.

"What do you mean?" Sean said. "Of course we should stay here."

"I don't know," David said. "Something's not right."

Sean spread his hands wide. "Like what? It's just a power outage."

"But the siren," David said.

"What siren are you talking about?" Sean asked.

"I'm going to look around a bit," Natalya said, turning away from them.

"Me too," David said, joining her.

Sean looked at Grace, his mouth halfway open, brow creased, and she knew what he was thinking. This was exactly what had gotten them into trouble once already, and he didn't want to get kicked out of the Aerie. She didn't, either.

"I am not a part of this," he said, shaking his head, wheeling back into his room. "And I will not go down with you guys." With that, he shut his door.

Natalya and David had stopped a few feet away and turned around.

"Are you coming, Grace?" David asked.

She didn't want to. But unlike Sean, she had heard the alarm, and now with the power out, she knew something was definitely going on, and a moment later, she made up her mind that she didn't want to face whatever it was by herself.

"Where are we going?" she asked as she joined the other two.

"Not far," Natalya said. "I just want to see what's going on in the other buildings. If the power's out in them, too."

That made some sense. So they crept along, tiptoeing, whispering, until they reached the first walkway, which was dark, and it seemed the main building on the other end of it was dark, too.

"Let's check the other one," David said.

They returned the way they had come, and then took another hallway toward the far side of the building. Grace had her ears and eyes so open they started making stuff up, convincing her that she could hear people shouting outside in the woods. Or maybe that was real, which felt even more disconcerting. She couldn't see anything out there.

When they reached the second walkway, its door was closed,

and unlike the locks on the doors to their rooms, this one had remained secure, but Grace could see through the windows that the lights were out in the next building over.

"What is going on?" David asked. "Where is everybody?"

"Maybe it was a fire," Natalya said. "That's why the siren went off, and it caused the power outage."

"Maybe," Grace said. "But—"

The door to the walkway clunked, and then it flew open. Before Grace could run, a flashlight shone in her face, and then the bright spot jumped to Natalya and David. The three of them froze as a figure stepped through the opening.

"There you are," he said.

Grace knew that voice. Its deep resonance had strummed the inside of her mind.

"Monroe?" David said.

The spotlight went to the ground, lighting the hallway indirectly, and they saw that it was him. He wore the same para-military gear as the Abstergo agents, his long hair pulled back in a ponytail, his goatee a bit longer, his face a bit more gaunt than it had been the last time they'd seen him.

"You kids okay?" he asked.

"We're fine," Grace said. "What—"

"Was this you?" David asked, gesturing wide around them.

"The power? Yeah, that was me. And now I'm going to get you guys out of here. Where are the others?"

"Sean's in his room," David said.

"Owen and Javier?" Monroe asked.

"We don't know," Natalya said. "They got away back when you did, weeks ago."

Monroe cocked his head and frowned for a moment. "Okay, it's just you guys then, after we get Sean—"

"He won't come," Grace said.

"What do you mean?" Monroe asked.

"He wants to stay here. I know he does."

"You sure about that?" he asked.

"I'm sure," she said.

Monroe paused, then nodded, once. "He has to make his own decision."

As for Grace, she didn't know what to think of Monroe anymore, not after what Isaiah had said about him. Monroe was unstable. He'd gone rogue. Grace didn't know whether she should trust him or turn him in, and she didn't like being in this position. "You shouldn't have come here," she said.

David turned to her. "Why is that?"

"It's okay," Monroe said. "I figured this might happen. Isaiah can be extremely convincing. He knows exactly what you want to hear, and he gives it to you exactly when you need to hear it."

"He told us about you," Grace said.

"I'm sure he told you something about me," Monroe said, anger stalking into his voice. "There's a lot more to the story. But there's no time to explain it right now. It seems each of you has a choice to make. Come with me, or stay here."

"I'm coming with you," Natalya said.

Her statement surprised Grace. She'd thought Natalya was working willingly with the Templars, toward the same goal as the rest of them, and right now, she was closer than any of them to achieving it.

"I'm coming, too," David said.

"What?" Grace spun on him. "No, you are not!"

"Yes, I am," he said. "I know you don't believe me, but it's only a matter of time before Isaiah turns on you. He's already locking you up at night. You need to come with us."

"She makes her own choice," Monroe said. "And we have to accept it. I'm not going to force anyone to do anything. But if you're coming with me, we have to go now."

"Where?" Natalya asked.

"I have a vehicle waiting," he said. "This way."

He turned around and crept back along the walkway through which he'd come. Natalya followed after him, and David took a few steps past the open door into the tunnel before he turned.

"Are you coming?" he asked.

Grace didn't know. She felt cemented to the ground. She didn't know if she could trust Monroe, but David was actually right, too. She did have misgivings about Isaiah. And yet, how could she walk away from everything Abstergo and the Templars offered her? And what about her brother?

"Grace?" David said.

"I don't—"

The lights flashed back on, clicking and popping. Grace and David both looked up, then at each other, but then the walkway door buzzed and began to swing shut.

"No!" David said, diving for it.

Grace did, too, but it slammed closed before either of them could reach it, and the lock engaged. She was separated from him. Grace tried the handle, but it wouldn't open, and the security touch screen was working now.

"David, can you get it from your side?" she called through the door.

"No!" came the muffled reply. "It won't open!"

"Damn," she heard Monroe say. "I'm sorry. But we have to move, now."

"Grace!" David said. "Break the glass!"

"She can't," Monroe said. "It's bulletproof. Almost unbreakable."

There wasn't any way around this door, and if those on the other side of it, including her brother, didn't move now, they would be caught. And if David and Natalya were caught with Monroe, Grace feared what would happen to them. She didn't want to believe that Isaiah would harm them, but now that her little brother was on the other side of this door, she couldn't take the risk that he was actually right.

"Go," she said.

"What?" David asked.

"Go. Get out of here while you can."

"I'm not leaving you."

"Yes, you are," she said. "I've always kept you out of trouble, and I'm not going to stop now. Now, go!"

"But—"

"David," she heard Monroe say, "it's now or never."

An endless second of silence.

"Go," Grace said.

"We'll come back and get you out, too," David said. "I promise."

Grace still didn't even know if that's what she wanted. If this door were open, she still couldn't say whether she would have walked through it. Maybe she and her brother were on different paths. Abstergo and the Animus had changed everything. She only knew she had to get David away from danger. After that, she would be free to take care of herself.

"Good-bye," she said. "Get going."

Another pause.

"Bye, Grace."

She heard footsteps racing away from the door. Then silence, and he was gone.

CHAPTER EIGHTEEN

Owen and Javier scouted around the outside of the Aerie building, avoiding the cameras and sentries, hoping Griffin would catch up with them soon. Owen still didn't understand what had happened with the alarm, but the Templars were on alert now. Abstergo agents patrolled everywhere, but fortunately, not all of them wore the Assassin-hunting gear.

"Why didn't that EMP grenade work back there?" Owen asked.

"Shielding on the electronic components," Javier said. "Copper would do it. They must have upgraded."

"Well, that sucks."

"So what's the plan here?" Javier looked around. "I say we go in."

Owen agreed. Griffin would probably freak out, but he wasn't there, and they still had a mission.

"There's a door on that building over there." Javier pointed, and Owen nodded.

They pressed toward it, evading the surveillance and security, and when they reached the door, Owen noted the electronic lock. It looked as though they would need a fingerprint or other biometric, as well as a code. Owen pulled out another EMP grenade.

"Again?" Javier said. "Is that the only song you know?"

"It's worth a shot." Owen armed the grenade and smacked it against the security console, but just like with the agents, nothing happened.

"Shielded," Javier said.

"I gotta find a new song," Owen said.

"We have to find a way in."

"How about we just break the glass?"

"Too noisy."

"The roof?"

"Worth a shot."

But it was hard to find a place to climb an entirely glass building, and Owen actually wondered if that was the Templar intent in its design. This place seemed built to be Assassin-proof. Eventually, they found a tree growing fairly close to one corner, and they scaled it to the height of a balcony on the building's second story, but the gap between their tree and the balcony was pretty wide.

"Got another zip line?" Javier asked.

"I think I can jump it."

"Really?"

Owen hoped so. In the Animus simulations, as Varius and Zhi, he'd made jumps that far, but those were the memories of fully trained Assassins, and he hadn't tested this particular Bleeding Effect yet. But they were running out of time and options. He braced himself, preparing to make the leap.

"Owen," Javier said. "That's a long fall if you miss."

"Got any other—"

"Shh." Javier held up his hand, and then pointed downward.

Owen looked, and saw a single Abstergo agent approaching their tree. A smile crossed Javier's face, and Owen could tell he'd just come up with another plan, and he thought he knew what it was. Javier motioned for them to climb down, which they did, silently, and when they were in position, Javier pulled out his crossbow pistol. Owen did the same, and when the agent walked right beneath them, they both dropped on her.

She went down with a grunt, and before she could get to her feet or pull her weapon, Owen and Javier pointed their pistols at her.

"Hands up," Owen said.

She complied, and Javier pulled off her helmet. She was fairly young, with straight blond hair, full lips, and a sharp chin. The badge on her chest read COLE.

"I've been looking for you two," she said.

Javier pulled out the pain grenade he'd taken. "You know what this is, Cole?"

She let out a little breath that wasn't quite a gasp, and nodded.

Owen smiled. "Do what we say, and maybe we won't microwave you."

"What's your plan?" she asked.

Owen pressed his crossbow pistol into her back. "Just move."

She nodded, hands still up, and Owen marched her forward. Her steps were slow and grudging, but eventually they reached the door.

"Open it," Javier said.

She resisted, and Owen jammed the pistol between her shoulder blades. "Open it."

Cole shook her head, her jaw muscles twitching. Then she placed her thumb on the door scanner, and entered a code. The lock clicked, and the door opened.

"What do you think you're going to do in there?" she asked.

"You'll find out what we did when you wake up," Javier said, and he shot her with a sleep dart.

She winced, and then two seconds later, her eyes rolled back and she slumped to the ground. Owen tapped her limp body with the toe of his boot. She was out.

He opened the door, and Javier followed him through. The building, brightly lit, was as made of glass on the inside as it was on the outside. They proceeded down a hallway, offices and rooms to either side, weapons at the ready, and Owen kept his Eagle Vision dialed in. The glass panes scattered their reflections, making it seem as if they weren't alone.

At the end of the hallway, they entered an enormous atrium. Owen looked up at the ceiling several stories above them, escalators and staircases climbing up from floor to floor, each level looking down on the open space below. While the Assassins hid in decrepit houses and storage units, the Templars worked toward their goals here, or in places like this one. The power and wealth disparity made the Assassin mission seem almost futile.

"Which way?" Javier asked.

"I don't know," Owen said. "Let's scout around a bit."

But after they'd taken three or four steps across the glossy atrium floor, the lights went out, all of them, and the building seemed to give an electrical sigh.

"Someone cut the power," Javier said.

Owen's eyes hadn't adjusted to the sudden darkness yet, but his Eagle Vision revealed his friend standing a few feet away from him. "Maybe it was Griffin."

"Let's hope," Javier said.

They decided to keep moving, and Owen actually felt a bit safer doing so without all the light falling around them, and eventually, his eyes did grow accustomed to the darkness. On the ground floor, they found only conference rooms and a large lounge area. They climbed a staircase to the second floor, but before they'd gone very far, they concluded it held only offices.

"This doesn't seem like the kind of place they'd hold Grace and the others," Owen said.

"Maybe one of the other buildings?" Javier asked. "I thought I saw one of those walkways down there."

"Let's go check it out."

So they descended to the ground floor and crossed the atrium to the walkway. This one had no lock, and the door opened. Javier looked at Owen, and Owen nodded. They entered the tunnel, encased in glass on all sides, and hurried through it to the other end, emerging into a new, smaller building.

The exterior walls here were still made of glass, but the interior walls were not. They passed down a few corridors, and Owen tried one of the doors. Inside, he found another, smaller lounge. But in the next hallway over, they found something that looked as though it might be an Animus, but a much more physical model. It had a harness suspended from a waist-high ring, with some kind of metal skeleton and all kinds of connections, including a helmet.

"I think we're on the right track," Owen said.

The next several doors revealed additional Animus machines, if that's what they were, each in its own room. The place was like some of kind of simulation factory.

"There are six of them," Javier said.

"There are six of us," Owen said, "if the Templars had caught us all."

They kept moving, and eventually found a kind of dorm room, but it was empty, the bed messed as if someone had left in a hurry, a pair of girl's pajama pants hanging over the footboard.

"This is them," Owen said.

"Then where are they?"

Before Owen could offer a possible answer to that, the lights switched back on. That meant anyone outside the building—and there were lots of agents out there in the woods—would be able to easily see them.

"We try the next building," Owen said.

Javier agreed, and they proceeded forward, keeping to the side corridors, searching for another passageway. Eventually they reached one, but this door had an electronic lock on it similar to the one Cole had opened for them. Only she was still outside, unconscious, and they had no way to open it.

"I hear someone coming," Javier said.

Owen did, too. Lots of heavy boots on the other side of the door. They ducked around a corner just as it opened, and a tall man in a charcoal suit walked through with several uniformed agents.

"Make sure they're still secured in their rooms," he said.

"Yes, sir."

"And find Cole!" he shouted as they marched down the hallway.

Owen didn't know who this man was, but it was obvious that he was in charge, and it seemed that he didn't know where Grace and the others were, either. In a few moments, he would also discover that they weren't in their rooms.

Javier tapped Owen and pointed at the door. It was open, but swinging shut, and they wouldn't reach it in time.

Owen whipped out his crossbow pistol and fired. The bolt lodged in the door's rubber seal, preventing it from closing all the way.

"It worked," Owen whispered, actually surprised.

They raced over to it, and Owen yanked his bolt free on the way through, then shut the door behind them. They hurried down the passageway, which proved longer than the first, and actually turned a corner that plunged down the mountain. They followed the stairway down, until the walkway leveled and led them to another door, this one set into the hillside.

"We going in?" Javier asked.

"We keep looking until we find them," Owen said.

"I wonder if Griffin got to them first."

Owen didn't know, but he opened the door and peered through. The hallway was empty, so they stepped inside. Down the corridor, two double doors opened into a kind of garage, with cars and vans parked in rows. Owen and Javier stalked toward it, wary of the side hallways they passed. Owen listened and sensed, letting his Eagle Vision warn him of threats. When they reached the doorway to the garage, they paused, and Owen scanned the room.

Over a dozen agents stood around the room in groups of three and four. But they weren't alone. Owen sensed others in the garage, and he searched until he found them by their sounds, and the almost imperceptible motion of the van in which they were hiding.

"It's them," he whispered to Javier, pointing at the vehicle. "It has to be."

"They're pinned down," Javier said.

The situation was only going to get worse, when those other agents realized their prisoners had escaped.

"We need to distract them," Owen said.

"We can't take them all out."

"We have to try. Use the pain grenade on that group of them over there. I'll use this laser pistol thing to blind the others, and then you take them out with your crossbow."

Javier shook his head. "I hope this works."

"Me too. Ready?"

Javier nodded and pulled out the grenade. Owen armed the laser pistol.

"Try to throw that away from us and away from the van with our friends," Owen said. "You give the word."

Javier readied his arm for a throw, and then he said, "Now."

Owen raised the pistol and aimed it as the pain grenade flew through the air and hit the cement on the far side of the garage. A quick, droning buzz could be heard, and then the four agents near the grenade dropped to the ground, rolling and screaming.

Owen charged into the garage while pulling the trigger on the laser pistol, flashing the searing light in the other agents' eyes while they were distracted by the grenade, and Javier raced after him, firing off rapid sleep darts from his crossbow.

The initial assault went well. Nine or ten of the agents were down within a matter of moments, but the others had already begun to regroup, taking cover.

"Hide!" Owen shouted, and then he and Javier dove between separate cars.

The agents' helmets allowed them to communicate by radio, which meant Owen couldn't hear them and anticipate their movements, and with the new shielding, he couldn't disable their electronics, either. But his Eagle Vision let him know that six enemies were converging on their location, weapons ready, and unlike he and Javier, the Templars used lethal means.

Owen braced himself, and then leapt out, hurling the sleep grenade, followed by a smoke grenade to cover his retreat. He heard two or three more agents hit the ground, unconscious, but then a gunshot cracked, the sound filling the entire garage. Owen wasn't hit, but the shock caused him to drop his crossbow pistol. He ducked away fast, throwing another smoke grenade to buy him more time, and reached the vehicles on other side of the garage.

Javier hadn't moved from his position, and as the smoke cleared, Owen saw there were still four agents active. They were closing in on his friend, boxing him in, and Owen fully expected reinforcements to arrive any minute.

He didn't know if the laser pistol had a long-enough range from where he was hiding, and besides, the Templars were facing away from him. He was out of smoke grenades, and without his crossbow pistol he had no way to help, other than to reveal himself and give the agents another target.

He was about to call out when he heard another gunshot. One of the agents fell, and the others scattered, dragging their wounded comrade with them.

The shot seemed to have come from another point farther down the row of cars, perhaps the van where the others were hiding.

Javier moved now, seizing the distraction. He threw his own smoke grenade and raced through the cloud across the open garage, to the point where the shot had come from.

"Owen!" a deep, familiar voice called.

Owen froze. "Monroe?"

"Can you make your way toward us?" Javier asked.

Owen crept out from his hiding place to get a better look, but as soon as he came out in the open, he heard a gunshot. The bullet struck the car near his head and ricocheted.

Owen ducked back. "I'm pinned down!"

There were three agents left in the garage, and any one of them could have made that shot. His Eagle Vision showed him their locations by the drumming of their elevated heart rates, and the stirring of the air by their rapid breathing. But Owen still had no way to fire back at them, and Javier and Monroe wouldn't have a clean shot, either. The agents had taken cover.

"Monroe?" Owen called.

"Here," Monroe yelled back.

"What are you doing here?"

"I came to help you kids escape. What are you and Javier doing here?"

"Same reason."

"Why is Javier armed like an Assassin?" Monroe asked.

"Because an Assassin has been training us," Owen said.

A moment passed.

"I see."

"So do you have a plan?" Owen asked.

"Maybe I—"

The pounding of footsteps charged toward them from the corridor, reinforcements arriving.

"You have to get out of here now!" Owen shouted. He was close enough to the door to use the laser pistol. "I'll cover you. Go!"

"No way!" Javier shouted.

"Go!" Owen said. "Get the others out of here!"

The first agents appeared, and Owen burned their eyes with the pistol. They fell back, and then another wave came, and Owen blinded them, too.

"Hurry!" Owen shouted.

He fired, and fired, and fired, pushing the agents back.

Then he heard an engine roar, and not the sound of a normal vehicle. Something much, much more powerful, like the rumble of an avalanche. Then a black car pulled out and sped toward the garage doors.

Owen kept up his laser fire until it seemed he'd drained the pistol's power source to empty. As soon as it quit working, a group of agents stormed into the room. But the doors to the garage had already opened, and the black car peeled away before they could shoot it or stop it. Then the man in the suit stalked into the room, his gaze sweeping back and forth.

"Report!"

One of the agents near him touched his ear. "Sir, you should find cover. There's still one, possibly two targets unaccounted for."

The man smoothed his blond hair back and raised his voice. "Whoever you are, come out now. We've realized the other Assassin is a distraction, and I've recalled my men here. I have another hundred agents on the way. Surrender and no harm will come to you."

Other Assassin? That must be Griffin, keeping the Templars occupied so Owen and Javier could find the others. Owen let out a long sigh. At least they'd gotten away.

"Isaiah!" Monroe shouted.

Owen whipped his head toward the sound of Monroe's voice. What was he still doing there? Why hadn't he escaped with the others?

"Monroe?" the tall man said. "Could that possibly be you?"

"I'm coming out," Monroe said. "Unarmed."

Then Owen saw him, walking out from between the vehicles, his hands in the air. A mob of agents rushed him and quickly bound his arms behind his back.

The tall man, Isaiah, approached him with a thin smile on his face. "This is unexpected."

"Tell your men to lower their weapons."

"Why?"

"Because he's a kid," Monroe said.

Isaiah looked around him at the cars to either side. "Lower your weapons."

The agents followed the order, pointing their pistols and rifles at the ground.

"You can come out now, Owen," Monroe called, never taking his eyes from Isaiah. "They won't harm you."

Owen couldn't see any other choice, so he did what Monroe asked, and stepped out from his hiding place.

At his appearance, Isaiah turned toward him, his green eyes sharp and wild. "You're Owen?"

Owen nodded.

"Then can I assume Javier is the one who just stole my car?"

Owen shrugged.

"Bring Owen to my office," Isaiah said. "Lock Monroe in a cell. I have to check on Grace and Sean."

That meant Grace and Sean were still there. Owen had assumed they were in the black car. "Where do you have them locked up?" he asked.

Isaiah's eyebrows came together in puzzlement. "Locked up? No, Owen. Grace and Sean chose to stay."

Owen didn't know what to make of that, or if it was a lie, but for now, he didn't struggle as an agent bound his wrists in zip ties.

CHAPTER NINETEEN

David sat in the back of the jet-car, Natalya in the front
passenger seat, Javier at the wheel. The engine rattled
David's teeth as they pulled out of the garage, and
when Javier gunned it, the force whipped David's neck
and threw him backward against his seat.

"Sorry," Javier said. "This thing's a beast."

He whipped them down a road that wound through the
Aerie complex, and David could see all five buildings. There
were Templar agents everywhere, but none of them dared get in
the car's way. A few agents shot at it, but apparently the jet-car
was bulletproof, and most didn't bother lifting their weapons.

As they rounded a bend, Javier put the brakes on, shoving
David hard against the front seat, smashing his glasses into his
nose, and throwing Natalya against the dash.

"Sorry," he said again.

"Why are we stopping?" Natalya asked.

"For him." Javier pointed at a man running toward the car wearing the same kind of leather jacket and hood that Javier wore. Some kind of electrical knife crackled from his wrist, but it disappeared.

Javier opened the front door and hopped out. "You're driving."

The stranger climbed into the front seat, while Javier jumped in the backseat next to David. A second later, the engine rumbled and the car jumped ahead.

"Now this is more like it." The stranger pushed back his cowl, revealing a shaved head, and surveyed the vehicle's dashboard. "Where's Owen?"

"Templars have him," Javier said.

The stranger cursed. "And who is this?"

"Natalya," she said, leaning away from him.

"I'm David."

The stranger nodded. "I'm Griffin."

Natalya looked back at Javier, and then at Griffin again. "Are you . . . ?"

"Yes," Javier said. "He's an Assassin."

"That bother anyone bad enough they want me to let 'em out?" Griffin asked.

David said nothing, and Natalya faced forward. If Javier hadn't been there, he definitely would not be going with this Griffin guy. But it seemed both Javier and Owen knew the Assassin, and had been with him, perhaps this whole time.

Griffin tapped some controls on the touch screens. One looked a bit like a radar screen, and another showed a basic GPS map, but with greater topographical detail. There were other displays that seemed to relate to the jet-car's systems. Griffin swiped through them, and engaged something that created a kind of ambient hum above the roar of the engine.

"What was that?" Javier asked.

"Stealth mode, I think," Griffin said. "For the helicopters."

"Helicopters?" David pushed his glasses up and looked out the window.

"There's three of them heading toward us," Griffin said. "But they won't be able to spot us. You guys picked a nice car."

"David's idea," Javier said.

"David has a good eye," Griffin said. "Tell me what happened before then."

So Javier explained how he and Owen had become separated from the Assassin, and decided to look for David and the others on their own. They'd broken in by threatening Cole, and then they'd searched the complex until they found everyone in the garage.

"What about you?" Javier asked.

"You guys did exactly what I hoped you'd do," Griffin said. "So I knew I needed to clear your path. I made my presence known to the Templars, and then spent the next little while keeping them occupied."

Javier turned to David. "Where's your sister?"

"We got separated," David said.

"I don't think she would've have come anyway," Natalya said. "Sean didn't come, either."

"Wait, they stayed by choice?" Javier asked.

Natalya nodded.

"I wish that surprised me," Griffin said.

"Why would they stay?" Javier asked.

"You don't know how it is there," Natalya said. "They're experts at getting people to do exactly what they want them to do. Controlling them."

She was right. Isaiah had even managed to turn David against his own sister, a little bit, and her against him. But in that last moment at the door, David would never have left her if she hadn't told him to. He worried about her, back at the Aerie. What would Isaiah do now that some of them had escaped? How would he explain things to their dad? Did Isaiah still need them badly enough to find the Piece of Eden that he would keep them safe?

"Monroe was there," Javier said.

Griffin nodded. "I wondered. That must have been him that started the fire, to do the same thing I was trying to do and distract the Templars. Isaiah probably had no idea what was going on."

The car sped down the mountain, and David kept glancing up at the sky. The helicopters circled overhead, but nowhere near them. Eventually, the car left the trees behind and reached level ground, and Griffin steered them onto the highway, heading south.

"So what do we do?" Javier asked.

"For now, we sit tight and stay low. There's no way we could stage a raid like that a second time."

"So we just leave Owen there?" Javier asked.

"And Grace?" David added.

"For now," Griffin said. "For now. We wait to see what Isaiah does, and then we make our move. Maybe Rothenberg will reach out."

"Rothenberg?" Natalya asked.

"An Assassin informant in the Templar Order," Javier said.

"Meanwhile," Griffin said, "there's the Piece of Eden. How close is Isaiah to finding the next one?"

"Ask Natalya," David said. "She's seen it."

Natalya went totally rigid, but David couldn't tell if she felt angry or scared.

Griffin glanced her way. "That true?"

"I've seen it," she said. "But I still don't know where it is."

"We can rectify that," Griffin said. "What about the third prong?"

"Isaiah has no idea," David said. "He's just sending us back into different ancestors, looking for it."

"That might change," Griffin said.

"How so?" Natalya asked.

"Isaiah has Monroe now. And Owen."

"Owen won't talk," Javier said.

"Isaiah can be very convincing," Natalya said.

Javier chuckled. "You don't know Owen."

"None of you know the Templars," Griffin said.

That brought a somber chill into the car, and no one talked for a while. They drove south on the highway, and then turned east, heading into hill country. Eventually, Griffin steered the car down a dirt road, and they followed that for a mile or so, until they came to a house that had DO NOT ENTER written all over it. The place looked as if it would collapse if you leaned on it wrong. David's dad would have said the only thing keeping it upright was the paint, except this rundown house didn't have any paint.

Griffin pulled the jet-car into a barn, and then led them all to the front door. The tall weeds and grass reached David's knees, and he could feel their tips brushing his calves through his pants.

At the front door, the Assassin entered a code into an unexpected electronic lock. "Let's be quick about this. We take what we need and we clear out."

"I told you," Javier said. "Owen won't—"

"Owen may not have a choice," Griffin said. "The Templars could use drugs to interrogate him, or even the Helix to poke around in his DNA. We have to assume this location is compromised."

Javier fell silent, and Griffin let them all in. David found the interior of the house matched the exterior. At one point in its distant history, this was probably a pretty nice house, and David imagined he could hear the echoes of that past life as Griffin and Javier walked through the darkness toward a door under the stairs.

"Watch your step," the Assassin said.

Javier led the way down into a basement that better matched the Aerie. Griffin had an Animus, with its computers and monitors, and a big conference table covered in files and papers, and, of course, an arsenal.

"Sit tight for a minute," Griffin said. "I have to make a call."

"Over here," Javier said, and motioned for David and Natalya to follow him.

He led them to a corner with some crates and a mini fridge. He pulled out several bottles of water, and the three of them sat down.

"So this is where you've been for the last few weeks?" Natalya asked.

Javier shook his head. "We only got here a couple of days ago. Before that, we were hiding out in a storage unit."

"You serious?" David asked.

"Unfortunately," Javier said. "It looked like you guys had it a lot better."

David had to agree with that.

"What have you been doing?" Natalya asked.

"Training," Javier said. "And Owen went into the Animus."

"Training?" Natalya asked. Her frown seemed worried.

"So you an Assassin, now?" David asked.

"Not if you ask him." Javier gestured with his water bottle toward Griffin, who sat with his back to them, talking to a bearded guy through a video chat.

"Who's that?" David asked.

"Gavin," Javier said. "I think he's a leader in the Brotherhood or something."

"Is that what they call themselves?" Natalya asked. "A Brotherhood?"

Javier nodded. "So you guys have been going into the Animus? Where?"

"I was a World War II pilot for most of the time," David said. "Natalya was a Mongol warrior."

"Owen fought the Mongols," Javier said. "He was a Chinese Assassin."

"He was?" Natalya set her water bottle down on the floor. "That . . . that was him?"

Something had just upset her, but she'd never told David many details about her simulation.

"What was him?" Javier asked.

Natalya shook her head, and her eyes got teary. "I . . . fought a Chinese Assassin. A young woman. I hurt her. Bad."

"Yeah, that was him," Javier said. "But not *really* him, and besides, you couldn't have known. You guys weren't in a shared simulation. Not like last time."

After he said that, Natalya seemed to calm down a little. "That's true . . ." she whispered.

"So what's the deal with Sean and your sister?" Javier asked David. "Are they Templars?"

"Maybe Sean is," David said. "But not Grace."

"Then why did she stay?"

Natalya picked her water bottle back up. "I told you, you don't know how it is there. You feel like you're in a prison, even though there aren't any bars."

"There were last night," David said. "They locked us in our rooms."

"That's what finally pushed me over the edge," Natalya said.

David had already figured that out. Her decision to stop cooperating with Isaiah had followed the director's announcement of the new security measures.

"But I feel bad for Sean," Natalya said. "Isaiah is manipulating him worse than any of us."

Griffin's screen went black, and the Assassin rose from his chair to face them. "Rothenberg already made contact," he said. "He's not happy about the raid. Not at all. He almost cut off further contact, but Gavin talked him down."

"What did he say?" Javier asked.

"Isaiah is mobilizing. He's pretty spooked now that we have Natalya, and he's mounting an expedition to Mongolia." Griffin stepped closer. "Does he know where it is?"

"Not exactly," Natalya said. "But he knows the area to look."

"And what is the area?" Griffin asked.

"The Burkhan Khaldun," Natalya said. "It's a mountain where some of the Great Khans were buried."

"That's a big area," Griffin said. "But it seems Isaiah is desperate now."

"Does Isaiah know about this hideout?" Javier asked.

"He's focused on the Piece of Eden. We're safe here, for now. Rothenberg will notify us if that changes." Griffin grabbed a water bottle from the fridge for himself. "Isaiah's force won't be ready to fly out to Mongolia for several days. I know this is a lot to ask, Natalya. I know the Templars have been using you. But would you consider going back into the Animus? We need to narrow down that location, and get there before Isaiah."

Natalya didn't answer. She got up and walked over to the table with all the files, and seemed to be thinking.

So everyone waited.

David realized then that it wasn't just about the Templars controlling her. She didn't want the Assassins controlling her, either. Maybe, like Monroe, she didn't want either group to find the prongs of the Trident. But what would Griffin do if she refused to help?

A moment later, she turned around and lifted her chin. "I'll help you, but under one condition."

"What condition?" Griffin asked.

"You take us with you to Mongolia."

"That—" Griffin grunted and dragged a hand down his face. "That's not my decision to make. *I* might not even be going to Mongolia. Gavin will make that call."

"You take us with you, or I won't help you." Natalya folded

her arms, her voice as hard and cold as steel. "And then Isaiah will find the prong. I promise you that."

While growing up, David had known better than to cross his older sister. She was immensely stubborn and strong-willed, like their dad. But now he was seeing a new side of Natalya, and realizing that she could rival Grace, and maybe even beat her at this game. He was impressed.

"Okay," Griffin said.

"Okay, what?" Natalya asked.

"You help me, and I'll take you to Mongolia."

Natalya turned to Javier. "Can I trust him?"

Javier nodded. "Yes. He'll keep his word."

"Then we have a deal," Natalya said.

Griffin sighed. "I don't know how I'm going to explain this to Gavin."

"Just let him talk to Natalya," David said. "He'll understand."

The Assassin actually smiled at that. Then he went to a closet door, opened it up, and pulled out several sleeping bags, inflatable mattresses, pillows, and blankets. "Before we do anything in the simulation, you kids need to rest. Especially you, Natalya. Fatigue and the Animus don't mix. I already lost Owen to the Templars tonight. I'm not going to risk Natalya's neural health. We can spare a few hours' rest and pick this up in the morning."

In the last hour, it seemed to David that Griffin had shown more genuine concern for them than Isaiah had in the past weeks. But that couldn't be said for Victoria. David had always believed her to be sincere, and he wondered where she had been during all the action at the Aerie.

David got up and walked over to the pile of bedding, where he grabbed a sleeping bag and a pillow, then used a hand pump to blow up an air mattress. The others did the same, and once again, David thought about the difference between this hideout and the complex from which they'd just escaped. Unless you had a thing for underdogs, David could understand why the Templars would seem so appealing. They promised a lot more than the Assassins did, namely prosperity, security, and stability.

Griffin had gone over to the conference table and started looking through the papers there.

"What is all that?" Natalya asked, spreading out her own bed. "I saw Owen's name."

Javier did the same as her and lay down. "That's the evidence they used to convict Owen's father."

"Of what?" David asked.

"Murder." Javier propped a pillow under his head. "During a bank robbery."

Natalya lay down next to him. "Why does Griffin have it?"

"Because I stole it from a police warehouse," Javier said. "Owen says his dad was innocent, and I believe him. We just have to prove it."

"Is his dad still in prison?" David asked.

"No. He died there."

David swallowed his voice and went quiet, unsure of what to say after that. His own dad had always been around, solid and loving, and he took that for granted.

"I had no idea," Natalya whispered.

"It's not something he talks about with just anybody. But you guys aren't just anybody anymore." Javier sighed. "That was how Monroe pulled us in. Owen wanted to go into his father's memories, but Monroe couldn't do it."

David remembered what Grace had said about the Animus not being a game. He had known she was right, on a certain level, but it wasn't until now that it really occurred to him how personal and important genetic memories could be. It was one thing to go to West Africa, or New York, or even pilot a plane. But this thing with Owen was something else. His father's memories mattered right now, in a different way than the Pieces of Eden.

Maybe that's what Grace and his dad had been trying to tell him. Maybe Grace's simulations had meant something to her, but he hadn't paid her attention. Maybe Sean's had meant something to him, too.

Maybe that's why they had stayed behind.

CHAPTER TWENTY

I t wasn't long after the others had left that Isaiah came with his agents to Sean's room. Sean had already climbed from his wheelchair back into bed, and was lying there on his back, with his hands behind his head, staring up at the ceiling.

"Is everything all right, Sean?" Isaiah asked, without turning the lights on.

"What's going on out there?" Sean asked.

Isaiah stepped into the room. "Everything is under control. Have you seen the others?"

Sean didn't want to betray them, but he also didn't want the director to think he was with them. "I don't speak for them, and they don't speak for me."

Isaiah paused. "Fair enough." He turned to the nearest agent. "Check the other rooms."

"Yes, sir."

The agent left, and Isaiah stepped closer to Sean's bed. "I believe this night will prove to be very decisive in many ways."

Sean waited in the darkness.

Isaiah continued. "Lines have been drawn and crossed. You have chosen well, Sean."

"I feel like I chose a long time ago." Sean looked down at his legs. "I just didn't know it."

"Perhaps that's true."

"But it's not about good and evil," Sean said. "They're still my friends. They're good people. That doesn't mean they can't be wrong."

"That is exactly right."

The agent returned. "Sir, Grace is in her room. David and Natalya are gone."

A moment of silence passed, and then Isaiah inhaled. "I have matters to attend to, Sean. Remain here, and try not to worry. All will be made right."

Sean nodded, and then Isaiah and his agent left, returning the room and the entire building to silence. The rain had stopped, but shouts could be heard outside. Sean ignored them, but made no attempt to sleep.

He couldn't take it personally that the others had left him. This wasn't about him to them, and it wasn't about them to him. This was about himself, and where his life had brought him. This was about the best way to make a better world for himself and others like him. The Assassins had their way, but Sean believed those methods could only ever lead to chaos. Vigilantes and rebels and terrorists trying to overturn the world. Abstergo and the Templars promised something better.

Someone knocked at his door.

"Yes?"

"Sean?"

It was Grace. "Come in," he said.

The door opened, and Grace stepped into the room. "Can I sit with you?"

Sean sat up. "Uh, sure." Then he maneuvered his legs over the side of the bed, so that Grace would have a place next to him.

"David's gone," she said, sitting down near enough to him that they shared the same indent in the mattress, falling slightly together.

"I heard." He folded his hands in his lap. "I'm sorry."

She started crying.

Sean didn't know exactly what to do, but he felt for her, and he felt like he knew her well enough to put his arm around her. When he did, she turned into him, and covered her face with her hands, her cheek against his shoulder, and he noticed that she smelled like sweet almonds.

"Maybe Isaiah will stop them," he said.

She shook her head. "I don't want him to." She leaned away, wiping under her eyes with her fingertips. "David wanted to go, and a part of me doesn't want to be responsible for him anymore."

Sean nodded. "I think I get that."

"You don't think it makes me a bad sister?"

"No, I think we all need to be responsible for ourselves. David too. He made his choice, and you made yours. It's okay that those choices are different."

Grace nodded. "I don't know what I'm going to tell my dad."

"Leave that to Isaiah," Sean said. Then he looked down at the floor. "Can I ask, why did you stay?"

Grace didn't answer for a few moments, and Sean waited.

"I think . . ." she finally said. "I think I'm still figuring that out."

"That's okay," Sean said. "I'm here if you want to talk about it."

After that, they sat there together for a while longer, neither of them speaking, until an Abstergo agent came to the door and knocked.

"Yes?" Sean said.

"Isaiah would like to see you both in his office."

Grace stood, and stepped aside as Sean heaved himself into his wheelchair. Then the three of them made their way down the hallways, but not to the office where they normally met with the director. The agent guided them to the main building, and across the atrium to an elevator. He scanned his fingerprint and entered a code just to call it, and then again when they stepped into the elevator and he selected the fourth floor.

Sean hadn't even known there was a fourth floor. He looked up at Grace, and she raised both eyebrows and shook her head.

When the elevator stopped, the agent got off and pointed to the right. "Isaiah is waiting."

Sean wheeled himself through the open doors into a circular hallway that wrapped around the rim of the atrium, glass ceiling above, the floor far below them. He turned to the right, and he and Grace made their way around the circle until they came to an open door. They heard Isaiah's voice inside, and they entered.

The long room felt almost like a modern church. Isaiah's desk formed an altar at one end, a stained-glass window in the shape of a cross behind it, the floor made of a polished, rose-colored marble. Numerous chairs stood arranged in rows, almost like pews, and a figure sat in one of them before the desk.

"Owen?" Grace said.

Sean looked again, and found she was right. It was Owen, wearing a leather jacket and paramilitary-style pants, his hands bound in his lap.

Isaiah stood before their friend, looking down at him. "Sean, Grace, thank you for joining us. Please, come closer."

Sean wheeled himself down the aisle between the seats, and Grace kept pace with him, until they reached Owen's row. He looked up at them and smiled.

"What are you guys doing here?" he asked.

"I was about to ask you that," Sean said.

"Owen staged an assault on the Aerie," Isaiah said. "Along with Javier and an Assassin named Griffin."

"What?" Sean said. Had Owen somehow become an Assassin?

"Is this true?" Grace said.

Owen nodded. "Absolutely."

"Why?" Sean said, sounding angrier than he intended.

"We were trying to rescue you," Owen said. "Clearly, we shouldn't have wasted our time."

"What's that supposed to mean?" Sean asked.

"Gentlemen," Isaiah said. "I did not bring you together to start a conflict. Quite the opposite. I was hoping that Sean and Grace might help Owen understand that we are not the enemy."

"Tell that to your boys downstairs who shot at us," Owen said.

"What else should they have done?" Isaiah said. "They didn't know who you were. They reasonably assumed your intentions to be hostile and your weapons to be lethal. I cannot fault them for their response."

"Neither can I," Sean said, even though he hadn't been there. But Owen made him angry enough, he didn't care. Who was he to think that Sean needed rescuing? Who was he to take that upon himself, as if Sean was helpless.

Isaiah went around the desk, opened a drawer, and pulled out a file. "Perhaps now would be a good time to give Owen a bit of truth."

Owen laughed. "Truth? From you? Isn't that what they call an oxymoron?"

Isaiah ignored him and came back around from behind the desk, holding the open file. "Your father," he said. "A terrible business."

That changed Owen's demeanor drastically. The smile and laugh vanished, replaced by a stare that carried rage with it. "You're gonna go there?"

"Oh, yes." Isaiah waved the file. "This is exactly where we are going to go."

"What is that?" Grace said.

"Evidence," Isaiah said. "The justice system found Owen's father guilty of a terrible crime, and sent him to prison where he subsequently died. And Owen believes his father was innocent."

"He *was* innocent!" Owen shouted.

Some of Sean's anger dissipated at the thought of what Owen had been through.

"Yes," Isaiah said. "He was. Your father was framed for murder."

Those words seemed to stop time for a few moments. Even Sean could feel it. He held his breath and waited, watching Owen as it seemed his friend's world turned on its side.

"What did you say?" Owen whispered.

"I have the evidence here," Isaiah said. "It's nothing that would have helped in court, but perhaps it will bring you some peace of mind."

"Show me," Owen said.

Isaiah closed the folder. "If I trust you and remove those restraints, will you trust me in return?"

"Show me the evidence," Owen said. "Then we'll talk."

Isaiah hesitated, and then said, "It appears I must take the first step." He pulled a knife out of his pocket, and with a deft stroke cut the ties from Owen's hands. Then he placed the folder in Owen's lap.

"What's in there?" Sean asked.

Owen's eyes scanned the file's contents frantically, and he said nothing.

Sean turned to Isaiah. "What's in there?"

"Owen's father was a puppet of the Assassins," Isaiah said. "They set him up to rob a branch of the Malta Banking Corporation, which is owned by Abstergo's financial holdings division."

"Why?" Grace asked.

"Convenience," Isaiah said. "To avoid drawing attention to their own activities. The Assassins will periodically target Abstergo's assets in an attempt to weaken the Order. In this case, Owen's father was meant to distract us from a much larger incursion. Similar to their strategy tonight."

"But how did they set him up?" Sean asked.

"It seems Owen's father had a gambling habit. The Assassins took advantage of that, and as soon as he owed them a large debt, they threatened his wife and son unless he paid. Of course, he didn't have the money, so they suggested the bank robbery as a way to wipe the slate."

Owen closed the folder and shook his head. "I don't believe you."

"Why not?" Isaiah said.

"Because you lie. That's what you do."

"Ask these two," Isaiah said. "Sean, Grace, have I lied to you?"

"No," Sean said.

Grace hesitated, but then said, "I don't believe so."

"What does that prove?" Owen held up the file. "What does this prove?"

"What kind of proof would you accept?" Isaiah said.

Owen reached into his jacket, as if for a weapon, and Isaiah lunged forward with his knife, suddenly and menacingly, stopping but a foot away.

"I'm trusting you, son. Don't disappoint me."

"I'm not your son." Owen pulled a ziplock bag out of his pocket.

"What's that?" Grace asked.

"My father's DNA. They took this sample after he was arrested."

Isaiah leaned away. "I see. You want something neither Monroe nor Griffin could give you. You want to use Helix."

"I want to get inside these memories," Owen said. "That's the only thing I'll believe."

Isaiah held out his hand. "I can offer you that. But that is a different device than the Animus."

Owen stared at the director for several moments, and then handed the ziplock bag over to him. "When?"

"Tomorrow." Isaiah slipped the evidence back into his own coat pocket. "It will take that long to extract the specific genetic memories you're looking for."

Owen narrowed his eyes, but then nodded.

Isaiah returned to the far side of his desk. "Perhaps after that, you will trust me."

"Not likely," Owen said.

"Sean and Grace," Isaiah said, "would you take Owen back with you? See that he gets one of the rooms near you?"

"Uh, sure," Sean said, and Grace nodded.

"Thank you. I'll meet with the three of you in your lounge in the morning, after you've had a chance to get some sleep and eat breakfast."

Sean was a bit confused by Isaiah's sudden casualness, and the way he was just letting Owen go free. But then it occurred to him that Owen wasn't really free, after all. The director had exactly what he wanted, and Owen wouldn't do anything to jeopardize that.

The next morning, Sean awoke, surprised that he had fallen asleep. The return to their rooms last night had been tense and silent, and he had lain in bed for quite a while, restless and uneasy. But now he got up, wheeled himself into the bathroom for a quick shower, and then dressed.

In the lounge, he found Grace having a breakfast of coffee and a bagel, Owen sitting next to her, eating nothing.

"What's the matter?" Sean asked. "Afraid it's poisoned?"

"What's your problem?" Owen said. "I'm just not hungry."

Sean shook his head. "Whatever."

"Look around you," Owen said. "David and Natalya are gone. Doesn't that tell you anything?"

"It tells me David and Natalya made a mistake," Sean said, but he looked over at Grace, worried about how she might be feeling.

She had stopped eating, but otherwise, her face remained impassive.

Sean turned back to Owen. "You think you have things figured out, but you don't. The Templars aren't what you think they are. The only thing you know is the simulation of New York. You're thinking of Boss Tweed and Cudgel Cormac. But we've experienced something totally different here."

"Is that right?" Owen said.

"Yes," Grace said, "it is."

Owen didn't reply, and then Isaiah walked in with Victoria. She looked tired, with red eyes and a smile that seemed to require effort.

"Good morning," Isaiah said. "After last night, I hope you were all able to get some rest."

"Is it ready?" Owen asked.

"Of course," Isaiah said. "I said it would be. I'll take you to your simulation, now."

"What will we be doing?" Sean asked.

"Given everything that has happened, Dr. Bibeau and I think that sticking with the routine might be helpful to you. So if you would like, you may return to your own simulations. But we certainly don't expect you to."

"I'd like to," Sean said.

"Very well." Victoria turned to Grace. "How do you feel?"

"I'm not sure," she said. "I'm still thinking about it."

"That's fine, take your time." Victoria motioned for Sean. "Do you want to come with me?"

Sean nodded and wheeled toward her, but as he passed Owen, he paused and spoke to him. "I'm not the bad guy, and I don't think you're the bad guy. I hope your simulation gives you what you're looking for."

Owen seemed a bit taken aback, but Sean didn't wait for a reply before rolling away, and not long after that, he was back in the Animus, in the memories of Styrbjörn, the events of the previous night in the Aerie now centuries distant from his mind.

He now marched toward the site of the coming duel, having challenged Palnatoke, chieftain of the Jomsvikings, to single combat. Such a challenge could not be refused, and was not lightly made. But Styrbjörn knew he would be victorious, even if his sister feared he would not.

She walked beside him, her head bowed with worry.

"What if you should be killed?" she asked.

"Palnatoke respects tradition," Styrbjörn said. "He won't try to kill me, and if I should lose, I will pay the ransom and we will depart. But Gyrid, I will not lose."

His words did not seem to appease her anxiety.

When they reached the crossroads, where all such duels took place, Styrbjörn found a crowd had already gathered to witness it. The trenches had been carved, marking the square ring, and the four hazel posts had already been planted. He removed his fur, and after handing it to his sister, he stretched his arms and his back, preparing himself.

Soon, men brought the duel cloak, nine feet square, and staked it to the ground within the hazel ring. Then Palnatoke appeared, attended by a dozen of his Jomsvikings, each of whom regarded Styrbjörn with open hatred. That was to be expected, and Styrbjörn studied their faces, so that he might remember them later.

Then it was time for the duel to begin. Styrbjörn had his three shields at the ready, one of his men standing by as his second, and he stepped into the ring. Palnatoke did the same, and their combat began.

Palnatoke struck first, his blade quick, landing hard on Styrbjörn's wooden shield, breaking it in half. The blow staggered Styrbjörn, and rang the bones of his arm like a bell. But he threw away the remnants of wood and received a new shield from outside the ring, and this time, he was better prepared.

Palnatoke lunged again, but Styrbjörn parried and counterstruck. Palnatoke dodged to the side, dropping low to slash at Styrbjörn's leg, but the strike missed, and then the two men were back on their feet.

Styrbjörn was not as accustomed to this type of ceremonial combat. It was slow, and methodical, and too close. He preferred the open battlefield, with its mud and blood and chaos, but he engaged in this ancient ritual because he had to. If he had simply killed Palnatoke, the Jomsvikings would never have followed him.

Styrbjörn lunged with a roar, and this time, it was Palnatoke's shield that broke, hanging from his arm in pieces. Sean felt the rush of adrenaline and rage that fueled his ancestor as combat ceased; the shield was replaced and then fighting began again.

Strike, parry, dodge.

Strike, shield, parry.

Their combat continued, and soon Styrbjörn had broken his second shield, and then his third, leaving him only with his sword for defense. Normally, this would mean a quick end to the duel, but Styrbjörn had always been a skilled swordsman.

When Palnatoke overconfidently charged him, Styrbjörn launched himself powerfully into the air, his feet at the height of Palnatoke's shoulders, and came down with his blade ready, slicing the chieftain's ear.

Blood fell from the wound and dripped onto the cloak beneath their feet, and by that red sigil, the duel was declared at an end.

Not a single person in the crowd cheered as both men left the ring, Palnatoke clutching a bloody rag to the side of his head, Styrbjörn cradling his battered arm.

"The Jomsvikings are yours to command," the chieftain said, breathing hard. "Where would you order us? Sweden? To fight your uncle?"

"No," Styrbjörn said as Gyrid came to his side.

"No?"

He took back his fur cloak and pulled it over his shoulders, while Sean relished the victory. "First we go to fight the Danes," Styrbjörn said, "for I would have the fleet of that Christian, Harald Bluetooth."

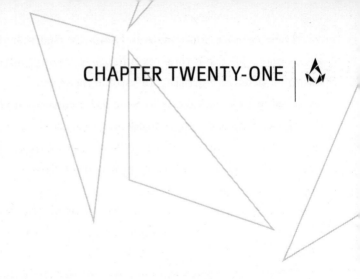

CHAPTER TWENTY-ONE

Natalya ate a granola bar for breakfast, and then took her place in the Animus chair. It was nearly identical to the one she'd been using at the Aerie, though not quite as comfortable. Griffin hooked her up to all the wires and connectors, and she closed her eyes.

"I hate this part."

"What part?" he asked.

"Going in."

"Why is that?"

"The Parietal Suppressor."

"Oh." He stepped away toward his computer console. "We're not using that."

"We're not?"

"No. And you'll be in the chair, so you might find this simulation a bit less robust. It'll be easier to desynchronize, if you're not careful."

"Got it." Natalya sighed, glad to be free of that discomfort, at least.

"Now," Griffin said, working the controls, "we know the date of Möngke Khan's death. How far out from that should I start you?"

"They had a lot of ground to cover," Natalya said. "Asutai marched them thirty to forty miles a day, so . . . a month? Five weeks?"

"We'll start at four weeks, and then if we need to jump ahead, we can. Are you ready?"

"Yes."

"Let's do this."

A few moments later, Natalya lay inside the envelope of black silence, and then Griffin's voice sounded in her ear.

I'm ready with the Memory Corridor whenever you are.

"I'm ready," Natalya said.

Okay. Here we go in three, two, one . . .

Blinding light shattered the darkness, but this time, it didn't feel like it broke through Natalya's skull, and a moment later she was standing in the void. Griffin was right, this didn't feel quite as *real* as the simulation with the Parietal Suppressor. There was a part of Natalya's mind that definitely knew she was still lying in the Animus chair in the basement of an old crappy house, and that part of her mind kept her from readily accepting the simulation.

I've got you all loaded up. One month out from the Khan's death.

"Okay."

The Memory Corridor blew apart, but again without her brain scrambling, and Natalya found herself astride a horse, moving along with a column of mounted Kheshig warriors, the wagon bearing the Great Khan's body in their midst. Natalya nearly lost her balance and fell from her saddle, and the simulation blurred.

Whoa, you okay?

"Yeah, I just . . ." Natalya calmed her thoughts. "I need to get my bearings."

This is going to be more like it was with Monroe's Animus.

Natalya was realizing that. It wasn't easy, but she forced herself to relinquish the stage of her mind to Bayan, as she had with Adelina, allowing him to right himself on his horse, sharing in his thoughts and memories.

Their small army moved north through the valley of the Black River, the air here blessedly cool and dry, the bright sky wide and open. Rice fields grew once more where engineers had altered the river's course, flooding the plains. Farmers with mud up to their knees watched in silence as the Mongol procession passed them, banners waving, war horns blaring. Chen Lun, that Tangghut conscript, had come from this region, and while it wasn't the same as Bayan's steppes, it felt much closer to home than the accursed valleys of the Song.

His shoulder and side had slowly healed, though they still gave him some pain, and he sometimes wondered about the Song warrior who'd defeated him. He was not so blinded by hatred that he couldn't admire her strength and skill, and with his awareness of the Sky-Father's displeasure, a part of him had begun to hope she had survived, and he sometimes even regretted the injury he had given her.

"Bayan!" Asutai waved him forward to join him at the head of their column.

He spurred his horse to catch up to the young prince, bowing his head as he approached. "My lord?"

"We approach the city of Iryai." He wore his ornately gilded armor, his helmet glinting in the sun. "I would have you by my side."

"Of course, my lord." Bayan did not yet understand why the Khan's son granted him such favor and attention, but he accepted it with the necessary humility.

"Ride ahead with me." Asutai urged his horse forward at a trot, and Bayan followed him, until they had put some distance between themselves and the main column, the advance archers and warriors still a dozen yards ahead. "Eighteen years ago, Genghis Khan's great general Subutai won a battle against the Kingdom of Poland."

Bayan nodded.

"Among the prisoners taken at Legnica was a young soldier who belonged to an Order called the Templars."

"A warrior society?" Bayan asked.

"Not solely a warrior society," Asutai said. "Our purpose and ambition transcend our military achievements. War is simply a very effective tool."

The prince had just named himself a member of this Templar Order, but Bayan refrained from commenting on that, allowing Asutai to continue.

"My father became a member of the Order before me. It is how he came to power, defeating and suppressing the treacherous heirs of my grandfather's brother, Ögedei. Now I take my father's place as a Templar, though not on the throne."

"What is the purpose of this Order?" Bayan asked.

Asutai nodded toward the valley ahead, where a city had come into view. "Iryai. The former capital of the Xi Xia Empire."

Bayan watched as the Kheshig column drew closer, remnants of the city's destruction still visible. Even after thirty years, lengthy sections of its walls had still not been rebuilt, and the burnt-out husks of its pagodas stood as blackened reminders of the consequence for betrayal.

Bayan had been a boy at the time, but he had heard the stories. The Horde had *nothinged* the city and slaughtered its inhabitants, here and throughout the countryside, nearly eradicating the Tangghut people. But the ruined city was no longer empty. The fields around it grew rice again. For now, tranquility reigned.

"We bring peace," Asutai said. "We bring order out of the chaos, with our government, our currency, our roads. We ensure tolerance among those who worship different gods, and our courts bring iron justice."

Bayan nodded, and behind his mind, Natalya felt horrified again. This Mongol prince discussed the murder of millions as though it was both necessary and justified. This was the world of the Templar Order, this city reduced to nothing, only returning to life decades later.

"Why do you tell me this?" Bayan asked.

"I would like you to join with us," Asutai said. "Most of the Kheshig are Templars, though not all of them. And as I said before, we need men like you."

Bayan hesitated, and in that moment, Natalya found the moral center in him. When Bayan had believed that divine will governed the conquests of the Horde, he had felt right with the killing, death, and renewal. But now that he had learned an Order of men controlled all these wars, he felt as though he'd been thrown from his saddle.

"You honor me," Bayan said. "Will you allow me to take time to consider this?"

"Of course," Asutai said. "I will ask you again when we reach Burkhan Khaldun."

"Thank you, my lord."

Bayan fell back, his head bowed, and rejoined the main body of the army. The column proceeded past Iryai, more the ghost of a city than a city itself. When Bayan looked at it now, he no longer saw the Sky-Father's retribution.

He saw only death.

I think we can jump you ahead, Griffin said.

Natalya agreed.

I'll bring you out into the Memory Corridor first, to make the transition easier.

"Thanks."

The road, the wagon with the Khan's body, and the column of warriors dissolved as if an impenetrable mist had rolled over the road, taking her horse with it, and then Natalya found herself standing on nothing.

Let's try five weeks out. They're still seven hundred miles from Burkhan Khaldun.

"Make it six," Natalya said.

You're the boss. Give me a second to recalibrate.

Natalya waited, growing anxious. It was very possible that in the next simulation she would learn the location of the Piece of Eden. That was exactly the point of all this, but the mission had become a kind of Doomsday Clock to her, first with Isaiah, and now with Griffin, counting down to the end of the world. Like Monroe, she didn't want *either* of them to have the prong. Both factions brought only death and destruction in their wake. But she wasn't sure how to prevent one of them from finding it.

We're ready.

Natalya sighed. "Okay."

The Memory Corridor blew apart, and the world came back together on another road. It was easier this time for Natalya to step back into the wings, allowing Bayan control. Through his eyes, she recognized the sacred mountains that had sheltered Genghis Khan when he was still called Temüjin, the peak of the Burkhan Khaldun rising, snow-covered, in the distance.

The funeral of Möngke Khan had begun days before, and now the small procession of his closest family members and selected Kheshig marched his body to its tomb in the mountain, bringing with it vast quantities of gold and silks and gemstones. The roads before them remained deserted, for the people feared that if they should chance to see the burial, they would be put to death, as had been done to any witness of the burial of Genghis Khan.

Bayan rode behind Asutai, who led the Kheshig up into the hills, behind his uncles, and eventually they broke from the roads and proceeded overland, following the river north along the valley floor. The pine trees here smelled of spice and oranges, and the green pastures and fields beckoned them inward through these sacred lands, the Burkhan Khaldun looming larger and larger.

Natalya felt a grim inevitability at her back, as mile after mile passed under the hooves of Bayan's horse. The dagger was with the Khan, along with several sets of armor, swords, and bows, and soon they would arrive at the tomb. She would witness the resting place of the Piece of Eden.

I think we're coming up on the moment of truth, Griffin said.

So he could sense it, too. Natalya said nothing.

You ready for this?

"Does it matter?"

That sounds like a no.

"I didn't say that."

You didn't say yes.

"I'm just trying to get through this and be done with it."

Okay, then. I'll leave you to it.

The Kheshig warriors reached a small valley at the base of the mountain, through which a river flowed. The gentle hills surrounding them had shaped this place into a shelter close to the gods. The column crossed the water at a shallow ford, and then started up the slope in reverent silence. Bayan looked up, toward the place to which they marched, and saw a natural formation of rocks in the shape of an ox's horn, and he knew with surety that was the site of the Great Khan's tomb.

"Bayan," Asutai said, drawing his horse near him. "We shall be there soon. I'm glad you are here."

"Thank you, my lord."

"If you had been made a Kheshig earlier, perhaps my father would still be alive."

Bayan didn't know how to answer that.

"Have you given thought to my offer?"

"I have, my lord."

"And what is your answer?"

Natalya knew that Bayan meant to accept it. That was the only honorable answer he could give. Whether the Mongols conquered for the Sky-Father, or for the Templar Order, or simply for wealth and bloodlust, they were Bayan's people. He was a man of the steppes, a warrior, a horse rider, an archer, and he would live and die that way, among the Horde.

"My lord, I—"

Natalya fought Bayan's mind to keep him from answering, and the simulation went sideways with distortion.

Rein it in, Griffin said.

Natalya didn't want to rein it in. She didn't want Bayan to become a Templar.

Natalya? You know you can't change this.

She did know that. But more important, she knew where the Khan would soon be buried, and Griffin didn't. If she were to desynchronize, right now, he would never know.

"I got this," she said, and turned back to Asutai, who peered at her from his horse, frowning through the warped simulation. "No," she told him firmly, and the world broke apart.

The Mongols scattered like leaves, and the Burkhan Khaldun collapsed on itself, taking the ox horn formation with it, and a storm with the raging strength of the Parietal Suppressor tore through Natalya's mind.

When it cleared, she stood in the Memory Corridor, gasping.

Griffin shouted in her ear, *What did you do?*

"I lost control."

No, you didn't! That was sabotage!

Natalya closed her eyes, her stomach heaving with the after-effects of her desynchronization.

I'm sending you back in.

"No," she whispered.

Yes!

"No!" she said. "If you send me back in, I'll just do it again."

Why? We're so close!

"Because I don't want you to know where it is. I don't want anyone to know where it is."

Griffin went quiet then, for a long time, and Natalya felt a chill creep through her, as if the Memory Corridor had heat, but someone had turned it off.

"Let me out," Natalya said.

Okay. Stand by.

A moment later, without warning, her mind lurched again. The simulation spit her out into the Animus chair. She pulled off the helmet and coughed, the force of it pounding the inside of her head with a barbwired baseball bat.

"You owe me an explanation," Griffin said.

Natalya was too dizzy and nauseous to reply.

"She doesn't owe you anything," she heard David say.

"Stay out of this, kid."

"No," David said. "We just left the Templars because they tried to control us. Now you're gonna do the same thing?"

"It's for a different reason," Griffin said.

David snorted. "You think that makes you better?"

"I do!" Griffin shouted. "We don't—"

"Stop." Natalya appreciated David speaking up for her, but she could fight for herself. "Just stop," she said.

"Was this your plan from the beginning?" Griffin asked.

Natalya shook her head. "No. I didn't have a plan. I just . . . ."

"Just what?"

"Leave her alone," Javier said.

Natalya rolled her eyes. If she didn't need David, she didn't need him, either.

"Why should I leave her alone?" Griffin asked. "For all I know, she's still working for Isaiah, and this whole thing was planned. For all I know—"

"I'm not working for Isaiah!" Natalya shouted, and then regretted it when the pain in her head surged. But she ignored it, refusing to back down, and sat up in the Animus chair. "I'm also not working for you. I'm not an Assassin, and I'm not a Templar."

Griffin shut his mouth and walked away, rubbing the knuckles of one hand with the palm of the other. "You sound like Monroe."

"Maybe he has the right idea," Natalya said.

Griffin pointed at the cement floor of the basement. "This is war!"

"It's not *my* war."

"That doesn't matter! You've been dragged onto the battlefield whether you like it or not, and now you're in the middle of it. Do you know what happens to people who freeze on the battlefield and do nothing?"

Natalya risked getting to her feet, but she managed to stay standing.

"They die," Griffin said. "If you want to make it out of this, you have to choose who you're going to fight alongside. You can't stay neutral. Monroe isn't neutral, no matter what he tells himself."

"What do you mean?" Javier asked.

"He used to work for Abstergo," Griffin said. "He was a Templar. You think that just washes off?"

Natalya hadn't really considered that. It didn't exactly make her rethink her own choice, but it did worry her.

Griffin continued. "Ask yourselves, why isn't Monroe here with us? Why didn't he get in that car with you?"

David looked at Javier and Natalya. "He said he was staying for Owen."

Griffin nodded. "Maybe he was. Or maybe he had his own reason."

The basement went quiet then, except for the hum of the computer fans.

But Natalya wasn't in the mood for more manipulation. It didn't matter what Monroe was doing or why he was doing it. She hadn't desynchronized for him, or anyone else. Griffin wouldn't get to her that easily.

"So what?" she said.

Griffin cocked his head. "So what?"

"Yes. So what if he had his own reason? What does that have to do with me?"

"Fine," Griffin said. "While you struggle with this case of adolescent rebellion, I'm going to Mongolia." He stomped over to the arsenal wall and started pulling down weapons.

"We're going, too, right?" David asked.

"Yes," Natalya said. "He gave us his word."

"A choice I now regret," Griffin said, and then he muttered, "Besides, you haven't kept your part of the bargain."

"I'll find the tomb when we reach Mongolia," Natalya said, careful of her wording.

Griffin just grunted, but she knew he would take them. She didn't actually want to go to Mongolia. But she had to somehow keep Griffin and Isaiah and anyone else from finding the Piece of Eden, and she knew she wouldn't be able to do that from the basement of an abandoned house in the middle of nowhere.

CHAPTER TWENTY-TWO

Owen stood outside the bank, watching the time. He had his instructions, and if he pulled this off, he'd be able to dig himself out of the hole and face his wife and son again. If he failed, they would lose their house and the life he had worked so hard to build for them. But no matter the outcome, they would be safe. He had been assured that much.

The seconds ticked away, and then it was 4:23, and he entered the bank. For a few minutes, he stood at one of the counters, as if filling out a deposit slip, resisting the fear that had already broken him out in a sweat and dried his mouth to sawdust. Then he walked to the restroom, and chose the middle stall, where he closed the door most of the way, leaving a two-inch crack, and perched on the toilet rim.

After that, he just had to wait.

And wait.

His thighs burned and his calves ached, but he stayed there, the tang of industrial cleaner and cherry air freshener sticking to the inside of his nose and coating his tongue.

At 5:03, he heard the bathroom door open, and he could tell by the jangle of keys it was the security guard. If the man followed protocol, he'd check each stall, but since the doors were all open, he skipped that step, just as Owen had prayed he would.

The guard cut the lights, and the bathroom door closed.

Owen climbed down from the toilet rim, and felt his way out of the stall in the dark, the only light coming from the red emergency exit sign over the door.

Then he waited.

At 5:17, he emerged from the bathroom and turned to the right, heading toward the bank's rear offices, where he opened the emergency exit, admitting his accomplice who had already deactivated that alarm. The man wore a black denim jacket over a hoodie, his face partially obscured.

Then the two of them walked toward the front of the bank, where tellers were still counting out before the safe had closed for the night.

There in the lobby, Owen's accomplice raised his voice, brandishing a pistol.

It didn't matter what he said. Owen wasn't really listening. Instead, he watched the tellers and employees, looking for any sign of trouble, finding only surprise and terror on their faces. He'd thought that, working in a bank, maybe they'd be better prepared for this. Tougher, somehow. But they all just put up their hands and cowered, except the ones who filled the sacks with money. Owen prayed again, this time that none of them would do anything stupid.

But then the security guard appeared, as if from nowhere.

"Freeze!" he shouted.

The fact that he had shouted the word *freeze* told Owen everything he needed to know about what would happen next, and he felt powerless to stop its unfolding.

The accomplice shot the guard in the chest, and everyone screamed. One of the men stuffing money into the bags just froze, and another employee swore at him, ripped the bags from his hands, and took over the job.

The security guard lay on the ground and moved for another minute or so, blood pooling beneath him, and then he lay still, and Owen went numb watching it. That wasn't supposed to happen, but he grabbed as many bags as he could carry, as did his accomplice, and then they bolted for the rear exit, where a car waited.

Have you seen enough? Isaiah asked.

"Yes," Owen said.

The simulation fragmented, like an ancient scroll that crumbled as soon as it was exposed to the sunlight and air, and Owen found himself back in the Memory Corridor.

"It wasn't him," he said.

He still robbed a bank, Owen, Isaiah said.

"Yeah, but they forced him to. He didn't have a choice. And he wasn't the one who shot the guard. He didn't murder anyone."

He would have gone to prison anyway.

"Maybe," Owen said. But that wasn't as important as the understanding he had just gained, the things he had learned about that day, because it all made sense now. His dad had been a victim as much as that security guard. No one would believe that, especially not Owen's grandparents, but that didn't matter. Owen knew the truth, and he realized that was what he'd wanted all along.

"Was that accomplice an Assassin?" he asked.

Perhaps.

"I'm ready to come out."

Very well. In three, two, one . . .

The Memory Corridor disappeared in a searing flash, and Owen opened his eyes back in Aerie, Isaiah standing over him, disconnecting him from the machine. Owen almost felt as if he should thank the Templar, but he couldn't bring himself to. Not yet.

Instead, he said, "I want to see Monroe."

Isaiah nodded. "I can certainly arrange that."

"What have you done with him?"

"What do you mean?"

"Where is he?"

"A holding cell."

"You haven't . . . done anything to him?"

"Like what?"

Owen knew that Monroe had information the Templars and the Assassins wanted. Monroe had decoded something in Owen's DNA, and the others' DNA, that connected them all to one another, and to the Trident of Eden. Owen just didn't know how far Isaiah would go to get that information out of Monroe.

"Have you hurt him?" Owen asked.

Isaiah scoffed. "Please. I may be angry with Monroe, but torture is always counterproductive. It inevitably damages the mind, and in my line of work, I find it pays to keep the mind intact. But you'll soon see for yourself that he's unharmed. Come, I'll escort you back to the lounge."

With that, he walked Owen back down the hallways and corridors of the Aerie to the room where Grace and Sean had eaten breakfast that morning. Grace was still there, talking closely with that Victoria woman from that morning. Isaiah left, and Owen took a seat away from Grace to give her privacy, facing the large windows.

The previous night's storm had left everything outside with that greener-than-green glow. The trees, the delicate underbrush, and the grass that grew in patches where the sunlight fell. It seemed very odd to him that only hours ago he had been freerunning in those woods to infiltrate this facility, and now he sat here on the inside looking out.

"Owen," Grace said.

She and Victoria were both looking in his direction.

"Did it work?" she asked.

"Yeah," he said. "It worked."

"And how are you feeling?" Victoria asked, and Owen figured she must be some kind of shrink.

"I'm good," he said. "Did you go into a simulation today, Grace?"

She shook her head.

"Last night was hard for everyone," Victoria said. "And everyone has to deal with it in their own way."

Definitely a shrink. Owen had seen a few of them after his dad had died.

"Are you okay if I go check on Sean?" Victoria asked.

Graced nodded, and so the woman left them alone. Then Owen got up and walked over to Grace's table.

"Do you mind?" he asked.

"Nope."

He pulled out a chair and flipped it around to sit in it reversed, his arms folded across its back.

"So," she said, "did the Assassins set your dad up?"

His shoulders tensed. "It looks that way."

"I'm sorry."

He'd never had anyone to blame for his father's death until now. The thing he didn't know was how involved Griffin had been, if at all, and that bothered him the most. "I guess it shouldn't come as a surprise," he said.

"Why is that?"

Owen told her about Zhi, and about how the Brotherhood had discarded her after her injury, even though she had single-handedly saved her empire. "It seems like that's what they do," he said. "They use people."

"That's wrong," Grace said.

"So much of this is."

"But at least she honored her father's memory, right? And that's kinda what you're doing."

That was true. Owen actually felt as though he owed something to Zhi for that. And he also owed Javier. Without the stolen DNA sample, Owen would still be where he was before, confused, alone, without answers. He wanted to tell Javier about everything he'd just learned, but he had no idea when he would see his friend again.

"So are you a Templar now?" Grace asked with a smirk.

He snorted. "What do you think?"

"I don't know," she said. "Isaiah can be pretty convincing."

Owen still found it hard to fully trust him, and it was impossible to forget the damage that Templars like Boss Tweed had done in New York, no matter what Sean said about the organization now. "I'm not a Templar."

"But you're not an Assassin, either."

"No. But I guess I'd started down that path."

"Me too. If you remember."

He did. His ancestor in New York had trained Grace's ancestor to be an Assassin. Varius and Eliza had spent a lot of time together, and they'd become close. A residual of that closeness and trust still lingered between Owen and Grace, if he paid attention to it.

Grace leaned back in her seat. "This situation messes with your mind."

"Yes, it does," Owen said. "It's like some kind of brain maze. It's hard to keep everything in its place. All the memories. The identities. You can get lost."

"You gotta find one true thing," Grace said. "Victoria was just telling me that. You gotta find one true thing and hang on to it."

Owen thought about that. "For me, it's my dad. What about you?"

"It's David," she said.

Owen dropped his gaze to the table. He still didn't understand what had happened between Grace and her brother, and how they had come to be on opposite sides of this conflict, but he knew better than to press her on it. If that was something she wanted to share, she would share it.

After that, a few Aerie staff brought in a tray of sandwiches and bags of chips, along with some fruit.

"Lunch," Grace said. "Not as nice as what we usually get."

"That's okay," Owen said. "Did I mention I've been hiding out in a storage unit?"

"For real?"

"Yes." He got up and went to grab a sandwich, roast beef. "Trust me, this is great."

As they were eating, Sean returned to the lounge. He greeted them, and joined them at their table, but seemed distant and distracted. A different guy than Owen had met weeks ago in Monroe's warehouse.

"How are you doing?" Owen asked.

"Huh?"

"How are you doing?"

"Oh, I'm good," Sean said. "I won a Viking duel."

Owen raised his eyebrows. "Seriously?"

Sean nodded. "I took control of the Jomsvikings, and now we're going to raid the Danish coast."

"That's cool." Owen put his sandwich down. "But how are *you* doing?"

Sean stopped chewing, and he looked confused, as if he didn't quite understand the question. "Me?"

"Yes, you."

"I—I'm fine," he said. "Better than fine."

Owen looked over at Grace, and she gave him a shrug. Sean seemed pretty lost in the brain maze, and Owen didn't think he wanted to be found.

The next morning, Victoria met them in the lounge by herself. She checked her tablet and suggested that Sean continue with the simulation of his Viking ancestor, who was apparently named Styrbjörn. Grace still wasn't sure she was ready to go back in, and as for Owen, Victoria said he could contribute to the effort through a simulation of his own. That only felt as if they were trying to distract him.

"I'm not doing anything to help you until I get to see Monroe," he said.

"I'm not sure that will be possible."

"Why not? Isaiah promised me I could talk to Monroe."

Victoria looked down at her tablet. "I'm afraid I don't know anything about that."

The Templar leader had lied to him. "Then go get Isaiah."

"I'm afraid Isaiah is occupied."

"Occupied?" Owen raised his voice a little. "With what?"

"That is none of your concern," she said, frustration cracking some of her shrink veneer.

"He's leaving, isn't he?" Grace said. "After what happened last night, he's going after the prong."

Victoria shook her head. "I didn't say—"

"Then he's going to China," Owen said. "Or Mongolia."

"How do you know that?" Sean asked. "You haven't talked to Natalya."

Owen looked directly at Victoria. "Because I was there."

With that, the woman dropped the rest of her forced gentility. "Do you know where the prong is?"

"No," Owen said. "My DNA was a dead end, otherwise the Assassins would already have it."

Victoria narrowed her eyes at him. "Your reunion with Monroe will have to wait until Isaiah returns. In the meantime, I will be here to guide you through further Animus simulations. Isaiah wanted me to tell you he is particularly hopeful about your current ancestor, Sean."

Sean looked up. "He is?"

Victoria tapped her tablet again. "Yes. We believe the Ptolemaic prong was the one you all discovered in New York. The Seleucid prong is the one we hope to find in Mongolia. That leaves the Macedonian prong. Our researchers have modeled some hypothetical routes it might have taken through history, and one of the strongest candidates puts the final piece of the Trident somewhere in Scandinavia."

Sean actually grinned at that. Like a fool. He had the look of an addict.

"When is Isaiah leaving?" Grace asked.

Victoria turned and walked toward the door. As she opened it, she said, "He may be gone already. Cole is in charge now." And then she left.

As soon as the door closed, Owen turned to the others. "Monroe is somewhere in the Aerie. Do you know where he might be?"

"Why?" Sean asked, but Owen ignored him.

"There are five buildings," Grace said. "We haven't seen them all."

"I think I saw three of them last night," Owen said. "I'm guessing they're keeping Monroe in one of the other two."

"Wait!" Sean leaned forward, his voice raised in alarm. "What are you going to do?"

"Relax," Owen said. "You just stay on your trip."

"What?"

"Nothing." Owen turned to Grace. "What about you?"

She looked hard at Owen, and took her time in answering him. "Why? Are you thinking of busting him out?"

"That's the idea," Owen said. "If Isaiah's going to Mongolia, I know I'm not staying here."

She chewed on her bottom lip, and Owen smiled. "We already know we make a good team," he said.

"Eliza and Varius made a good team," she said. "You and I? That's not a settled question."

But Owen could sense the frustration in her, too. He saw it in her face when Victoria told them that Isaiah might have already left. "I know you don't want to be left behind," he said. "Besides, chances are good Griffin is headed that way, too, and David will be with him. I know you're still worried about him."

"That is a low blow."

Owen held up his hands. "It's the truth."

Grace stared at him for another full minute, and Owen just left the question sitting there on the table the whole time, waiting patiently.

"Okay," she finally said. "I'm in."

Owen nodded. "Good." Then he turned to Sean, who'd been silent for a while now. "What about you?"

"Oh, I'm staying here," Sean said.

"Of course you are." Owen really hadn't expected him to say anything different. "Can we at least trust you not to rat us out?"

Sean shrugged. "I don't speak for you. You don't speak for me."

Owen decided that would have to be good enough. "Okay, then."

Grace leaned on one of her elbows. "You have a plan for how to pull this off?"

"I think so."

"And what am I going to think of this plan?"

Owen smiled again. "You probably won't like it."

CHAPTER TWENTY-THREE

Javier could tell that Griffin still boiled at what Natalya had done in the simulation, but apparently he'd accepted there wasn't anything he could do about it and he'd moved on to preparing them for the trip to Mongolia. He'd spent more time on the video chat with Gavin and some other members of the Brotherhood, and now Javier helped him pack up weapons and equipment, most of which Natalya refused to handle, while David had to be constantly reminded not to touch anything.

"So how are we getting there?" Javier asked. "Does that Templar car fly?"

Griffin didn't give him anything for that. Just silence. "I've arranged a plane."

"What, like a private jet?"

The Assassin stopped packing. "Yes. Exactly like that."

Javier nodded and returned to what he was doing, loading up a crate with anything he could fit inside it. Each of them also stuffed a backpack. They grabbed food, the sleeping bags, and also some warm gear, though most of the clothing in the basement was a bit large for Natalya and David. When they'd finished, Griffin had them bring it all out to the barn, and then he shut everything down and secured the basement lair.

The car had some storage space, in two rear compartments on either side of the jet turbine. They loaded what didn't fit in those into the backseat, or carried it on their laps. Javier sat up front with Griffin, while Natalya and David sat behind them.

It was nearing evening as they pulled out of the barn and down the driveway, and Javier took one last look at the ghost house before they rounded a bend and it disappeared in the trees. Griffin drove them to the highway, and then turned them south, toward the airport, which was a good hour away. Fellow travelers stared at the car as it passed them. Javier smiled at that for a little while, and then watched the sun's slow-motion fall to the horizon, and had almost drifted off to sleep when Griffin took an exit, waking him up.

"This isn't the airport," David said.

"Sure it is," Griffin said.

David pointed out the window. "No, I can see the terminal over there."

"We're not taking that kind of plane."

Javier frowned, but decided to keep quiet, wait, and see.

Griffin drove them through a series of warehouses and other industrial buildings, finally pulling into a small, empty hangar.

Two men waited inside with an airport luggage truck. Griffin stopped the car but left it running.

"Keep it somewhere safe," he said to one of the men. "I'll be back for it."

"You got it."

The second man helped them load all their bags and gear onto the luggage truck, and after they'd emptied the car, Javier watched the first guy pull it back out of the hangar and drive away.

Griffin motioned them all to climb onto the luggage truck, and the stranger drove them out onto the tarmac. Javier breathed sulfurous exhaust the whole way, the engine of the truck both loud and obnoxious after the purr of the car. There weren't many jets waiting that Javier could see, and he tried to figure out which one they might be headed toward. But when the luggage truck came to a stop in front of a big cargo plane of some kind, Javier realized the flight would probably not be what David had hoped for.

"What is this?" David asked, pushing up his glasses.

"This is your private jet," Griffin said.

David shook his head. "That is not what this is."

"Sure it is." Griffin pointed at the plane's wings. "Those are jet engines, and we'll have the entire thing to ourselves. Unless you count all the packages."

"Packages?" David asked.

"Packages."

"You're mailing us to Mongolia?" Javier said.

"By way of China." Griffin clapped his hand on Javier's back. "Hide in plain sight."

The inside of the plane matched the idea of a private jet even less than the outside. Their seats were made of canvas sewn around a metal frame. Basically, deck chairs bolted to the bulkhead. But the hold was pressurized and heated, and there was actually a bathroom. The drone of the engines made it a bit difficult for Javier to talk without raising his voice, but they weren't so loud he couldn't think.

After they'd been in the air for a few hours, and Natalya and David had both somehow fallen asleep, Javier leaned over and asked Griffin who the men back in the hangar were, and how the Brotherhood had arranged this flight.

"Abstergo has many enemies," Griffin said. "Not all of them are Assassins. We sometimes work together toward a common goal."

"The enemy of my enemy is my friend?" Javier said.

"You could say that." He regarded Javier for a moment, nodding to himself. "In spite of your recklessness, you've impressed me."

"Is that hard to do?"

"Very."

Javier nodded back, but he hadn't made any of his choices to impress Griffin.

"I've spoken to Gavin about you, and he agrees. If you're looking for a place and a purpose, you may have found it."

"In the Brotherhood?"

Griffin nodded.

"Is this a formal invitation?"

"If you want it to be."

Javier found the idea appealed to him more than he would have expected it to. The Assassins represented choice. Equal rights for everyone, everyone free to exercise their individual agency. That vision of the world seemed better than the world in which Javier lived, where he didn't yet feel free to openly be himself.

"Is there an initiation?" he asked, half joking.

"An induction," Griffin said. "Then your real training would begin."

Javier nodded. "I'll think about it."

"Do." Griffin closed his eyes and leaned his head back against the bulkhead. "But try to get some rest, too."

Javier was tired, but after that conversation he found it difficult to sleep. He wondered what Owen would say about all this, and then he wondered if that should even matter. This was Javier's choice. This was about finding the place where *he* belonged.

Many hours later, the plane landed in Beijing, and Griffin led them out onto the tarmac. A persistent, gray haze stole the horizon away in every direction. They might have been surrounded by mountains, or on an island, and Javier wouldn't have known it.

Before they'd gone far, an SUV pulled up, and a woman got out. She appeared Chinese, approaching middle age, with long black hair, and she wore a fitted white outfit that looked like a cross between military and Olympic athlete. Unlike the two men from before, she seemed to Javier exactly like an Assassin.

"Griffin?" she said.

Griffin nodded and shook her hand. "Pleasure to finally meet you, Yanmei."

"Please." She gestured toward the SUV. "Come with me?"

"Let us grab our gear."

"Of course."

Yanmei helped them load their bags and crates into the back of her vehicle, and then they all piled in, Griffin in the front passenger seat, Javier and the others in back, while Yanmei drove. Javier noticed her scrutinizing all of them in the rearview mirror.

"Gavin didn't explain what this is about," she said. "Why are you here?"

"A Piece of Eden," Griffin said.

Yanmei whipped her head toward him, and then slowly returned her gaze to the road. "He could have mentioned that," she said. "He didn't think we could retrieve it on our own?"

"It's a unique situation."

"How so?"

Griffin turned around. "Natalya, here, has seen it."

Yanmei paused. "In the Animus?"

"Shaun obtained blueprints and a processor in Madrid," Griffin said. "We're actually trying to locate three different Pieces. The prongs of a Trident. These kids, and three others, are connected to it. You've heard the name Isaiah?"

"Yes."

"He's tracking something he's calling an Ascendance Event, and the six of them are a part of it."

"I see."

"Isaiah is probably on his way here now. Have you seen any increased Templar movement?"

"No," she said. "It's been quiet."

"That's odd." Griffin ran a hand over his shaved head. "That's very odd. You'd think they'd be raising an army . . ."

"Gavin said I need to get you to Mongolia. The Burkhan Khaldun?"

"That's right."

"I have a private jet standing by."

"Finally!" David said.

Javier and Natalya laughed at that, and even Griffin chuckled.

When the SUV reached the far side of the airport, Yanmei pulled it up to a plane that would probably make David very happy. Javier didn't know much about jets, but this one looked fast, with the sleek lines of an arrow. They unloaded their gear from the SUV, and then they boarded. Inside the cabin, the leather upholstered chairs welcomed them with wide arms and reclining backs. The seats ran down the sides of the plane, grouped in two's that faced each other.

"Where's the rest of your cell?" Griffin asked.

"Tibet," Yanmei said. "I didn't have time to recall them. Gavin didn't give me much notice."

"He didn't have any. This has really developed over the past thirty-six hours."

Yanmei headed up to the front of the plane. "Let me make sure all the preflight checks are done, and we can be on our way."

Javier settled into a chair facing Natalya, while David sat farther down from her, on his own, staring out through the little window at the runway. Before long, the plane moved, and Yanmei returned to the cabin. She buckled into a seat opposite Griffin, on the other side of the plane from Javier and Natalya.

"Introductions?" she said.

"Sure." Griffin pointed at Javier, Natalya, and David in turn, giving the Assassin their names.

She smiled at each of them. "And Natalya, you've seen this prong from the Trident?"

Natalya nodded.

"What does it look like?"

"A weird dagger," David said. "We saw the first one in New York."

"The first one?" Yanmei frowned. "Perhaps you should brief me from the beginning."

So the three of them took turns, Javier doing most of the talking, David doing most of the interrupting, in explaining first Monroe, and the Draft Riots simulation, followed by the events of the past few weeks. Natalya described her memories of her Mongol ancestor, and Yanmei listened to it all patiently, without asking questions until they were through.

Then she sat for a moment with her index finger pressed to her lips. "One thing you didn't say is whether you know where Möngke Khan was buried."

"We don't. No one does." Griffin grunted. "Natalya elected not to find out."

"What do you mean?" Yanmei asked.

"She intentionally desynchronized."

"Why?"

"Because she believes that no one should have the Piece of Eden," David said.

Natalya turned around to face him. "I can speak for myself." Then she turned to Yanmei. "I just think it might be better if it stayed hidden."

Yanmei nodded. "I don't actually disagree with that. But I don't think that's the situation we face, is it? That's not a choice we have. From what you have said, it doesn't seem to be a question of if it's found, but by whom."

This older Assassin had a much better bedside manner than Griffin did. Natalya actually seemed to be listening to her, thinking about what she said, instead of arguing and shutting down.

"You know where it is," Yanmei said, "don't you, Natalya?"

She paused. "Not exactly."

"I have an idea," Griffin said. "I saw enough before she killed the simulation, I think I'll be able to get us pretty close."

Yanmei nodded, but she didn't take her eyes from Natalya, who had pulled her feet up onto her seat, hugging her knees. She stayed that way for the rest of the flight, as the Chinese countryside passed beneath them, and they flew up, over mountains, above a wide and rugged plateau.

"The Mongolian steppes," Yanmei said. "I don't know what it is about this land, but it breeds conquerors. Attila the Hun. Genghis Khan—"

"Isaiah," David said, but fortunately thought better of adding Griffin to that list.

"We should land at Möngönmorit in another hour or so," Yanmei said. "Burkhan Khaldun is another fifty miles or more from there."

"Maybe we should circle around the mountain," Griffin said. "Get a look at things."

Yanmei nodded. "I can instruct the pilot." Then she unbuckled and walked up toward the front of the plane. A few minutes later, she returned. "We've updated the flight plan for a slight detour over the target."

Not long after that, the steppes gave way to hills, and the hills became tree-covered mountains with winding rivers and wide valleys.

"This region is sacred to the Mongolian people," Yanmei said. "It has been since before Genghis Khan. Foreigners aren't even allowed to climb the Burkhan Khaldun."

"I don't think Isaiah will respect that boundary," Javier said.

"No," she said. "But it would be wise for us to tread lightly."

Not long after that, the plane dipped in its approach over the mountains, and everyone found a window from which to look out. They flew low enough, the trees appearing to look like individual, green brush strokes against a canvas of gray rock and snow. The mountain range had almost endless peaks and ridges, dips and valleys, rivers, its terrain spreading for miles in all directions.

"That is the Burkhan Khaldun."

"Which mountain?" David asked.

"That one, there," Yanmei said.

She pointed to one of the highest peaks. It wasn't an Everest in size or height, but something about it struck Javier as singular, imposing, and even regal, with its crown of white ice and its throne of green.

"Look for any sign of a Templar camp," Griffin said.

Javier strained to bring the distant ground into focus, but trees grew everywhere, and the camp would have to be pretty big to be visible from their elevation.

"Can the pilot take us down any lower?" David asked.

"Perhaps," Yanmei said. "I can go—"

Something exploded outside the plane, and the cabin jerked hard enough to throw Javier's face against the window, bashing his nose. He tasted blood, and his eyes watered, the ground outside the window racing closer to them.

"We've been hit!" Yanmei shouted.

Javier looked out a window on the other side of the jet, and saw one of the engines blown partially away, trailing a thick black smoke.

Javier felt the sudden loss of altitude pressing him into his seat, the rattling shaking the air from his lungs. They were going to crash. Javier had been training with an Assassin, he'd broken into a police warehouse, and he'd raided a Templar stronghold, and he was going to die in a plane crash.

"I'm going up front!" Yanmei shouted. She unbuckled and pulled herself out of her chair, then walked through the cabin, arms spread wide, and disappeared into the cockpit.

"Hold tight, everyone!" Griffin shouted. "We'll make a landing. We've still got one engine."

"Unless they shoot at us again!" David said.

The damage to the plane didn't look like mechanical failure, and Yanmei had called it a hit. That had to be the Templars. They were down there, and the flyover had been a mistake. Even if they survived, the Templars now knew they were there.

Yanmei lurched back down the aisle and dove into her seat. "We're going to make an emergency landing! The pilot spotted an open field!"

"Brace yourselves!" Griffin shouted. "Heads down and stay down!"

Javier obeyed, and then he waited, listening to the howl of the one remaining engine, and the deafening rattle of what sounded like every single part of the plane. From the corner of his eye, to the right, he could see the mountains out the window, not below them, but alongside them. The tops of the pine trees looked close enough to smell.

They were about to hit.

CHAPTER TWENTY-FOUR

Grace did not like Owen's plan.

So far, it consisted of him searching the lounge, and their dorms, and finally one of the Animus rooms, looking for things he could use to make something that resembled what he called a pain grenade.

"But you're not making an *actual* grenade," Grace said.

They sat in the bathroom of Grace's dorm, hoping that was the one place Abstergo hadn't installed surveillance.

"No," Owen said. "It just has to look like one."

He held up a canister he'd assembled from the can of an energy drink, some wires, with an outer shell of electrical tape, and that is exactly what it looked like. "You seriously think that's going to fool anybody?"

"It's close enough it'll work," Owen said. "Come on, let's go."

He tucked the taped-up can inside a pocket, and they left the bathroom. If someone, somewhere in the Aerie had watched them go in there together, Grace wondered about what that person would assume, and then realized she didn't care.

They left her dorm, and went out into the hallway. It was late, well after midnight, and the hallways were deserted as they headed toward the main building. They already knew how far they could get by going in the other direction, but wondered if there could be a better way to access one of the two remaining buildings they'd hadn't yet explored.

They reached the glass walkway and crept along it, into the large atrium, which they then crossed toward another walkway on the other side. No doorways had been locked so far, and they'd encountered no security.

"You'd think after what happened, they'd have tightened things up," Grace said.

Owen looked over his shoulder, behind them. "Maybe they've all gone with Isaiah to Mongolia."

"Maybe," Grace said. "But still. This seems strange."

When they reached the new walkway, they found it opened without a fingerprint or key code, and they entered it carefully, unsure of where it would lead them. The trees here grew closer to the building, and the walkway hunkered in their shadows, making the passage darker than the rest. When they reached the far side, they entered a building that seemed different than the others. There were fewer doors, with occasional windows that offered views inside large laboratories full of computers and robotics.

"This looks like the place Abstergo cooks everything up," Owen said.

"They told Sean they could build him prosthetic legs."

Owen scowled. "No wonder Isaiah's got him hooked. But it's hard to blame him for that side of it."

"Why?"

"You don't think you'd want to walk again?"

"Of course I would, but that's not the problem."

"Then what's the problem?"

"Sean needs to know that he's fine either way. That he's not defined by his legs or his ability to walk."

"Did you get that from Victoria?"

"No. I got that from myself."

They walked on in silence, through more hallways of laboratories, until they came to another glass walkway. That passage would most likely take them to the fifth building, but this door had a thumbprint scanner and required a key code.

"Does that fake pain grenade open doors?" Grace asked.

"Maybe we should search the labs for something we could use to open it."

"You won't find anything," said a woman's voice behind them.

Grace spun around, her neck on fire. A Templar agent stood behind them, cutting off their escape the way they had come.

"Cole," Owen said.

The woman pointed a gun at them, and looking at her, Grace had no doubt she would use it. "I've been watching you since you left your dorm," Cole said. "What are you doing here?"

"Just looking around," Grace said.

"Remember me from the other night?" Owen asked.

Cole's eyes narrowed. "You think it's smart to remind me of that right now?"

Owen pulled out the fake pain grenade, keeping it mostly obscured in his fist. "How about I remind you of this?"

Cole stared at the grenade for a moment, and Grace waited for her reaction.

"Doesn't look familiar," Cole finally said. "But maybe that's because you just made it."

Grace wanted to swear at Owen. This whole plan had been stupid and ridiculous from the beginning, but she had gone along with it, thinking that an almost-Assassin might have learned a thing or two in the past few weeks.

Owen looked at the fake grenade, and then dropped it on the floor. "So what happens now?"

"First, pick up that trash."

"Seriously?"

"Pick it up!"

Owen bent over and recovered the fake grenade.

"Now, you are going to march through that door, and I am going to take you to the holding cells." She kept the gun on them and marched up to the control pad on the door, where she scanned her thumb and entered her code. The door opened.

"Move," she said.

Owen led the way, and Grace marched behind him. They entered the walkway and followed its track through the woods, where it eventually followed the mountain slope downward, like the walkway to the garage on the other side of the Aerie.

"You're going to lock us up?" Grace said to Cole.

"Keep moving."

"Going to be hard to explain that to my dad," Grace added.

"Not my problem," Cole said. "We can make your dad think what we want him to think. We've got enough surveillance of you sneaking around, I could shoot you both and say it was self-defense."

Grace fell silent then. The Aerie suddenly felt very isolated, the night outside very cold.

Next to her, Owen walked with his head bowed, but she could tell his mind was racing. She wanted to think of a way out of this, too, but she still wasn't exactly sure what this was. What could the Templars really do? She knew what they'd done in the past, in New York, but she didn't think they could get away with that in the modern world. She had also begun to trust Victoria, and wanted to believe she wouldn't hurt any of them. But Grace didn't know anything about Cole.

They reached the bottom of the slope, and the passage reached a door into the mountain, also secured with an electronic lock. Cole opened it, and they entered the fifth building. This part of the Aerie had a very different feel. It was colder, and had none of the touches that made the rest of the facility inviting or impressive, giving Grace the impression that this wasn't meant to be seen by many.

"Proceed down the hall," Cole said.

They marched past a series of secured doors until Cole ordered them to stop. Then she opened up one of the unmarked doors with her key code, and spoke to someone inside.

"It's time," she said.

Monroe stepped out into the hallway. "Good to see you both."

"Monroe?" Owen moved toward him. "What—"

"Stop talking and march," Cole said. "Straight ahead."

Monroe nodded, made eye contact with Grace, and smiled. Then the three of them moved down the hallway and followed Cole's orders until they reached a vaulted room that resembled a warehouse, the walls and ceiling made of rock, with tall shelves and several of the large shipping containers Grace had seen stacked on ships. Cole directed them toward one of them.

"Is everything prepared?" Monroe asked.

"Yes," Cole said. "This unit is carrying sensitive equipment, so it's climate-controlled and oxygenated. I made sure you have water, food, and a couple of lanterns. I'm afraid there's only a bucket for . . . other things."

Grace looked over at Owen. What the hell was going on?

"Are you sure you won't be in danger?" Monroe asked.

"Yes," she said. "Surveillance is deactivated, but I made it look like it was done by someone hacking into one of the Animus rooms." She turned to Owen. "I'll take that piece of trash now."

Owen smiled and pulled out the fake grenade. "You're Rothenberg."

She took the grenade from him. "I don't know what you're talking about."

It had now become obvious to Grace that Cole was some kind of double agent, or a mole, and she was helping them escape. Grace didn't know why, and she didn't know who Rothenberg was, but in that moment, she didn't care.

"Better get inside," Cole said. "Surveillance will be coming back online, and I need to get in position. The hardest part will be convincing them that I fell for this thing." She held up the fake grenade.

"I owe you," Monroe said.

"Call it even," Cole said. "Supplies in the far left corner."

Monroe nodded and stepped inside the shipping container. Owen followed him, and then Grace took a deep breath and did the same. Then she turned around toward the opening as Cole pulled the doors closed.

"Settle in," she told them. "It's twenty-four hours to Mongolia."

Then she shut the doors, causing total darkness, and Grace heard the latch engage. Then she heard the sounds of someone moving, thumping and tapping along a far corner of the container, until a light bloomed.

"There," Monroe said, lifting a lantern onto a nearby crate.

"Is she Rothenberg?" Owen asked.

"Cole is an old friend," Monroe said. "I helped her once, and she promised to return the favor. I called her weeks ago. If she wanted you to know more about her, she would have told you. Leave it at that, or you might put her in danger. She's risking her life for you two."

That statement made Grace question her assumptions about the limits of the modern Templars. She looked around for a place to sit down, and landed on a cardboard box. Then she let out a long sigh and leaned forward.

"Where have you been?" Owen asked Monroe.

"Hiding out," he said. "Preparing. From what I saw in the garage, you and Javier obtained some training somewhere."

Owen nodded. "We were with Griffin. The Assassins."

"Ah." He looked at Grace. "And the rest of you were here at the Aerie."

Grace nodded.

"What does Isaiah know?" Monroe asked.

"He knows about the Piece of Eden in Mongolia," Grace said. "And we just found out they think there's another one in Scandinavia."

Monroe sat down on a crate, the lantern lighting one half of his face. "What about the one in New York?"

"What do you mean?" Owen said. "I thought you had it."

Grace had assumed that, too.

"No, I don't have it," Monroe said. "You didn't find it?"

"We found where it was hidden," Owen said. "But someone else had beaten everyone to it."

"I hope that doesn't mean there's a third player." Monroe tugged the ponytail out of his graying hair and scratched his head. "So that means there are still two missing prongs, assuming they eventually find this one in Mongolia."

"We're going to stop them, right?" Owen said.

"We're going to try," Monroe said. "Does Isaiah know about the Ascendance Event?"

"He mentioned it," Grace said. "But I don't think the Templars understand it."

Monroe nodded. "Good."

Grace waited a moment, and when Monroe failed to elaborate, she said, "We don't understand it, either, by the way."

Monroe looked into the lantern, lighting up his whole face. The glow deepened the wrinkles around his eyes, his mouth, and his forehead, making him seem older and more tired. "I'm not sure now is the time."

"We're going to be stuck in this thing for twenty-four hours," Owen said. "Can you think of a better time?"

Monroe nodded. And kept nodding, as if thinking. "Okay. Okay, maybe you're right. I wish the others were here, but . . . The thing you have to understand is that even though I discovered the Ascendance Event, I don't know exactly what effect it will have. Isaiah believes it will hold great power. A weapon. But I'm not convinced. I think it's a source of wisdom. Enlightenment."

"But what is it?" Grace asked.

"You already know about genetic memory. I spent my time at Abstergo researching it, decoding it, taking it apart, trying to make sure we understood everything there was to know, so that we could better exploit it. But in my analysis one day, I found something unusual. A subcode in the DNA beneath the primary code. It was like a background signal buried in the main transmission."

"What was it?" Grace asked.

"At the time, I didn't know, but once I knew what to look for, I found more of it. In fragments. Snippets here and there. Not everyone carries it, although I suspect at one time, everyone did."

"Did you figure out what it is?" Owen asked.

"I think so. I believe it's the collective unconscious of the human race."

"As in psychology?" Grace asked.

"Yes," Monroe said. "Carl Jung coined the term. He believed that all of humanity shared the same collection of fundamental images, symbols, and archetypes, passed down from the beginnings of the *Homo sapiens* species, during the Paleolithic era."

"You believe that?" Owen asked.

"I think the theory has been overinterpreted," Monroe said. "Some people see the mystical in it. They think the symbols are magical in some way, with esoteric power. But I'm a scientist. I didn't want mysticism, I wanted to understand the mechanics of this sub-DNA. So I dug deeper, and I started running proto-simulations with it, just to see what would happen."

"What's a protosimulation?" Grace asked.

"In the lab we would sometimes run a kind of . . . simulated simulation, using a rudimentary artificial intelligence as the subject, just to see if the simulation would hold, and what it looked like. And this new sub-DNA . . ." He rubbed his goatee. "Are either of you afraid of spiders?"

"Not really," Grace said.

"Yes," Owen said. "Why?"

"That's what the collective unconscious is like," Monroe said. "Some people are *born* afraid of spiders. It's an unconscious fear."

"Like an instinct?" Grace asked.

"In a way, but more complex than that. Have you wondered why so many of us have that fear? I think the answer is that somewhere in our ancient past, we learned that spiders can be deadly, and that memory got passed on. It's like a genetic memory, but it's not specific to one lineage or one ancestor. Well, it is, but it comes from a time so far back we were barely human, so that whole notion loses meaning. But now, all these millennia later, some people have that fear of spiders, and some people have lost it."

"So what does this have to do with the Ascendance Event?" Owen asked.

"I'm getting there." Monroe stood up and took a few steps away from them. "I started analyzing every strand of DNA in Abstergo's possession, looking for more fragments. It became an obsession, I admit. I wanted to re-create the entire collective unconscious sub-DNA. It would be like going back in time to the birth of humanity. But I made the mistake of telling Isaiah about it, and after that, it became his obsession, too. But like I said, he saw power in it. Something he could hopefully use in some way, not learn from."

"So do the rest of us have some of this sub-DNA?" Grace asked.

Monroe turned around to face her. "You don't have some of it. Between the six of you, you have *all* of it. That is the Ascendance Event. The collective unconscious, rising up."

Grace looked over at Owen. He looked puzzled, with eyebrows pinched, sporting a frown. She felt the same confusion. "Okay," she said. "But what does that actually mean for us?"

"I wish I could tell you," he said, turning Grace's confusion into frustration. "That's what I was doing in all of your schools. I'd left Abstergo, but I hadn't given up my research. I was trying to gather more fragments of the sub-DNA. It was purely scientific. But after I found all of you, I learned that your Genetic Memory Concordance goes beyond that, to the Pieces of Eden. That was . . . unexpected. I'm still trying to figure out how the relics and the sub-DNA are connected."

"So is Isaiah," Grace said.

The sound of a vehicle engine approached the shipping container from outside, and the three of them stopped to listen. Then the whole unit shifted suddenly, and Monroe dropped to the nearest crate, almost losing his balance.

"We're on our way," he whispered.

Owen pretended to look at a watch on his wrist. "Twenty-four hours to go."

CHAPTER TWENTY-FIVE

When the plane struck the ground, the impact hurled David forward, but his seat belt kept him in his seat, bending him in the middle, while his glasses flew the length of the cabin. The entire plane shook, grinding against the earth, and then bounced back up into the air for a moment, before crashing again. The next few moments seemed endless, and terrifying, but eventually they slid to a stop, and David looked up around the cabin. Its smooth lines all looked bent and crooked now.

"You kids okay?" Griffin asked. "Give me a name and a yes."

Natalya, yes. David, yes. Javier, yes.

"I'll go check on the pilot," Yanmei said. "And then we need to move out quickly." She staggered forward toward the cockpit.

David blinked, rubbing his head and his neck, feeling as though he'd just been a mountain's chew toy. "Why do we need to move out so fast?"

"Because the Templars will try to find the crash site," Griffin said. "We need to not be here when they do."

"Forget the element of surprise," Javier said.

"Unless you count their surprise that we're still alive," David said.

Yanmei returned from the cockpit. "Pilot's unharmed. He's already radioed the crash."

Griffin unbuckled and got out of his seat. "Let's move, people."

David did the same, along with Javier and Natalya, and after he'd recovered his glasses, unbroken, he followed Griffin to the rear of the plane. There they pulled on their warmer clothing, and loaded up as much of the weapons and equipment as they could carry, leaving the rest behind. David didn't really know what most of it did, except for the obvious flashlight, and he both wanted and didn't want to find out for himself. After they'd prepared, Yanmei pulled the emergency exit hatch, and a yellow inflatable slide exploded from the opening.

Griffin went down first, then Natalya, then David, squeaking his way down. At the bottom, on the ground, he was able to get a view of the wide track the plane had carved through the field, ripping up the grass and vegetation to the dirt, and he saw just how far they had slid. Hills stood to both sides, covered in pine trees, and beyond the rise on the right, the Burkhan Khaldun climbed up to its icy reaches.

Well below the snowline, just visible over the nearer ridge, a rock formation stood out, shaped like the horn of an ox. David turned to point it out to Natalya, but she was already staring right at it. When she noticed David looking at her, she quickly turned around and faced a different direction.

David looked back up at the horn and realized that Natalya probably recognized it from her simulation. Maybe she had even stood in this same spot before. But she also didn't seem to want anyone to notice her recognizing it, which meant the horn might be connected to the Khan's tomb.

"Did you see where the shot came from?" Griffin asked Yanmei.

She pointed. "It came from the west, near those mountains, but I'm not certain beyond that."

"What does your gut tell you?" Griffin asked.

Yanmei turned to Natalya. "I'm more interested in her gut."

Now everyone else turned toward Natalya, and David had to decide whether to talk about what he'd just seen her do, or let Natalya reveal it in her own time. He thought he knew what Grace would probably do. She'd say something about it to the others, not wanting to waste time with secrets, to get it all out in the open so they could deal with it. But David wasn't sure that was the best idea in this situation, because he wondered if Natalya was right. Perhaps the Assassins weren't any more trustworthy than the Templars.

David had to think about who he *could* actually trust, and right now, that was Javier and Natalya, and wherever she was, his sister.

Natalya pointed toward the south side of the mountains. "I think that way."

Yanmei nodded. "Sounds good to me."

"Okay, then," Griffin said. "Let's try to keep quiet."

"And watch out for wolves," Yanmei said.

She led the way forward, up the slope to the west, and before long they entered the forest. A persistent wind whipped up the thin, cold air, and the pine trees grew tall and narrow, as if they'd pulled their branches in tight. Tough grass and moss covered the ground, with very little undergrowth. They proceeded without talking, and when they reached the top of the ridge, David saw they still had a few more ridges just like it before they would actually reach the Burkhan Khaldun. Below them, another small valley spread out with a fairly wide expanse of open grassland.

"I haven't heard any helicopters," Griffin said.

Yanmei looked up. "They might have drones we can't hear." She turned to the left. "We'll skirt around and keep to the trees."

"This is your territory," Griffin said.

So they followed Yanmei around the bowl of the valley, and managed to stay mostly hidden under the forest's canopy. Another silent mile went by, and then another, with still more valleys and draws. At one point, David saw a fox dart away from them, and later watched an eagle missile-dive into a meadow, where it then pulled apart and ate whatever animal it had just skewered with its talons.

At last they reached what David hoped would be the final ridge before the Burkhan Khaldun, and as they crested it, he looked down into the widest valley they had yet encountered, a sweeping plain at least a half mile across, running far to the north and to the south, with a shimmering river right down the length of it.

"This is the source of the Kherlen River," Yanmei said. "According to legend, this area is one of the possible burial places of Genghis Khan. One story claims they diverted the river to flow over his tomb, so that it would never be found."

"What's that down there?" Javier pointed to the south, where the valley nearly doubled in width.

David strained, and thought he saw something glinting, either metal or glass, near the river, as well as some structures and possibly vehicles. "It's them!" he said, and wondered if Grace was down there with them.

Griffin pulled out a pair of binoculars and looked through them. "It's a camp," he said, and passed the binoculars to Yanmei. "David's right. It's Abstergo. They beat us here."

Yanmei turned to Natalya. "Are they searching in the right place?"

Natalya didn't answer.

"They're way off," Griffin said. "I saw enough of the simulation to know that much. I think the tomb is farther west, across this valley and up the slopes of the Burkhan Khaldun."

But David wasn't worried about that anymore. "What about my sister and Owen and Sean?" he asked. "We need to rescue them."

"That would be too risky," Griffin said. "Besides, didn't your sister and Sean choose to stay behind?"

"She got trapped," David said, getting angry. "She would have come."

He noticed that Natalya frowned at that, but she said nothing.

"I agree with Griffin," Yanmei said. "The Piece of Eden is the mission. If we locate that, then we can discuss a rescue." She looked to the west. "It's going to be difficult to cross this valley. There's no cover at all. They could easily spot us."

"That's it?" David said. "We're just pretending like our friends aren't down there?"

"I get it," Javier said. "Owen is my best friend. But we don't even know if they *are* down there."

"Even if they were," Griffin said, "the Piece of Eden has to come first. Look, don't you guys think Owen and Grace would want you to stop Isaiah before saving them?"

David knew he was probably right, so he couldn't argue with that.

Javier turned back to Yanmei. "I think I could get across without being seen."

"You've had training," Griffin said. "These two haven't."

David didn't like being referred to as one of the ones holding them back, but he didn't have the skills Bleeding through that Grace had talked about. In the New York simulation, he'd been an old man, while Natalya had been an opera singer.

"What if we cross at night?" Javier asked.

"That's a possibility," Yanmei said. "We should wait for the moon to go down, and then make a decision."

"Then for now, let's get some rest." Griffin looked around them at the ground. "Make a camp in the trees, sit tight, and watch."

They all agreed, so they unpacked a bit of food and their sleeping bags. They lit no fire, and bundled up with whatever they had. A few hours later, the sun went down, and the ridge grew frigid. David leaned against a tree, chin tucked into his coat, breathing out puffs of air that turned to steam and fogged his glasses, and then watching the fog slowly retreat. He listened to the wind that had yet to weaken, and over it heard the warble of an owl or some other night bird.

Yanmei had been right to worry about the moon. It lit the valley floor and polished the river to silver. Away to the south, the lights of the Abstergo camp shone even brighter, and David wondered about Grace. If she really was down there, or if she was still back in the Aerie. He felt as if he'd let her down in some way, taking so long to understand why the Animus mattered to her. He had to get her away from Abstergo, somehow. He had promised her that.

Something moved in the trees nearby. Something big, but it was too dark in the shadows to see what it was. Yanmei had mentioned wolves.

"Everyone hold still," Yanmei whispered. "Griffin?"

"Stun grenade armed."

"My crossbow is loaded, too," Javier said.

David's breath came in short gasps as the thing got closer to him with the sounds of feet much too big and heavy to be a wolf. His mind leapt to a bear.

"What is that thing?" Natalya asked.

"I'm not sure," Yanmei said.

The animal's breathing came in long, deep snorts, and seemed to be just a few yards away from David now. He thought he could smell it, a musky odor. His hands trembled as he reached for his flashlight.

"Stay calm," Griffin said.

But David couldn't. When it took another step toward him, the sudden shiver up his back jerked his arm, and before he thought better of it he'd switched the flashlight on, pointing it toward the sound.

It was enormous, a towering moose with antlers five or six feet wide. Its eyes glowed back at David.

"Kill that light!" Griffin hissed.

David switched the flashlight off, and then waited. He'd heard that moose could be very aggressive, and listened as the animal took a step, and then another, but realized it was moving away from him, off into the forest. He sighed.

"That thing was huge," Javier said.

"That light was bright," Griffin said. "Bright enough for Abstergo to see if they happened to be looking up this way."

That was David's fault. "I'm sorry. I just didn't know what it was."

"It's done," Yanmei said. "Let's be silent."

So David went quiet again with the rest of them, but now he watched the Abstergo camp not only thinking about his sister, but also waiting for signs of movement toward them. None came, and the cold night got colder.

As the moon fell, first gilding the peak of the Burkhan Khaldun, then sliding down behind it, the valley grew much darker, and the river turned to ink. The others directed their attention west, but David kept his eyes on the Templars. He couldn't move past the idea that Grace might be down there, in need of help.

"What do you think?" Griffin asked.

"I think maybe we should try," Yanmei said. "This might be our best chance. That Abstergo camp is only going to expand. So is their surveillance."

"Let's do it, then," Griffin said.

They packed up their sleeping bags and the other gear they'd pulled out, and then moved slowly down into the valley, staying low, using the uneven swells of ground to hide as best they could. They all kept the Abstergo camp in sight, looking for any indication that they'd been noticed, and soon they reached the valley floor.

As they started across—Yanmei first, then Javier and Natalya, then David, followed by Griffin—David noticed a new red light shining from the camp. But then it changed and became a green light. Then it changed again, and became an amber light.

Red, green, and amber.

The light went out, and David stopped. Those were the colors of the aircraft recognition lights on the P-51 Mustang, the plane David had flown in the memories of his great-grandfather.

Was that a coincidence?

The light blinked in sequence again. Red, green, and amber. Then went out.

David knew he had told Grace about those lights, and he wondered if it was some kind of code from her. Even though she'd given him such grief about how much he enjoyed the flight simulation, maybe she'd been paying attention to him, after all. And maybe she had seen David's flashlight earlier, and she was sending him back a message.

"David, what's going on?" Griffin whispered behind him.

"I think it's Grace," he said.

"What is?"

"The lights. Red, green, and amber. They're from my simulation back at the Aerie."

Griffin glanced toward the camp.

"They're gone now," David said. "But I saw them. It's Grace. It has to be."

"We can't know that for sure," Griffin said. "And our mission is the same. The Piece of Eden comes first."

"But—"

"I'm sorry." Griffin pushed past David. "Let's keep moving."

The Assassin prowled ahead across the field, though still trailing behind the others, but David stayed where he was. He couldn't dismiss what he'd seen, or rid his mind of the feeling that the lights had come from Grace. She needed him. He knew it. He'd left her behind once before, and he wasn't going to do it again, even if it meant going in on his own.

He turned around and ran back toward the hill and the trees. He had to get closer to the Abstergo camp without being seen, and he wouldn't be able to do that from the valley floor.

As he ran, he half expected Griffin to tackle him, or maybe get one of those Assassin sleep darts in his rear, but none came. He wasn't even sure if they'd noticed he was gone, but they would any moment. Would they just let him go, or keep to their own mission? He didn't turn around to find out.

When he reached the base of the hill, he climbed it back out of the valley to the trees, and only then did he stop, chest heaving, to turn around.

He could barely see the dark shadows of the others against the open field down below. They hadn't moved far from where he'd left them, which probably meant they'd stopped to figure out what to do about him. But now they seemed to be moving again, slowly westward.

David turned to the south, toward the camp, and crept forward through the trees. With the moon down, he stumbled several times over roots and rocks he couldn't see, but he kept moving. It felt as though a clock had started ticking, counting down to something. Counting down to something happening to Grace. Counting down to one of the groups finding the Piece of Eden. Counting down the time that David had to do something about it.

Along the way, he kept his ears and eyes aware of the woods to his left, and he didn't venture any deeper into them than he had to for cover. The moose had freaked him out, and again he remembered Yanmei's mention of wolves.

The cold wasn't as bad now that he was moving, but his breath still fogged his glasses up, which didn't help with his stumbling. Eventually, he reached a close-enough point to see more of what was going on in the camp.

There were five very large tents, shaped like simple cartoon houses, with straight walls and peaked roofs. David also noticed a few large shipping containers, as big as semitruck trailers, and many SUVs. They also had two helicopters, one smaller, and one with double propellers, front and back, for carrying heavy loads. Bright floodlights lit the entire camp, and several Templar agents patrolled the perimeter.

David searched for any sign of Grace, but saw none. He also couldn't see a point from which the colored lights might have come. His best guess was one of the tents. Some of them had windows. But which one?

He didn't know how he'd be able to find that out, with the floodlights and the agents everywhere. But he had to try, and he figured the middle of the night would be the best chance he would get.

He took a deep breath, about to sneak down the hill, when he heard a footstep behind him. He spun around, fearing an animal.

"Freeze!" The agent wearing the full uniform with the black helmet and SWAT gear pointed a gun at David. "Tell Isaiah the girl's plan worked," he said into a radio. "Her brother came."

CHAPTER TWENTY-SIX

For the last part of the journey to Mongolia, Owen could hear helicopter rotors overhead, and gusts of wind that set the shipping container swaying and trembling. Motion sickness rolled down to his stomach from his head, and then came back up through nauseous tingles in his cheeks. But before he threw up, the helicopter set the container down, and the floor stabilized beneath his feet.

"We should hide," Grace whispered.

They all moved to one of the far corners and crouched down behind a stack of crates. Monroe switched off the lantern, and then they waited.

A few minutes later, the latches rattled, and then the wide doors squealed open, flooding the container with almost blinding light from the outside. Owen squinted, and it took longer than usual for his eyes to calm down.

"Get these ground-penetrating radar units off first," someone said. "Isaiah wants us up and running by dawn."

"Yes, sir."

Owen heard the sound of crates being dragged, multiple footsteps, the occasional grunt. The commotion lasted for several minutes, but no one came far enough into the container to see the three of them hiding there, and before long they heard nothing at all, except for the voices and sounds of vehicles outside the container.

Owen risked a glance over the nearest crate. The bright light came from floodlights attached to mobile generators, like those he'd seen construction crews using at night. He glimpsed the edge of a large tent, and Templar agents periodically marching by.

"Looks like we're right in the middle of their camp," Owen said. "Do we just make a break for it?"

"Maybe we should hide in here until things calm down out there," Grace said.

"What if they don't calm down?" Owen asked. "What if they come back to unload the rest of this?"

"We should try to get out of here," Monroe said. "But cautiously. Not charging out of here like Billy the Kid and the Regulators."

"Huh?" Owen said.

Monroe shook his head. "I'll show you in my Animus sometime." He crept out from behind the crates. "But for now, let's go."

They moved toward the shipping container's doors, staying hidden as much as they could, until they reached the opening. From there, Owen could see the camp was even bigger than he'd thought. There were three, maybe four other tents in addition to the one he'd seen, as well as numerous vehicles. There didn't seem to be as many agents as Owen had feared, and he thought they might stand a chance of getting away.

"That way." Monroe pointed to the right, where the ground rose up beyond the camp floodlights to a line of trees. "Make for the trees."

"Sounds good," Grace said. "I'm ready."

Owen nodded. "Me too. We—"

But then he saw Isaiah emerge from a tent.

The director walked directly toward the shipping container with a contingency of a dozen agents outfitted for combat. Two other, smaller units closed in from the sides.

"I think we missed out chance," Monroe said. "Back up, back up."

So they retreated farther into the shipping container until they were out of sight again. Owen closed his eyes and held perfectly still. He sensed Grace doing the same next to him, and a memory landed on his shoulder with the light touch of a hand, a memory of Varius and Eliza outside Tweed's house. It lingered for a moment, and then the memory pulled away.

"You can come out," Isaiah said into the container, his voice echoing off its metal walls. "There's no use delaying the inevitable, is there?"

Monroe looked at Owen and Grace, shook his head, and nodded.

Owen stood up, then Grace, then Monroe.

"Victoria contacted me hours ago," Isaiah said. "She's on her way here now." He cast his gaze around the container's interior. "Very resourceful of you. I expected you'd try to escape the Aerie, of course, but I didn't anticipate this method."

"There've been many things you didn't anticipate," Monroe said.

Isaiah nodded. "That is true." He turned to the agent nearest him. "Bring them."

Then he walked away, and the agents with him closed in. They ordered the three of them out of the container, and they complied. Then, at gunpoint, they marched them in the direction Isaiah now stalked, toward one of the tents. Owen noticed now that the camp appeared to be situated in a long valley, with a large mountain range on one side.

"Sir!"

Isaiah turned around, and one of the agents pointed north.

Owen looked, and saw a light flickering in the trees some distance away, up along the valley's edge on the right. Grace looked, too, and then she looked at Owen, but her thoughts seemed to be churning. A moment later, the light went out.

"Now this, I did anticipate," Isaiah said. "We knew they survived."

"Who survived what?" Monroe asked.

"The Assassins survived the crash of the plane. We shot it down earlier today." Isaiah pointed to where the light had been. "Target that location."

"Yes, sir."

Another Templar agent walked up with a shoulder-mounted rocket launcher. Owen had never seen one, and it didn't seem real, more like a toy. It did look heavy, though, and took two additional agents to load it with the grenade and prepare it to fire. Then the shooter sighted through the large scope, and Owen realized this was actually happening. He didn't know who was up there, but if it was the Assassins, there was a chance it was Griffin. Possibly Javier, too.

"Target acquired," the shooter said. "Ready to fire."

"Don't!" Grace screamed, before Owen could do the same.

Isaiah held up a hand, and the shooter pulled his eye away from the scope.

"Why?" Isaiah asked.

"My brother could be up there," she said.

"What?" Isaiah frowned. "I would never have brought children to Mongolia. I highly doubt the Assassins would."

"And I know my brother," Grace said. "If that Assassin came here, David wouldn't want to be left behind. Please, if there's even a chance he's up there—"

"Very well," Isaiah said. "We'll send in a strike team."

"No," Grace said. "If David is up there, I think I can get him to come to us. Here."

"I'm listening," Isaiah said.

Owen wondered what Grace was doing, but hoped she had some kind of plan.

"You don't know what's up there," Grace said. "If I can get David down here, he'll listen to me. He can tell us what the Assassins are doing. What they know. Maybe Natalya gave them the location of the tomb."

Isaiah looked at her for a moment, frowning, and then motioned the shooter to lower the rocket launcher. "I'll give you an hour to get him here. After that, I send in my team."

"Thank you," Grace said.

"How do you propose to signal him?" Isaiah asked.

Grace looked at the ground for a few moments, and paced the few steps the agents surrounding them allowed. Then she looked up. "I need three colored lights. A red one, a green one, and an amber one."

Isaiah paused, and then smiled. "The Tuskegee Airmen."

Owen had no idea what that meant, but several minutes later, an agent brought out a large camera bag filled with different lenses and filters. Grace pulled out three different colored filters, and then asked for a flashlight, which she then switched on and pointed in the same direction the rocket launcher had targeted.

One by one, she placed the filters in front of the flashlight. Red, green, amber.

Then she did it again.

"I hope this works," Monroe said.

"Actually, so do I," Isaiah said. "Far fewer casualties than sending in a strike team." Then he gestured to one of the agents. "Take them inside."

The gun pressed against Owen's back and again he marched ahead. When they reached the first tent, the agents behind him shoved him inside, and Owen entered what he assumed was the camp command center. Computers and several large monitors stood around a wide table with a digital map of the area. The agents prodded Owen, Grace, and Monroe past all that, to a separate conference table in a far corner of the tent.

"Sit," one of them ordered.

Owen took one of the chairs at the table, and so did Grace and Monroe.

"You think David's going to come?" Owen asked.

Grace nodded, staring at the agents watching them.

"Are you sure?" Monroe asked.

She nodded again. "Masireh counted on his brother, and I am counting on mine."

Owen had no idea what that meant, wasn't going to ask for an explanation in front of the Templar agents. So they sat there silently, waiting. As the minutes went by, Owen grew more nervous, but from the outside, Grace remained calm, sitting there in her chair with her hands folded in her lap.

Then Isaiah walked in, and he crossed the room to their table. "I've got men positioned up on both ridges of the valley. They'll catch him if he comes this way."

"He will," Grace said.

More minutes passed, and Monroe showed signs of nervousness, fidgeting and glancing around the tent. But Grace kept her face blank, her body still, and her stare hard. Owen thought he probably looked more like Monroe.

Eventually, an agent walked in. "Sir, we have him."

Owen felt both surprise and relief, after which he wondered if David's presence meant Javier was out there, too. With everything Owen had learned about his father, he felt the need to get his friend away from the Brotherhood.

"Excellent," Isaiah said. "Bring David here."

The agent nodded and left.

"I told you," Grace said. "I knew I could count on him."

"Yes, you did," Isaiah said. "Let's see about the rest of it though, shall we?"

Several moments later, two agents dragged David into the tent. He was wearing a warm coat, with a large pack on his back.

"Let me go!" he shouted.

Grace flew out of her chair toward him. "David!"

But before she could reach him, a Templar agent grabbed her around the neck and pulled her back, dumping her into her chair.

"Time for that later," Isaiah said. "Right now, I have some questions for this young man."

The agents brought David up to the table, and he yanked his arms free of them. "Let me go," he said. "Grace, I—"

"I'll do the talking," Isaiah said. "But I should first mention that your sister said you could be relied on to tell the truth. I hope you won't disappoint her."

"It's okay," Grace said. "I did."

David looked at her a moment, and then nodded. "What do you want to know?"

"How many Assassins are there on the ridge?" Isaiah asked.

"Two," David said. "And Javier and Natalya, also."

That answered Owen's question about his friend. Now he just needed to figure out a way to get a message to Javier the way Grace had signaled her brother.

"If Natalya is with them," Isaiah said, "do they know where the Piece of Eden is located?"

"Yes," David said.

"Then why have they not claimed it?"

David glowered, his lips clamped tight.

"David," Grace said, "please, just tell him."

"Fine." David folded his arms. "This camp is in the way."

"What do you mean?" Isaiah asked.

"I mean, the tomb is south of here. Griffin was trying to think of a way to get past your camp without being detected."

Isaiah leaned forward, his eyes wider than Owen had ever seen them. "Do *you* know where the prong is?"

David said nothing.

Isaiah's voice dropped almost to a whisper. "You do."

David shook his head. "Natalya is the only one who's actually seen it. But . . . she said the tomb is near a big rock shaped like a turtle. Several miles from here. That's all I know."

Isaiah sighed. "That is enough." He turned away from the table and strode toward the command center. "We're not waiting until dawn! I want all teams ready with radar and excavation equipment! We're moving south in fifteen minutes!"

Owen was a bit surprised that David had given that up so easily, when he had supposedly turned against the Templars when he left the Aerie. But after Isaiah's orders, the action in the tent grew frenzied, agents rushing in and out, the sounds of vehicles revving up outside. Fifteen minutes later, Isaiah returned to the table, now suited up in his own paramilitary gear, with the exception of a red cross emblazoned on his chest.

He spoke to two armed agents guarding them. "Keep them here."

"Yes, sir."

Then he left, and within a few moments, the engines of one of the helicopters could be heard whining slowly to life, and the sound of it thumping the air rose up before fading into the distance. After that, the camp went very quiet.

"Why did you do that?" Monroe whispered to David.

"It's better than the Assassins getting it," Owen said. His anger at them had begun to slowly turn to hatred. They had ruined his life, his mother's life, and taken his father's life.

"Why do you say that?" Monroe asked.

"After what they did to my dad."

"What did they do to your dad?"

"I got a sample of his DNA. Isaiah let me go into those memories. I saw the bank robbery."

Monroe sat up. "And?"

"The Assassins set him up. It was a way to get into Abstergo's bank. My dad didn't kill the guard, and he didn't really have a choice."

Monroe looked at the guards. "Isaiah showed you that, did he?"

"Yes."

Monroe pressed his hands together in front of his mouth and chin. He looked really disappointed, or perhaps just sad, and that wasn't the reaction Owen expected or wanted.

"What?" he asked.

"I worked on DNA and simulations for years." Monroe kept his voice low and even. "Abstergo can easily manipulate them. Isaiah can almost literally show you anything."

Owen did not like what Monroe was suggesting, or the twist it gave his stomach. "But he didn't. He showed me the truth."

"Did he? Or did he just show you what you wanted to see?"

Owen's anger flashed, and he slammed the table with his fist. "You weren't there. This was why I came to you in the first place, but you wouldn't help me. Remember?"

"I remember I couldn't help you."

"Well, Isaiah did. I'm not saying I'm ready to sign on with the Templars, but I am going to get justice for my dad with the Assassins. Somehow."

That sad, disappointed look remained in Monroe's eyes. "I warned you," he said.

"I need to use the bathroom," David said.

One of the agents scowled at him. "Hold it or go in your pants."

"Come on," David said. "You've got a porta-potty around here somewhere, right?"

The agent ignored him.

"You seriously want me to go right here?" David stood up and reached for the zipper on his pants. "You prepared to deal with cleanup?"

The agent wrinkled his nose. "Fine." He turned to the other guard. "You want to take him?"

The second guard shook his head.

"I have no preference," David said.

The first guard rolled his eyes. "This way."

He led David away from the table, past the command center, and out of the tent. Owen looked at Grace, and she was looking at him. The determined expression on her face touched his mind with another memory, Eliza, preparing to strike. He felt the mind of Varius descending upon him, almost as if he were in the Animus, but without nearly that weight. Owen made eye contact with Grace again, and she nodded, almost imperceptibly. So Owen rose to his feet, and gave his mind over to Varius in the same way he would to stay synchronized.

"Sit back down," the agent said.

"I need to stretch," Owen said. "I've been trapped in a shipping crate for twenty-four hours."

Grace also got to her feet.

"Sit down, both of you!"

When Owen attacked, the strikes and defensive moves felt automatic, as much Varius as him, and it seemed as though

Grace was as much Eliza. Within a moment, the two of them had the guard disarmed and down on the ground, unconscious.

"Let's go," Owen said.

"What the hell was that?" Monroe asked.

"Bleeding Effects," Grace said. "I've been feeling them a lot stronger with Owen around."

"Me too," Owen said.

They took the guard's gun and left the tent, searching for David through the camp. They encountered a few more agents along the way, but dealt with them without even having to fire the Templar weapon. When they found the porta-potties, they surprised the agent guarding David, and took him down, too.

"Is that you guys?" David asked from inside, his voice echoing.

"Yes," Grace said.

David stepped out, the spring-loaded door slamming shut behind him with a bang. "Took you long enough. It stinks in there."

Monroe looked back and forth between all three of them. "Would someone please tell me what is going on?"

"We'll explain on the way," Grace said. "Right now, we need some shovels."

"On the way where?" Monroe asked.

David pushed up his glasses, his eyebrows pressing down, as if the answer should be obvious. "The real location of the Piece of Eden."

atalya didn't want to leave David behind. Javier didn't, either, but Griffin and Yanmei decided it would draw too much attention to go catch him, and cost them time and energy to keep him from running off again. They also feared he would soon get himself caught by the Templars, putting the entire mission in jeopardy, so they insisted on pressing ahead with even greater urgency.

Natalya still hadn't decided what she would or could do about the Piece of Eden. Griffin had seen enough of the simulation to get them close to the burial site, but not all the way. They would soon look to Natalya to reveal its specific location, but her entire purpose in coming here had been to prevent them, or anyone, from finding it.

"Are you doing okay?" Javier whispered.

"No," she said.

"Why won't you cooperate?"

She wanted to ask why he *was* cooperating. "I'm afraid of putting a weapon of absolute power into the hands of anyone serving an ideology. I think Monroe was right. Neither the Assassins nor the Templars should have it."

Javier said nothing.

They soon arrived at the river, which appeared to run deep and probably freezing cold, though its current wasn't in a hurry. Yanmei turned them north, and they followed the water up through the valley, looking for a sound place to ford it. Perhaps a quarter mile on they reached a spot where the river wrapped around a rocky point, and the water riffled wide and shallow. They crossed over the wobbly stone bed, and at its deepest, the icy water only reached Natalya's knees.

The ox horn rock formation now lay slightly to the south of them, and Griffin redirected them toward it. Not long after that, they finished crossing the second half of the valley floor, and then ascended the opposite slope. When they reached the upper, western edge of the valley, the sound of engines rumbled faintly in the distance, and they turned to look south at the Templar camp.

Multiple sets of headlights came on and circled around, forming a train, and there seemed to be a lot of activity. The larger of the helicopters actually lifted off, its spotlights pressing down on the ground.

"Do you think that has anything to do with David?" Natalya asked.

"Most likely," Griffin said.

"Are they coming for us?" Javier asked.

Griffin pulled out his binoculars. "They're moving out, but not toward us." He passed the binoculars to Yanmei. "They're heading farther south. In a hurry."

"Where are they going?" Natalya asked.

"You tell us," Griffin said. "Do they know where the Piece of Eden is located?"

"How would I know that?" Natalya asked.

Javier turned a bit angry. "He wants to know if they're headed in the right direction."

Natalya hesitated, and then shook her head.

"Well, something has them on the move," Yanmei said. "I wonder what it could be."

"It doesn't really matter," Griffin said. "As long as they're not headed this way, we'll use the distraction to our advantage."

So they turned and kept going, but Natalya periodically glanced back over her shoulder, watching the convoy of Abstergo vehicles moving down the valley, a string of twinkling lights. It seemed too coincidental that they should mobilize like that, in the middle of the night, shortly after David had fled. He had taken note of Natalya as she peered up at the ox horn rocks, which might have given him a clue as to where the Möngke Khan had been buried. She wondered if he had somehow sent the Templars in the opposite direction, to perhaps give her and the Assassins time. But time to do what?

She had to get away from Griffin and Yanmei, somehow, to find the Piece of Eden on her own. But that didn't seem possible. At least not easy. She wished she had Javier on her side, but he seemed to have found something within the Brotherhood that appealed to him, the way Sean and Grace had both found things within the Order.

The slope upward rose unevenly, with dips and washes choked with brush and a few trees. The ox horn rocks were still some distance above them, but they were getting closer every moment that passed.

They had almost reached the point where Natalya had desynchronized when Griffin paused. "This is as near as I can get us." He turned to Natalya. "I admire your will, but I'm almost out of patience. You need to step up."

Natalya stood up straight, feeling the mood shift against her.

"Please," Javier said. "It's the Templars or the Assassins. It has to be one or the other."

"Does it?" Natalya asked.

"Yes," he said. "And I think you stand for free will."

"My grandparents lived under Communist rule. Of course I stand for free will. And that's exactly the reason I'm not giving my blind allegiance to the Assassins."

"You are right," Yanmei said. "But our Creed does not command us to be free. It commands us to be wise."

"What does that mean?" Natalya asked.

Griffin shook his head. "We don't have time for the Ironies, Yanmei."

"What Ironies?" Natalya asked.

Yanmei offered a gentle smile. "They were written down by one of the wisest and greatest Assassins in history, Altaïr Ibn-La'Ahad. Our Brotherhood seeks to promote peace, but we commit murder. We seek to open the minds of men, but require absolute obedience to the Creed. We seek to reveal the dangers of blind faith, but practice it ourselves. These are the Ironies."

"So how do you reconcile those?" Natalya asked.

"By being wise." Yanmei laid a palm against her chest. "I surrender some of my free will so that I might bring it to the world. As an Assassin, I stand apart."

Natalya understood that, but she wasn't ready to surrender any of her free will, and she didn't think anyone should be asked to. Next to her, Javier had gone quiet. He looked at Yanmei and Griffin, and he seemed to be thinking about what Yanmei had just said. Natalya wondered if he agreed with her and was prepared to sign on. She hoped not.

"The Templars must not acquire the prong," Yanmei said. "Please. Help us."

Natalya knew she had to make a choice. It wouldn't work to keep putting them off anymore. But Javier was wrong. It wasn't just a choice between the Templars and the Assassins. Monroe had said from the beginning that there was a third choice.

"It's this way," Natalya said, and she turned back to the south, away from the ox horn formation. She walked toward a distant mound of earth near one of the stands of trees.

"Is that the tomb?" Griffin asked.

Natalya nodded, but she had begun to breathe harder, and struggled to maintain her outward calm. Her plan required more from her than a lie.

Javier came up beside her as they walked. "Thank you," he said.

She glanced into his eyes. "Are you ready to give up your free will to be an Assassin? Is that really what you want?"

"I . . . don't know," he said. "But I can't figure that out right now. The prong comes first."

She nodded, and they closed the distance between them and the hillock. When they reached it, Griffin dropped his pack to the ground and pulled out a narrow, foldable shovel. He locked it open, and surveyed the mound.

"Where should I start digging?"

"I'm not sure." Natalya pointed at a spot near the base of the hill. "I think the tomb opening might be somewhere near there."

Griffin nodded and dropped to his knees, his back to Natalya, and Yanmei went to stand next to him. The rhythmic sound of the shovel scraping dirt filled the night, and she let Griffin dig for several minutes.

"This will take a while," Natalya said to Javier. "What if Abstergo finds us?"

"I'll be ready," he said.

"With what?" she asked.

He pulled out his crossbow pistol. "With this. Sleep darts drop them in seconds."

"Can I see it?"

Javier handed her the weapon, and it felt heavier than she was expecting, solid, the grip warm from Javier's hand.

"How does it work?" she asked.

"Pull back here." He pointed to the spring mechanism. "Pull the trigger. Reload with this lever, and then do it again."

"And these are sleep darts?"

"Yeah."

Natalya pulled back on the spring mechanism, raised the pistol, and shot Yanmei in the back. The scrape of the shovel stopped as Natalya reloaded and raised the weapon again. Griffin had almost reached her when she shot him in the chest. Javier had done nothing to stop her in the seconds it had taken, too stunned to move. Both Assassins now lay on the ground, unconscious.

She handed Javier back his pistol. "I don't want to shoot you, too."

His mouth hung open. "Why did—"

"Come on, we don't have much time."

She snatched up Griffin's shovel and ran back the way they had just come before turning up the mountain toward the ox horn formation. Javier caught up with her, growling.

"Natalya! What the hell was that?"

"The third choice!" she shouted back. "I think David bought us some time, and I'm not going to waste it."

The rock formation grew in size as they got closer, and by the time they reached it, Natalya almost couldn't tell its shape anymore. But this was the place Bayan had seen. She knew it, and she knew the tomb entrance had to be somewhere nearby. The total darkness of night had passed, dawn just hours away.

"Okay," Javier said. "Let's say you find it. What then? How are you going to get it out of here on your own? What if Abstergo catches you?"

"I'll deal with that problem next," she said. She didn't want to admit she hadn't planned that far. "Help me look around."

"What are we looking for?" he asked.

"Something that might indicate an opening." She walked along the edge of the formation, scanning the ground where it met the stone, periodically glancing toward the south, hoping to see the others coming. But that would depend on David.

"What about this?" Javier said from several yards away.

Natalya hurried over to him and saw what he'd found. A carving of the Templar cross in the stone, small enough you'd have to be looking for it to find it.

"This is it." She dropped to the ground and plunged the shovel into the ground beneath the symbol, prying up chunks of cold, hard turf and dirt. Javier knelt down next to her, helping to scoop it out and away with his hands. They'd managed to dig about a foot down when Javier suddenly jumped to his feet.

"Someone's coming." He already had his crossbow pistol in his hand.

Natalya turned to look, hoping it was who she thought it was.

Four figures approached, distant and vague, but as they drew closer, Natalya smiled. "It's them."

"Who?" Javier asked.

But that question was answered a moment later when the party arrived. Owen, Grace, David, and Monroe. But no Sean.

"I knew it," David said.

Grace laughed. "My brother swore he knew the location of the tomb."

"He was right," Natalya said.

"He's been right about a lot of things." Grace smiled at her brother in a way Natalya hadn't noticed before. There was a new pride in it, and respect.

Natalya turned back to the hole. "The tomb entrance is here. We just have to uncover it. I put Griffin to sleep, but he'll only be out for a couple of hours."

"Then we better get started," Monroe said.

So they all took turns digging and scooping, pushing hard until their shoulders and arms ached before turning it over to the next in line. While they dug, they caught one another up on what had happened to them. Natalya felt disappointed and sad that Sean had chosen to stay at the Aerie, but Grace and David seemed to have come back together with a new understanding of each other. It had something to do with one of Grace's simulations, the memories of a man named Masireh and his brother.

Owen then told what he'd learned about his father and the Assassins, mostly aiming the explanation at Javier.

"I have to say I agree with Monroe," Javier said after his friend had finished. "I think Isaiah tricked you."

"What?" Owen took a step away from his friend. "Do you realize what you're saying? If Isaiah faked it—"

"That still doesn't mean your dad did it," Javier said.

"It means he *might* have done it," Owen said. "Is that what you think?"

Javier scowled. "Of course not. How can you say that? Why do you think I broke into that warehouse for you?"

"I got something," Monroe said, his arms deep in the hole.

"What is it?" Natalya asked.

"A stone slab. It could be a door."

"Let's dig it out," Owen said.

They all crowded around the opening, trying to help, trying to get a look. Dawn was closer now, the light around them pale and blue, and Natalya felt a thrill that in spite of everything, they had all come back together to pull this off.

But then a low thumping reached her ears, and she pulled away from the opening, looking up into the sky. "It's the Templars," she said.

The others all glanced up.

"Run," Monroe said.

"Run where?" Owen asked.

In the next moment, the helicopter charged over the hill above them, blinding spotlights pinning them against the slope.

Black uniformed figures leapt from the aircraft, sliding down ropes to the ground, weapons drawn. Owen, Grace, and Javier charged them, but it was clear they were outnumbered, and a machine gun soon fired from above, tearing up the ground around them.

"Cease your opposition!" Isaiah's voice assailed them from a loudspeaker. "It is pointless, and it might regrettably get you killed!"

A second wave of agents stormed over the same hill on foot, and there no longer seemed to be any way out. They couldn't run, they couldn't hide, they couldn't fight. Natalya looked up into the spotlight, raging inside, but powerless.

"Put your hands up, everyone," Monroe said. "I want you all to make it out of this alive."

Agents had already subdued Owen, Grace, and Javier. Natalya put her hands up, along with David and Monroe, and soon they were completely surrounded.

Isaiah descended from the helicopter then, zipping down a line to the ground. The helicopter pulled away, taking with it the roaring storm of wind it churned, and the hillside grew quiet. The director strode over toward David, hands clasped behind his back.

"A very clever attempt to throw us off," he said. "But of course, I knew what you were up to. It was simply more efficient to allow you the freedom to lead me to the location of the tomb, which you have done, saving me weeks if not months of labor."

"Isaiah, don't hurt them," Monroe said.

Isaiah turned toward him. "Why would I do that? I might still need them, just as I may still need you." Then he stalked over to Javier. "Where are the Assassins?"

"I have no idea," Javier said. "We left them behind."

"So it seems," Isaiah said. He turned to one of the agents. "Get to work! I want that tomb open! And stay sharp!"

"Yes, sir!"

The Templars set to work digging and clearing, and Natalya could only watch as the hole she'd started grew wider and wider, revealing more of the stone door. It didn't seem real to her that this could be happening. Her plan had failed, they had lost, and she had to wonder now if Javier had been right all along. Perhaps it really had only been a choice between the Assassins and the Templars, and in fighting that decision, Natalya had let the Piece of Eden go to the worse of the two.

When the Templars uncovered the edges of the stone slab, they brought forward two large crowbars and pried them against the door, several agents throwing their weight against each side. Slowly, the door shifted, and then tipped forward until it fell outward, slamming into the hillside.

The opening was small and narrow, perhaps four feet tall and two feet wide. Isaiah stood for a moment with a smile, and then stepped toward it.

CHAPTER TWENTY-EIGHT

Two agents had Javier's arms restrained, with Owen and Grace similarly immobilized, as Isaiah strode calmly toward the tomb. But before he reached the opening, men shouted and gunshots cracked. Javier turned toward the commotion and saw Griffin and Yanmei charging in, hoods over their heads, electric hidden blades crackling.

Javier seized the moment of distraction and threw off his captors. Then he pulled out a smoke grenade and smashed it against the ground, giving him the chance to bolt away. He glanced back and saw that Owen and Grace had done the same.

The Templar agents near the two Assassins had regrouped, but Javier fired off his crossbow pistol into the thick of them until he ran out of darts. Then he tossed the weapon aside and reached into his coat for his throwing knives.

At the appearance of the Assassins, Isaiah had bolted for the tomb, and he'd almost made it inside. Javier charged after him.

"Owen!"

"I see it!"

The two of them barreled ahead. Javier did what he could along the way, throwing grenades and knives to help Griffin and Yanmei. Grace had recovered and stood near her brother, defending him.

Isaiah made it through the doorway first, and Javier ducked through the narrow opening, into a low tunnel. Owen came in right behind him, and they heard Isaiah's footsteps racing off into the darkness, his flashlight shaking off shadows around his silhouette.

Owen and Javier darted after him. The tunnel appeared to be made of brick and earth, and smelled of clay. Ahead of them, it opened into a chamber that Isaiah had already reached, and when they entered it, Owen and Javier both held knives, ready to throw them.

Isaiah arched over a stone sarcophagus, bent under the low dome ceiling. Near him, on the ground, lay piles of artifacts and the tarnished remains of several suits of armor, and in his hand, he gripped a dagger. Javier recognized it immediately. He had held one like it in the memories of Cudgel Cormac.

Isaiah now possessed the Piece of Eden.

Javier was about to throw his knife, but before he could, Isaiah looked into his eyes, and a wave broke over his mind. He had only ever felt a sensation like it once before, in the presence of Cortés in his first experience with the Animus.

On the back of the wave came an unstoppable torrent of thought. Javier imagined his parents, as if they were there in front of him. His mamá sobbed and told him she wished he'd never been born. His papá told him it would have been better if Javier had murdered someone. And then his brother appeared, screaming at him, calling him a faggot, and then he started beating him.

Javier fell to the ground under the blows, crying at the pain, only vaguely aware that he was still in the tomb. Owen crouched nearby, rocking, holding the sides of his head. Beyond Javier's brother and his parents, he saw Isaiah calmly walking by, out of the chamber.

After he'd gone, Javier's parents and brother slowly retreated into the shadows of the tomb, their eyes and their hatred fixed on him until they'd vanished completely. Javier choked and rubbed his eyes before staggering to his feet in the darkness.

"What the hell was that?" he said.

"I think," Owen said, "that was the fear prong. I . . . couldn't fight it."

"We have to try," Javier said, and he stumbled forward, still clutching his knife, out of the chamber and down the narrow passage, the light of dawn visible through the opening.

Outside, Isaiah stood triumphant on the mountain slope. Everyone around him knelt or lay on the ground, consumed by their own worst fears, trapped in their personal hells. Isaiah surveyed them with an expression of ultimate satisfaction, his mouth set in a hard smile.

Javier raised his knife once more to throw, but his parents stepped into view again, between his blade and its target. They walked toward Javier, glaring, wagging their fingers and spewing vile insults that he covered his ears against.

But over them, Javier heard a scream, and looked up to see Yanmei rushing at Isaiah, tears streaming from her eyes, her hidden blade ready. But Javier could see her attack was desperate. It lacked control. Isaiah stepped easily aside and thrust the point of his dagger, the Piece of Eden, up into her stomach. She screamed again, and he tossed her aside.

"Listen to me!" he bellowed. "I am no longer a Templar! I am become death, the destroyer of worlds. All of you who once served the Order now serve me, and all others shall perish! Come!"

He turned and strode down the hill, and after he'd walked some yards on, the Templar agents all dragged themselves to their feet and followed after him. Javier managed to raise himself and rush to Yanmei's side.

She winced and clutched her stomach where she bled. So much blood. Too much. Javier used his own hands to put pressure on the wound as Griffin staggered over to them.

"Yanmei," he said.

She looked up at him. "He showed me something I'd buried a long time ago."

"You were the only one who got close," Griffin said.

She coughed. "Not close enough."

The others had drawn nearer, standing around the Assassins, and Javier could see they all suffered the aftershocks of their own fears, just as he did, even as they worried about Yanmei. Monroe's face had lost all color.

"What can we do?" Grace asked.

"We need to get her out of here," Griffin said.

"How?" David asked.

"One of the helicopters. Help me carry her."

Griffin moved to Yanmei's shoulders, and the others stepped in to take her arms and her legs, while Javier kept pressure on her stomach. They lifted her together and shuffled along together down the mountain.

The sun rose above the peaks and valleys to the east, throwing its light on the Abstergo camp, and Javier could see the vehicle convoy moving away, Isaiah with his army. But Javier despaired when he saw and heard both helicopters also flying away with the ground troops.

"Stay with us," Griffin said, looking down. "Yanmei, stay with us."

But her eyes had mostly closed, her eyelids fluttering.

"Put her down," Griffin said. "Put her down, and keep pressure on that wound."

They gently set her limp body on the ground, and Javier leaned into her, while Griffin shook her gently.

"Yanmei, stay with me. Come on, you have to fight."

But Javier could sense that a change had taken place beneath his bloody hands. Her chest no longer expanded with her breathing. She no longer winced or moved. Even the bleeding seemed to have slowed to a stop. She was gone.

"Damn," Griffin said, eyes closed, digging his knuckles into the ground.

Natalya started to cry, and Javier felt tears coming to his own eyes. Owen and Grace and Monroe hadn't really known Yanmei, but they stood by, somber and silent, and they all remained that way for some time.

Eventually, Griffin rose to his feet and lifted her body by himself, cradling her in his arms. He resumed his march down the hill, and Javier and the others followed him, much slower now. When they reached the valley floor, they trudged toward the Templar camp, now abandoned. Griffin set Yanmei down again, and looked around.

"I need to find a way to reach Gavin. Or at least the rest of Yanmei's cell."

"This is my fault," Natalya said. "If I had just told you where the Piece of Eden was—"

"Stop that," Griffin said. "This is war, and war takes lives. I happen to know Yanmei respected you for your principles. She wouldn't blame you. She would blame Isaiah, and so do I. We can't forget who the real enemy is."

"I agree with Griffin," Monroe said. "This is not your fault."

"What did he mean?" Javier asked. "Isaiah said he wasn't a Templar anymore."

"I don't know," Griffin said. "One problem at a time."

He walked over to one of the tents, poked his head inside, and then walked to the next, most likely looking for something he could use to radio or connect with the outside world. Javier pulled Owen aside.

"Are you okay?"

Owen nodded, but it wasn't convincing, and Javier knew exactly what the dagger had shown his friend.

"It wasn't any more real than Isaiah's fake simulation," he said. "You have to put it out of your mind. Focus on finding out the truth."

Owen nodded. "What did you see?"

"My parents," Javier said. "They . . ." But he broke off, unable to finish.

Owen put an arm around his shoulder. "Never mind. Like you said, it's not real."

Javier looked over at the others. Grace and David huddled close together, and Natalya stood next to Monroe. "I wonder what they saw."

"Probably better not to ask."

Javier thought that was probably true. He and Owen walked back over toward them, but in that moment the thumping of a helicopter reached them. They all looked up as Griffin bolted out of one of the tents.

"Take cover!" he said.

They scattered. Javier went for one of the open shipping containers with Owen and Monroe, while Grace and David dove inside one of the tents with Griffin and Natalya. Then they waited, and Javier wondered if Isaiah was coming back for them. He believed Isaiah meant it when he'd said he needed them all alive, but that didn't mean he intended to leave them free.

When the helicopter came into view, roaring overhead, it circled the camp once before setting down in the field, next to the river. The rotors slowed, shutting down, as the side door opened and a woman climbed out with a few Abstergo agents.

"Victoria," Owen said.

"Who?" Javier asked.

"That's Victoria. She was at the Aerie. Isaiah said she was on her way here."

The woman wore the same uniform as Isaiah and looked around the camp as she walked closer, her face worried and confused, her posture defensive.

"Doesn't look like she knows what happened," Monroe said.

"Nope," Javier said.

"Victoria!" Grace called as she emerged from the tent, waving her arms.

"What is she doing?" Owen asked, and Javier wondered the same thing.

Victoria turned and waved back, and rushed to meet Grace in the middle of the camp. Then David and Natalya came out, and Monroe looked at Owen and Javier with a shrug.

"No sense hiding now."

So they left the shipping container and crossed the camp to join the others. Javier kept a wary eye on the agents, ready to pull a weapon if needed, as the helicopter's blades came to a complete stop.

"Where is he?" Victoria asked. "Where is Isaiah?"

"Gone," Grace said. "With the Piece of Eden."

"But where is everyone else?" she asked.

"He took them with him," Monroe said. "He's gone rogue."

Victoria closed her eyes, as if something she feared had just been confirmed. "He sent something to me just now." She held up her phone. "It's some kind of . . . manifesto."

"What did it say?" Grace asked.

"I haven't read it all yet. But he's broken from the Order, that much is clear. And he claims to have two of the prongs."

"Two of them?" Owen asked.

Victoria nodded. "He found the one at Mount McGregor before you got there."

"So he's one away from the Trident," Javier said. "The world is one prong away from another Alexander the Great."

"Or worse," Natalya said.

"I'm still trying to make sense of this," Victoria said. "But so much is becoming clear. He and I disagreed often, about all of you, and now I know that's because he was working toward his own agenda. Not the Templar vision."

"We have to stop him from finding the third prong," Javier said. "He was practically unstoppable with the fear prong. If he completes the Trident, he'll be invincible."

Victoria seemed to notice him for the first time, tilting her head. "You're Javier."

"Yes."

"So the Assassins were here?"

"They *are* here," Grace said.

At that, the Templar agents went into a defensive position, scanning their surroundings with weapons raised.

"Seriously?" Natalya said. "After what just happened, you're still ready to fight? We need to work together. Isaiah has become bigger than the Templar Order or the Assassin Brotherhood, and I think he wants to destroy both of you."

Victoria looked at her through narrowed eyes for several long moments. Then she turned to the agents at her side. "Put your weapons on the ground."

They hesitated and she repeated the order. After they'd complied, she stepped away from the group with her hands spread wide and open.

"I am Dr. Victoria Bibeau! I know you can hear me! As you can see, my agents have put down their weapons!"

A moment passed. Javier wondered what Griffin would do.

"I'm calling for a ceasefire! I would like you to come out so we can talk!"

Another moment went by, and then Griffin emerged from the tent, his hood up, hiding half his face in shadow. He strode toward them, confidently, even aggressively, but kept his blade hidden.

"I'm Griffin," he said. "And you, Dr. Bibeau, are probably the only Templar I would ever trust."

"Those days are long past," she said. "I am a Templar, now, make no mistake of that. But it is true that I am probably the only Templar who would even consider speaking with you. Or working with you to defeat Isaiah."

It seemed there was more to Victoria's history than any of them had known. Griffin seemed to know *of* her, at least, and she had apparently not always been loyal to the Templars. But Javier put his questions about that aside for the moment, hoping that Griffin would keep his cool, and Victoria would keep hers.

"I believe this might be unprecedented," Griffin said. "A Templar asking an Assassin for help."

"I'm not interested in which one of us is asking the other, and I really don't care if that matters to your pride. What matters to me is stopping Isaiah."

"Fair enough," Griffin said. "The ceasefire will hold until the third prong is found, and Isaiah is stopped."

"Maybe the world won't come to an end, after all," Monroe said.

"Do we have any idea where it is?" Javier asked.

"Scandinavia," Victoria said. "We had very strong indications that it was in Scandinavia."

CHAPTER TWENTY-NINE

Styrbjörn stood once more with Gyrid at the prow of his *drakkar*, but this time, he had a fleet of two hundred long-ships behind him. They had been raiding the Danish coast for months, and the Jomsvikings had proven their reputation well-founded. No village or town had resisted them, and every fleet sent to stop them had been sent to the bottom of the sea.

Palnatoke stood at Styrbjörn's side, his second-in-command. "I look forward to seeing Harald's rotten tooth as he smiles away his kingdom."

"I don't want his kingdom," Styrbjörn said. "I want his army."

"I want his kingdom," Gyrid said.

Styrbjörn turned to his sister. "Are you sure about this?"

"I am sure," she said. "You will have Sweden, and I will have Denmark."

Styrbjörn nodded and turned his attention back to the harbor as his fleet moved in. The currents of the ocean and the wind flowed through Sean's mind, and he relished the smell of the salt, the cry of the gulls overhead, the freedom.

Are you doing okay, Sean? Anaya asked.

"Yes," he said. Victoria had wanted to take him with her after Grace and Owen had escaped with Monroe, but Sean had refused. How could he give this up? This was where he belonged. "I'm doing great."

The *drakkar* eased up to the harbor's main pier, and Styrbjörn saw a welcome party waiting for him there, prepared to offer him gifts and friendship to prevent the pillaging of their city. Among them, Styrbjörn saw Harald Bluetooth standing with his sons and daughters. The king of Denmark did not smile but seemed resigned, wearing a thick fur with an ornamented belt, and from his belt hung a peculiar dagger.

Sean leaned forward through the current of Styrbjörn's mind, straining to get a closer look at the weapon, and realized with an almost overwhelming excitement what it was. He didn't want to take his eyes from the weapon, for fear it would vanish.

"Anaya, I found it! I found the Piece of Eden!"

Silence met him.

"Anaya!"

Still more silence.

That seemed odd. "Anaya?"

Hello, Sean, came Isaiah's voice.

"Isaiah?" Sean said. "You're back?"

I am.

"I found it," he said, almost finding it hard to breath. "The Piece of Eden. My ancestor just saw it!"

That's incredible. I'm going to pull you out now so we can discuss it, all right?

"Okay," Sean said, working to steady himself.

He then endured the discomforts of his transition to the Memory Corridor and then the extraction of the Parietal Suppressor, impatiently, and shook his head after the removal of the helmet, feeling slightly dizzy, but elated.

Isaiah stood next to the Animus ring, smiling. "Well done."

"I just need to stay with this ancestor," Sean said. "Styrbjörn will show us what happened to the Piece of Eden."

"Excellent," Isaiah said. He turned to the security woman standing next to him. She had blond hair, and the name badge on her uniform read COLE. "Bring the processor from Sean's Animus."

"Yes, sir."

"Bring?" Sean said. "Are you leaving again?"

"Yes," Isaiah said. "And this time, you are coming with me."